"A subtle, fascinating collection of exquisi[te] respects, exquisite and painstaking attention. [...] restored here, each relationship cultivated or h[...] [...], elegantly dense with the projections of the people implicated. I love too that Gregory Spatz reveals most of these people to be unexpectedly good and interesting, without becoming sentimental, and without sacrificing acknowledgment of a full spectrum of human behavior. In Gregory Spatz's *What Could Be Saved*, the violin—in the most unexpected landscape for so old and storied an instrument—is a magnificent container for and mirror of the best and worst of humanity; is a vehicle for our greatest capacities for the eternal verities, and a currency of deception and evil. This book is a new favorite."
— Bonnie Nadzam, author of *Lamb and Lions*

"Gregory Spatz has an extraordinary ability to get at what lies beneath the surface and put words to the ineffable—music, yes (even his violins speak!), but also the under-currents of emotions, unconscious urges and inchoate longings that form and deform our lives. *What Could Be Saved* is as fiercely seeing as it is ultimately generous in its gentle vision of human frailty and the desire to connect."
— Elizabeth Graver, author of *The End of the Point*

"If good fiction is a bringing of the news from one world to another, then Greg-ory Spatz, with this radiant book, is bringing us news of the violin, giving voice to its makers, its players, and even the instrument itself. What a rare gift it is to be im-mersed in this world and emerge from it changed, with not only a richer under-standing of music and those who make it, but a whole new way of listening."
— Sarah Shun-lien Bynum, author of *Madeleine is Sleeping* and *Ms. Hempel Chronicles*

"Intricate and formally daring, Gregory Spatz's *What Could Be Saved* unshrouds the secret lives of high-end violins and their dedicated and impassioned makers. With their loves, losses, and obsessions spanning generations, we can't help but root for these perfectionists in an imperfect world. Like the venerable instrument at the center of these linked tales, Spatz's prose produces a beautiful tone."
— Leland Cheuk, author of *The Misadventures of Sulliver Pong*

"The novellas and stories of Gregory Spatz's *What Could Be Saved* teem with notes of human discord and connectivity, a constant surge of dissonance and melody, crushing a concert in your head of subtle, tortured character, of lyrical language languishing in the ear, of sadness and triumph wringing your heart. This tightly woven series of connected tales reminds us of what good literary writing is for, and why it will never fade out of tune."
—Jamie Iredell, author of *The Fat Kid*

"*What Could Be Saved* initiates the reader into the mysteries of a secret society of artists and artisans, thieves and treasure hunters, forgers and true believers, all of whom idolize the nearly supernatural powers and traditions of the violin. Those old, priceless instruments are like keys that unlock the quintessence of music and beauty, but they are also 'the devil's box,' just as often counterfeits that sow delusion and disenchantment as they pass from acolyte to acolyte – player to player, luthier to luthier – through the centuries. Gregory Spatz has conjoined these stories into a masterly quartet that casts the same spell on the reader as on its characters. This collection is magical, hypnotic, brilliant."

— Paul Harding, musician and author of Pulitzer Prize winning *Tinkers*

"*What Could Be Saved* is a vivid, engrossing portrait of luthiers and musicians, of fathers and sons, and of family lore fueling life-long obsessions. Gregory Spatz has written a love letter to both violins and to the artists and craftsmen whose lives, however briefly, intersect with them. Above all, these perfectly tuned stories convey the pathos of inheritance: the difference between what we think we're leaving behind, and what's actually left."

— Alexis Smith, author of *Glaciers* and *Marrow Island*

What Could Be Saved
Bookmatched Novellas & Stories

WHAT COULD BE SAVED:

Bookmatched Novellas and Stories

T|P

Tupelo Press
North Adams, Massachusetts

Library of Congress Catalog-in-Publication data available upon request.
ISBN paperback: ISBN: 978-1-946482-17-4

Cover and text designed by Bill Kuch.

First edition: June 2019

Tupelo Press
P.O. Box 1767
North Adams, Massachusetts 01247
(413) 664-9611 / Fax: (413) 664-9711
editor@tupelopress.org / www.tupelopress.org

Tupelo Press is an award-winning independent literary press that publishes
fine fiction, non-fiction, and poetry in books that are a joy to hold as well as
read. Tupelo Press is a registered 501(c)(3) non-profit organization, and we rely
on public support to carry out our mission of publishing extraordinary work
that may be outside the realm of the large commercial publishers. Financial
donations are welcome and are tax deductible.

For Caridwen,
        who made three violins in the time it took me
        to write one book.

Contents

What Could Be Saved
Bookmatched Novellas & Stories

WHAT
COULD
BE
SAVED
GREGORY
SPATZ

One

Leather apron, pot belly, and eyes that went in two different directions. Later, picturing him, Paul would start with the beard, close-cropped but not so close that it didn't mostly conceal the ravages of a repaired cleft pallet, and he'd realize this had confounded his judgment by preventing him from ever gauging the man's age. Older than him, for sure. Younger than Paul's father. Maybe. He wore blue alligator-skin loafers with a gold buckle, khakis and a dress shirt, horn-rimmed glasses, and he walked in a way that hinted at effeminacy but this was instantly offset by the bluntness of his fingers and his potbelly. Not gay, Paul thought. Probably. This impression was further supported by the man's energetic attention to the young woman, May, with whom Paul had come to help look for a new instrument. A violin tasting, she'd called it. No commitment. Just looking. Violin after violin the owner brought to them in the trial room, each offered with the same close-mouthed smile and head tilt, as he spun the instrument once by the neck to show front and back before laying it on the leather-topped table, never naming a price, often stuttering or hesitating at the starts of sentences. "H-h-here's one to look at, since you said you liked the Gemünder. Also American. So these ones here are still of interest, and these are not?" and out he went again. "Th-this one is French. Turn-of-the-century. Also a little oversized, like the Scottish one you liked. Scale length is standard of course—but you'll have a reach. M-m-my guess is the Scottish one would be a challenge, but maybe worth trying a while before ruling out. We don't want you sustaining a playing injury." Between tests, and most notably when the owner slid open the door to bring another violin, letting in sounds from the shop as he entered—voices, a door jingling open and shut, and from down the hall sounds of another ongoing trial, a concert cellist whose notoriety the owner had mentioned in passing (and in a manner Paul felt certain was meant to assess his and May's worldliness or humility with regard to concert cellists)—he had to realize that he was back where he'd sworn to himself he'd never be: in a violin shop. In a room surrounded with violins. A very nice, formally but austerely appointed room, formerly the den or sitting room of a grand-style miner's mansion, he guessed, with pocket doors and a plaster floret at the center of the ceiling like an upside-down cake, floors thickly carpeted to deaden overtones . . . but still, a room full of violins. Months ago, not quite a year, he might reflexively have tried to construct the phrase in Chinese, forever practicing and memorizing, mediating all meaning and sense through Chinese, beginning first with the inside-out grammar—*I am violins-full-of room inside*—but no more. As quickly as his short-term memory had bloated with thousands upon thousands of Chinese words, characters, and grammatical constructions, the knowledge had drifted away. Spiraled like water down a drain. Gone. Room . . . What was the word for room, even?

The woman with him, playing and tasting violins, he didn't know, exactly. May. Since fall quarter, he'd been hearing her through the walls and floors of the off-campus house they shared with three other students. He was pretty sure which food items were hers in the fridge and freezer—tubs of mint chocolate chip and pistachio ice cream gummed with fingerprints, diet cottage cheese, noodle and spice packages labeled in kanji—and he knew which studies and pieces would follow which in her daily practice, where she'd stumble or soar through passages. He'd seen her on her way out the door for morning classes and sometimes walking from the shared shower down the hall to her room wearing only a towel, black hair in a shiny rope down her back, shoulders beading water and pink heels pounding the floor with a surprising volume. "Your girlfriend," Melissa, his closest friend at the time, the one who'd gotten him into the house and then promptly moved out to take over the lease on a one-bedroom apartment of her own, sometimes called her—because of his family connection with violins, he supposed, or an expression of abstracted absorption and distracted longing he couldn't conceal if he happened to hear her through the walls of the house, practicing, and Melissa was there to witness.

"Please! You think I haven't had enough of violins and violinists to last a few lifetimes? I don't even know her name. May something. Whatever."

"And she's Chinese, Paul."

"You don't know that. How do you know what she is? Anyway, so what."

He knew how May's present instrument held her back as a player, and a few days earlier he'd helped by adjusting her bridge and rewinding her strings so the pegs would turn smoothly.

"That should help." They were at the dining room table, a rare intersection in their schedules, and rarer that she wasn't in her room practicing or studying. She'd been taking advantage of the extra table space and additional light from the west-facing picture windows, since no one had been at home—marking bowings and fingerings in a lengthy photocopied score spread across the table top.

"You know about violins," she said.

"I should. I should know more, really. My father builds them."

"Really! Do you play?"

"God, no."

"I don't believe you."

He shrugged and shook his head, and because she wasn't saying anything further and her eyes had an effect that was hard for him to ignore or control his reaction to—attentive, probing but not unkindly, so he wanted only to look back and be wordlessly absorbed in them—he picked up her violin again and turned it front to back. Plucked the strings. Strad copy from the mid fifties or forties. German, probably. Maybe Czech. Crazed yellow orange varnish that instantly made him want to set it back down on the table and not touch it again, though he liked the tight flaming in the back wood. "Pretty," he said, looking at the back. He set it with a resonant thunk back on the dining room table.

"It's shit, if you must know. But what are you going to do?"

This was not a question he felt in any way able to answer. "It's just overbuilt. I mean, it'll never be more than what it is, but if you could . . . if someone who knows what they're doing cut some wood out of the plates, you might be surprised how it sounds."

"You could do that?"

He shrugged. He wouldn't dream of trying. Wouldn't even know how to begin. "Maybe. Sure."

"But you don't play. How can you be so sure?"

"We were just all about making them. My dad, that is. I guess I don't know why I never played. I must never have wanted to. But I love . . ."

"Is he alive still?"

"My dad?" He nodded. "Very much so. He can't . . . he can play just enough to hear, like, fundamental tones. That's it. But hearing you sometimes . . ." The words escaped him. "It's just great. You're getting pretty much as good of a sound out of this thing as anyone could. Seriously. Which is saying a lot."

She gave him a look he couldn't read. One that seemed to see through his attraction and to discredit or disbelieve it, to discredit him for having it, as if his feeling were some alien third party they might agree to tolerate and acknowledge for the moment though they both knew better than to believe it. "In your humble, expert opinion."

"Well. Expert. I don't know——"

"Relax, Paul. I'm just giving you shit."

This was when she'd mentioned the trip into town and named the shop she'd be visiting.

"They're good. I hear. Reputable, anyway." And because she hadn't quit looking at him in that way he found so disarming, he continued, staring back until his eyes felt as if they might dissolve from the pressure and unrelenting pseudo-sincerity. "Not that I know them or anything."

"I'm only tasting. Not shopping. Looking and trying. My teacher says I should, but he's too busy. So you could be my chaperone. Chaperone and 'expert' consultant. If you're free, that is? Want to? Help me figure out what's crap and what isn't. "

He knew from his father that money-talk should come later in the sequence, so he didn't ask, and he wasn't surprised when the shop owner didn't name his prices. You established a price range (in this case, up to six thousand) and then you didn't talk again specifically about cost until sounds had filled the air. Until music had eased the boundaries, leveled the field between buyer and seller, between love and intention, faith and objective value.

One with boxwood fittings; one with a low neck angle and hodgepodge of string tails (consignment piece, he guessed, since the others appeared to have immaculately standard if unimaginative setups—all strung with the same string sets, bridges crowned a little thick and high with minimal tapering to the inside points, all ready for customization); one French, narrow-waisted and long; one Maggini copy, also slightly oversized, with double purfling extending into a fleur de lis pattern around the button; one that was only a few years old, with thick red varnish, made by a woman in the Southwest; one English, with an obvious button graft; another Scottish; a modern Italian . . . Each in its way suited her differently, and failed to suit her. He watched from his seat in the corner of the room, fingers on his forehead, and tried to understand what worked and what didn't. The room felt permeated with smells of her hair and skin, and of violins—linseed oil, spruce, Sacconi and rosin—enough so he felt on the verge of tasting each. When she was able to relax into the bow strokes and become one with whatever instrument she was playing, all the air in the room seemed to be drawn into the vibration, string noise and bow noise vanishing, likewise any evidence of a material world—strings, wood, any sense of time passing—so he was aware only of the fluctuations of his inner-ear in correlation with some feeling just below the surface of her playing that kept slipping aside as words attached to it—*flight, dream, song, love* . . . But what allowed her most consistently to break through and stay there, he couldn't quantify. One violin bottomed out too easily, another seemed too weak in the mid-range, another had the sweetest e-string sound of the lot but not enough clarity on the low end.

"OK, so a little Violin 101," he'd told her on the ride over. "In terms of formal valuation anyway, the last thing to consider is sound. I know that seems ridiculous, crazy even, but it's true. Because sound is actually the most subjective, unmeasurable piece of the equation. For valuation. If you think you sound better on a certain Holy Grail instrument, then you probably will. You adjust your playing or just convince yourself to overcome whatever the shortcomings are. It's been proven over and over. Someone else, on the other hand, without the same feeling or expectation or with a different playing style or whatever, might make the same violin sound great, or like nothing. So it's too subjective. Mostly. So we look at other factors. Varnish, proportion, quality of the wood, carving, purfling, arching. All stuff you can measure quantitatively, and which, weirdly enough, does sort of dictate sound in the end. So we never get away from sound, really, but we never talk about it either. With regard to value."

All of this had been by way of cautioning her on how to talk to the owner—how violin dealers could trick you into believing one instrument was essential and another wasn't. "Any player," he said, "is more or less at the dealer's mercy, because what you care about is this totally subjective thing, right? Sound. It's all you know and care about. It's your whole, like, reason for being. And the shop owner knows this. And knows that you don't know much about violin construction or valuation. Which makes you totally vulnerable. Because . . . whatever. It's all about trust." He'd wanted to explain further, to help buffer her and serve as an ally in keeping things fair and above-board, but sensed that his words were somehow not getting through. How could she believe him that she was at anyone's mercy where sound was concerned?

Now, watching her—her bare arms and shoulders, the strap of her plaid print dress under the shoulder-rest on one side, the violin nestled at her jaw, black hair tossed back, and then the moment as the bow sank and found its groove, gravity weighting her arm through the stroke into sound vibration . . . all objectivity and reason went out the window for him too. He wondered if he knew anything at all; if he'd told her anything like the truth.

"This one's darkest," he said. "Tonally."

"The French one?"

"I like it."

"Me too!"

"But you're fighting it on the fast passages."

She lifted it. "I could adjust." Flicked the strings and flew into a passage of spiccato bowing and stopped. "Or not. I don't know. I don't know!" She set it down again and picked up the consignment instrument.

"Not so much."

She bent to tune, peghead pressed to one side of a knee.

"Not that one," he said. And when he noticed her looking questioningly at him, not having heard, he repeated himself, shaking his head. "Not that one."

"Agreed." She set it back on the table. "So what now?"

The tasting had wound to an end without her coming to any sort of conclusion. On one end of the table were two of the instruments she'd tried initially, and two from later in the session, each imperfect for her, yet each indisputably better than her own violin. At the other end, not quite a dozen violins on their sides: rejected. He tilted his head and pretended to think it through, studying the violins she'd ruled out, plucking the g-string of one, lifting the scroll of another, but knowing there was nothing more to be said. The best violin for her was not in this room. "Keep trying, I guess? I mean, you learned what you came here to find out and what you probably already knew anyway, which is that you need something different. A better violin. But . . . here. Play this one a second." Without thinking, he reached and chose the violin that had seemed to him most interesting at a glance—unusual or unclassifiable—one she'd put aside with a sour face after a single scale and arpeggio. No label, though the shop owner had assured them it was probably mid-century English. "Might warm up, I don't know," he said. "Try. All I can tell you is that whoever made this knew what they were doing. The corners, the scroll and arching—it's for real. Very Strad-like. It's 'of a piece,' as my dad would say."

"Yes, but it doesn't sound like anything. No soul."

"Agreed. But maybe it needs time. He said it hadn't been played in years. Maybe we need to mess with the soundpost."

When the shop owner returned, Paul understood from his expression that he'd instantly taken their measure: having chosen four favorites they were now backtracking through other violins because none of the four bests stood out sufficiently to close a deal. But moments later, when she mentioned his father, mispronouncing the last name and explaining again how Paul was not her boyfriend, husband, buyer, relative of any kind, only a friend—roommate actually, but not like that—here to listen and evaluate on the basis of his *expertise*, the look changed again. "Denis LeFault," the owner said, getting the name right. "I thought you seemed somehow familiar. I know your father well. Exquisite work. You should have said something! And he's still out there on the island? Where was it again?" The eyes were impossible to read, each going slightly in a different direction and magnified behind dusty lenses, green or brown (even the color was hard to judge), inviting, fond, calculating, amorous, revealing nothing. "In fact ..." He stood straighter, finger to his bent lips as if hushing them. "In fact, if I'm remembering right and it's not out on approval, I do have one of his instruments—took it on trade a while back. Somewhat beyond the range you quoted," here he winked in Paul's direction, "but let me just see. If you don't mind? And h-h-how is your father doing, Paul?"

"So far as I know—"

"Still trying to burn down his shop cooking his own batches of varnish? Hang on one little second while I check. Such a fine, fine builder. Both he and Karl Marcowicz. Worked for us, years ago, must have been the early '80s. Not that you'd remember. The first time I saw one of his instruments . . . outstanding. I said so even then."

The violin he returned with was not one Paul remembered, though the work was clearly his father's. He touched one shoulder, an f-hole, turned it to see the back, and spun it again when he saw, for the first time, like being let in on a joke: how knowingly and exactingly the front plate was constructed in the likeness of a human face. As his father had said, years ago. Either because of his personal connection with it—with the days and hours of its construction—or because of some special care his father had taken with the carving, he didn't know, but this violin more than any of the other twenty or so he'd seen and touched that afternoon, wore a human face. Made him want to laugh, though the face in the violin was anything but humorous. Sad mainly. Also dignified. Withdrawn or withdrawing. And looking from the instrument—dark, rust brown finish, slab cut back with antiquing in its midsection like a froth of caramel and melted butter, wearily elegant points, and Guarneri-patterned shoulders—and back again to May, he knew that if he was asked to choose between them, her face or the one in the violin, to say which was more beautiful, he'd pick hers: less perfect, but more magnetizing because of its imperfections and because its hold on beauty wouldn't last, unlike this violin's. "I don't remember it," he said. "But I kind of remember when he was using that pigment in his finish and that sort of Kreisler pattern. Maybe early middle school for me, so like ten-eleven years ago? Can that be right?"

"Smart kid. It's exactly that old. You have an eye."

There it was again. The thing his father had told him occasionally and which he knew to be true but still didn't have a good response for—only stopless, blushing pride and pleasure in himself for the centuries of violin knowledge that seemed to have come to him through the air or maybe genetically, and confused longing for more praise and approval, all of which he needed somehow to force back under a cover of not-caring, or else risk giving away too much of himself and looking a fool. No, *being* a fool. "I don't know." *Wǒ bù zhīdào.*

"Your dad's violins are as handsome and easy on the eye as they are on the ear and this one, if I remember right . . . Well, I'll leave you to it. See what you think. I said it was out of your price range, but . . . I always tell folks, hey, what you can't buy won't hurt you. Right?"

In the seconds before her bow went across the strings, he already knew—as if invisible forces had aligned around her, planes of energy converging at her bent wrist and forearm determining the outcome in advance, so the moment she drew a downward bowstroke, the sound felt to him as if it were already there. As if it had always been there and the movement of her arm was only causing them both to remember. With that, all other awareness of the world vanished. The hair from the back of his neck to the top of his scalp tingled and stood forward, and his throat tightened . . . No. Because it could be done, because he'd heard it done often enough, he tried analyzing his experience of the sound as quantitatively as he could, like a listing of ingredients, separating and describing for himself the tonal properties, fundamental and overtone, warm and cold, sweet and bracing, strong, deep, thin—tried to understand how each pitch seemed comprised of weight and light simultaneously in its center and not one fundamental but layers within layers of fundamental which opened further the longer she played and adjusted her playing to get more from the instrument. "Oh," she was saying now. "Wow. Paul. Why . . ."

She went across all the strings for the opening double-stops of Bach's First Partita and continued—the only piece she played in full, start to finish all afternoon. As she played, he leaned forward in his seat, drumming his fingers at his temples and watching his feet on the carpet to keep from feeling too much: the familiar scuffs on the toes of his shoes from days walking to campus, catching buses, kicking into curbs, aimless stupid afternoons missing classes, a black smudge across one from running over his foot with the tire of his bike the other day walking it up the front steps, in a rush because it had begun to rain and he was hungry, one sole beginning to delaminate at the toe . . . that day he remembered as well, rain and sunshine, and a lucky five dollar bill on the sidewalk with which he'd bought a double latte and biscotti he'd ended up giving away to a friend. What did any of this matter? Still, for moments at a time all of it looked to be unified, connecting through some meaning or pattern also expressed in the music, a form of hieroglyphics not unlike the pages of Chinese writing in his own hand now mostly unreadable to him because of the instant short-term memory drop, a message to be read backwards toward an essential meaning leading him—

"This. Oh my god, I think I'm going to cry. Or maybe laugh. Am I crying? What the hell! Paul. This . . ." She flipped the violin around and held it at arm's length to look again. "This is how I imagine sounding in my dreams. Jesus, I could play all day and never get tired. Seriously. It's perfect. So what do we do now. I'm ruined!" Here she did laugh. "Can we steal it? Seriously, did you come here with me today specifically just to destroy the entire rest of my life?"

"There's other violins in the world." What else was he supposed to say.

—

Growing up, he hardly touched a woodworking tool. For one thing there was his father's sovereignty. No sense competing against a man whose trade had so fully defined him and that he in turn had helped to define, and in which he'd spent his entire adult life in a state of complete and selfless absorption. The notion of comparison or competition was irrelevant. His father had already won. He'd pre-won. He had always and would always have pre-won. And anyway, he wouldn't have consented to competition, if challenged in the first place. *You want to build?* he'd say. Too happy, too willing to share. Paul knew. *We'll start with scraping some ribs. Let's go!*

There was more to what kept him out. Still he hadn't found the right words for it. Only a shrug, when customers of his father used to ask about his plans and whether he might someday try his hand, take over the business. *Sure. Doubtful. I don't know.* At first, he felt he was saving the option. Why, or what he was saving it *for*, he couldn't have said. He'd seen what his father had gotten for his sovereignty and dedication: a room full of molds, models and tools, rare violin books full of color plates, mentions in *The Strad* magazine, medals and certificates. A daily activity to engross him without any break, ever. A clientele that hung on his words and trusted him in all matters violin-related, treated him with the deference of a sage or guru, but without understanding what he did and without fairly compensating him. Fingers that reported back to him in ways he could neither describe or calibrate, yielding knowledge of how a piece of wood was going to respond under pressure. Orders that came all at once or not at all.

When he was younger, he'd spend afternoons and slow times on weekends in the shop. He learned the names of tools and processes and occasionally helped his father to select wood blanks for a new instrument; in retrospect, he supposed his father could only have been humoring him. Once, when he was nine, he surprised them both with an ability to identify differences between the scrolls and corners of various old Italian makers in one of the books of color plates his father kept in the workshop. "That one's a Strad. And that's a Guarneri. Right? The shape of this, whatever it's called. And this is a Maggini," he flipped more pages and kept going, "Strad . . ." How he knew, he couldn't say—the names were already familiar, he'd been seeing and hearing them for as long as he could remember. The shape to go with each seemed only a natural, logical extension, and an easier way to tell one thing from another.

"Isn't that interesting. You figured that out all on your own? Really? Hey, look at me. You're cheating. You read the chapter titles?" And when Paul shook his head no, his father asked, "What's this one, then?"

"Amati."

"Excellent, that's excellent. Great eye. And this? And this?"

His father flipped randomly to a page in another book, the paper scuffed and dented with ghosts of his own handwriting—letters, numbers, lines transferred through tracing paper; a brown half-ring of varnish or spilled blacking floated to one side of the image like a cookie with a bite out of it. The finish of the violin in the picture, blown open in the middle, pigmentation darkest at the edges, reminded Paul of the uneven film of suds and color left in his parents' beer glasses after dinner.

"Look here. No guesses?"

"I don't know."

His father tapped two fingers on the page and traced the outline of the c-bout. He drew in his lips and puffed air through them in a way that normally indicated amusement but here seemed to mean something else, while his fingers continued moving up and down, as if the violin's shape corresponded with some unspoken longing or mystery. "Late Guarneri. Spent a lot of time with this one, as you can see." He ended by brushing his fingers along the spilled varnish. "I don't know. Fairly atypical for the rest of his work, right? You might say he was slipping a little in his old age. Dipping into the sauce or rushing to get the orders out? Messing up his blocks? Still, so uniquely beautiful. It's a paradox. What do you think? Would we let an instrument go out of the shop looking like that?"

Being included in his father's attention to violins this way was like standing under one of the high-powered lights by his workbench and seeing all the grains in your fingernail and the bits of dead skin on the surface of every wrinkle in the back of your hand. Such clarity it was a form of erasure. If he said any more, he'd fail them both. The look on his father's face now too was so much the same as when he first examined an instrument he'd recently finished, lifted at arm's length: he'd angle his chin to one side and the other, nodding, grunting, spinning the instrument back to front, front to back, nodding some more—*not bad, not bad*—measuring against some internal standard, until it dawned on him. The imperfection. The flaw or flaws. Whatever inscrutable details or misbegotten choices among all the better details and choices caused the final product to fall short of some ideal.

It was all Paul could do to remember to keep breathing.

"I don't know."

"It's OK. I was actually trying to trick you. Never mind. Not fair. I'm impressed though! A real visual sense. I wonder where you came by that!"

The next several days after this, his father was busy varnishing new instruments and, between coats, finally getting serious about an overdue restoration job on an old violin that had been mostly destroyed in a house fire. Paul watched from the leather chair by the window and tried not to interrupt with questions or suggestions. "Please," his father would say. "Please, not today." The restoration job was a torment for him, not only because of the painstaking work of building the plates back, splinter by splinter, but because something about agreeing to take it on put him at odds with a dealer in the city. "Double for nothing," he explained. "Oldest trick in the business. You total the instrument, scam the insurance and sell the customer a new violin with the claim money. Later, whenever you feel like it, when no one's looking, you fix the so-called totaled violin. Write some papers so no one's the wiser, and off it goes. It'd be like," here he paused, hands on his hips, "say I owned a toy store and I took one of your Transformers, broke it—well, maybe I don't break it, but it gets broken somehow—and then I tell someone to pay you to buy another one from me, top dollar, by swearing that the first one can't ever be fixed, and . . . Never mind." This made no sense to Paul. "No," his father said, bending again to his work, "of course not. Because as soon as anyone decided it was a good idea, charging crazy money for old Italian violins, as soon as that happened, it became the most corrupt business in the world. It doesn't make sense." And before and after dinner, more of the same, complaining to his mother: "Can you even imagine? All she wanted was her Obici back."

Still, for weeks afterward, hoping his father might remember—*a visual sense! I wonder where you came by that!*—he went around mumbling the names of builders, hoping his father would overhear. *Obici, del Gesù Guarneri, Tononi, Bergonzi, Stradivarius.* A kind of incantation . . . recitation to invite attention, to get his father to lift his eyes like that again, full of wonder, really seeing him. But this never happened. Eventually, he stopped waiting. Let the few little projects he'd begun—a clumsy top of wide-grained spruce; a neck blank of flawed wood nicked and scarred around with rasp marks; a handle for his own knife—gather dust, kicked aside in a box under the bench. Who had spurned or forgotten whom he couldn't say, but long after the visits stopped and other afterschool activities took up his time—chess club, swimming, track—the cedar-chip walk between the house and his father's workshop felt raw to him: a nightmare tightrope walk past a chasm, a place not to let your eyes linger.

—

Back at home, he unstrung May's old violin, slid tail gut from endpin and removed the endpin. Gingerly, cradling it in one hand at the c-bout, he lifted the violin so it was inches from the light over the kitchen table, closed an eye and looked in though the endpin hole like seeing into a spyglass. "Yeah," he said

after a moment, and stood back, holding it to the light for her. "Have a look."
He felt her breath on his wrist. Imagined the touch of her eyelashes, blinking,
brushing the violin's ribs. "We always called this candling. I don't know if it's the
official term for it or whatever. But that's where . . ."

"What am I looking for?"

"Here." He lowered the violin to the table, pushing aside receipts, a pot-
holder, newspaper sections folded in quarters, a dirty napkin and a spoon. "So
wherever you see light seeping in through the top plate, so it looks like orange
candlelight in those gouge or scraper marks you probably noticed, right about
here? And wherever it's thinnest, like it's blushing—especially here and here
around the upper bouts? That's all showing you the graduation of the carving
on the top plate—where it's thinnest you see light, where it's thicker, no light
gets through. And what you notice, actually, is it's mostly just graded pretty
thick on that top plate. Dark, everywhere. Like, there's no light at all here,"
he outlined areas around the f-holes. "Not that *light* equals *tone*, exactly, or thin
equals good, but if it's too thick in these areas especially, where the plates need
to move the most and sound really gets amplified then you have kind of a thin,
weak response like . . ."

"Wow. Can I see again?"

"Careful."

She raised the violin to the light and peered in through the endpin hole. Un-
watched and watching her, he felt the tension build in his fingers and throat
again, a longing just to lose himself in smelling and touching her—trace the
outline of her wrists and forearms, the delicate fold of skin where her upper
arm and shoulder joined, the crescent outline of her shoulder muscles. She
rocked the violin to one side and he shifted closer to her, smelling her hair and
perfume, sweat and whiffs of garlic from the late lunch they'd stopped for on
the way back—burgers and onion rings, her treat, at her favorite Phinney Ridge
diner. He was back there again in the red-upholstered booth, enclosed by smells
of milk and fryer oil as she probed him with more and more violin-related
questions. *But eighteen thousand dollars! Paul, how am I supposed to come up with eighteen
thousand dollars! I have, like, eighteen dollars in savings. Do you have any idea? Your dad must
be a freaking genius*—the refrain of the meal, her excitement from having played

his father's violin ebbing as food vanished and whatever had been set loose in her from playing retreated to the more familiar quizzical, skeptical boundaries demarcating her personality.

"Careful," he repeated, touching her arm. "Hey. May? Keep it flat like I said. I have no idea how tight that soundpost fits and if it falls over, we don't have anything like a soundpost setter here so . . . In fact, we should end this little demonstration . . ."

"The sides are totally glowing though!"

"The ribs. Yes, they would do that. They're always super thin, or should be, like a millimeter, but that's not the issue. Tone comes from the top and bottom plates. Not the ribs."

"Why?"

He shrugged, though she wasn't looking away yet to see it. "Surface area, I guess? The top acts like a speaker cone. The ribs, not so much." Still, these questions he couldn't help himself from answering in too much detail. And then questions to follow the questions. It was how he'd gotten to this point, agreeing to strip down her violin so she could look inside.

"It'd be awesome to have a room like this though, wouldn't it? With those sort of stripes of light coming in along the sides? Like a space ship." Again she tipped the violin sideways, stumbling forward slightly and extending a hand toward the table top. "Like *Serenity*."

"May? Really, seriously. If that soundpost falls . . ."

"OK, OK, the soundpost, whatever."

A fallen soundpost would expose him for this bit of deceit he was in the midst of putting over on her. He couldn't set a post, even with the tool for it—had never as much as tried, though it was among the most basic and necessary tasks of violin setup and maintenance; worse, it would ruin days of playing for her until she could get to a violin shop, canceling any romantic potential between them as well. "The French word for it is actually the same word for *soul*, if that gives you any idea. *L'âme*. It's just a cheap piece of wood, really—a plain old spruce dowel, that's it—stuck between the plates at exactly the right spot and held up by the pressure of the top and back plates, and yet without it your violin will sound like nothing at all. Like, seriously nothing. Like a transistor radio, and your top . . . well not this top. But a top with less meat to it? It'd collapse from the pressure. Where the soundpost sits and how well it fits, it actually does more for your violin's sound than just about anything else." He said this all between shallow breaths as he went about re-inserting the endpin, sliding the tailgut back into its slot and the string tails through their grooves in the tailpiece. Tasks he'd witnessed his father doing dozens of times but had only infrequently tried on his own. Lastly, in silence, he inserted the bridge under the slack strings, stood it up, and wound some tension into the outer strings to hold it in place. A few adjustments to the bridge placement, more tension through the strings, and he was able to register the hammering of his heartbeats through his solar plexus. The queasy tunneling of his vision. Sweat bloomed under his arms and at his hairline. A few more deep breaths and he handed the violin to her. "You finish," he said. "Tune up."

"Cool! You're really good with this stuff, Paul. Thank you."

He kept his eyes from hers. His father, if he were here, would be laughing in disbelief or disgust, hands on his hips or flung up suddenly around the top of his head. *You had the nerve to do what? Just because you're foolish and willing to take a risk that doesn't end in total disaster does NOT make you good. Jesus. Dumb luck.* But the plates were so thick, he'd counter. That soundpost wasn't going anywhere . . .

"Why not do more with it? Like, work-wise. I mean, the other day, if you hadn't started talking to me, I wouldn't have even known. Why not start your own shop or something? You totally could."

He snorted. "I totally could not. Not even close." Still, he couldn't resist adding more. "These," he said, pointing to the cuts in the f-holes, as he took the violin back from her, "Like I showed you the other day. See? They actually indicate where the bridge feet are supposed to be aligned. They're not just for decoration. So if your bridge ever gets knocked down or pushed out of place like before . . ." He gripped the bridge feet on both sides between his thumbs and fingers and slid until they lined up with the inner cuts. "That's it." He set the violin on the table. "That's how you put it back in place. Tune again, and you're good."

In his mind's eye, as he felt a shift and she turned toward him rather than the violin, swaying closer, her feet coming between his so his arms could go around her, he still pictured the red-orange light inside her violin. The dumb luck and dumb risk of having gotten her to this point, believing he knew so much more than he did. *Wŏ bù zhīdào. Wŏ dō bù zhīdào.* As if the picture of her violin's interior correlated with some irregular hollowness caught between them now—some poorly graduated, overbuilt aspect of the way in which she would hereafter have to think of him and see him—he kept returning to it: the dark floor of the bottom plate, the glowing gouge marks and sideways stripes of firelight coming in, bass bar like a beam overhead, dirt and dust, a puff of lint up beside the neck block, the soundpost standing to the side like a column in a dream . . . until her mouth found his, slid lips over and under his, tongue touching the corner of his mouth, creamy, dispelling all images and leaving him with no awareness other than his desire for her.

"Hey," she said after a moment, tipping back in his arms. "I have a thing tonight, dinner, but . . ."

He nodded. "We should stop."

"OK." Now she was laughing. "I was going to say . . ."

"What?"

"Whatever. I like you though. You're . . ."

A fraud, a poser? From one perspective, his pretentions to knowledge were nothing. A little posturing and glibness. From another (his father's, his own) they were falsifications of the most soul-damning kind.

"I'll have to think. Get the right word. I want to say gentle, but that's not it. A gentleman? Prince Charming!" She giggled. "Am I right? Have I got you exactly?" For an answer he slid his hands from her waist up to her ribs, lifting her closer. Her arms rose around his neck as she crushed herself to him again, mouth enveloping his, hair catching in the stubble on his cheeks. The moment was now, or very soon anyway, if he wanted to set the record straight, explain. Say that he didn't know the first goddamned thing, actually; that he'd fooled her to get them to exactly where they were. He should do so now, before this went any further.

—

One afternoon in the boat on Bishop's Pond, his mother asked if he thought she was an ascetic, a term she first had to explain—he was in middle school at the time. By the nature and tone of the explanation, he felt invited to confirm that, no, in fact, she was not. Not an ascetic. She loved her walks in the woods and along the beach, her drink before and after dinner, her weaving, singing, collections of beach rocks in jars of water on the windowsill, occasional Sunday nights at the symphony. Her plants and garden. Earthly, sensual pleasures. She was anything but an ascetic. They'd been drifting in a patch of calm, through tree shadows close to the shore. He watched her hand on the gunwale, stroking up and back again along the refinished wood before dropping over the side, underwater, the shape of her hand so familiar because it so exactly matched his own, though more fully formed, older—same nails, same taper, same thickness of muscles at the base of the thumb. *What other earthly pleasures*, he wondered and leaned hard into his next oar-strokes as if to pull them away from the thought— her hand caressing the gunwale and dipping underwater—to reset the moment and undo her question's effect on his mind.

"More than forgoing earthly pleasures," she continued, "actually . . . maybe I'm overemphasizing that aspect of it. An ascetic is a person who cuts themselves off in order to clarify perception. To really see. Someone who forgoes pleasure relating to the senses in order to be better tuned in with . . ." She waved a hand. "Everything. Minus all the noise. Like a mental cleansing. Sensory fasting."

"Sounds boring."

"Boring! Anything but. It's fascinating. Fascina*ted*, maybe more like."

He watched the water eddy and flatten in whorls behind them where his strokes had broken the surface. "What? Is this something Dad's asking about?"

"Denis is such a natural ascetic himself it would never occur to him to talk about it, much less ask."

He had no response to this except to stroke again and feel the tension through his wrists and forearms, the slight tug as the oars came up and released, and again as they went underwater. The glug-glug of water rushing under them and the eddies of different smells and shifting temperatures along the water's surface—not quite spring, not yet summer.

"That would be like asking . . . a bird about wind." She shook her head. "A snowman about ice crystals."

"A maggot about dead flesh."

"Well . . ." She laughed. "But what about you?"

She held a hand over her eyes like a visor, in the shadow of which he was able to make out individual flecks of color through the irises—gold, green, gray. *A violin is a face*, he remembered his father telling him once, years ago, or maybe it was more recently. Maybe last spring. *Think about it. Eyebrows outlining the shoulders. Mouth like a bridge. Right? It's constructed, somewhat anyway, according to the same geometrical principles by which we know a face is beautiful—the golden mean—and therefore it is, actually, just another reconfiguration of a perfectly beautiful, perfectly perfect . . .* here he'd changed his voice to indicate some self-mocking awareness of his overseriousness . . . *perfectly noble human face.* But Paul hadn't wanted to think about it any further because the only face he might have imagined, in connection with such a principle, was his mother's. A thought as aberrant as it was impossibly absorbing.

"What about me, what?"

"I dunno." She said it in a tone to mock him. Mulish and indifferent. A tone to draw him out by teasing, he knew. "Come on! Anything at all. What makes you tick? What's the world like for you these days? Speak!"

He rowed harder for the middle of the pond. This had to be something his father had put her up to. *Find out what the boy's doing and what he wants. I'm worried.* Or was it something else going on between her and his father and manifesting as strange, new attention to him and questions about asceticism? He couldn't be sure. Was she trying to distract herself, or really concerned? Guilty maybe, for having let him slip from them as far as he had recently? Too many games after school. Too easy to hack past their rudimentary sense of parental controls on the internet in order to see whatever he wanted, game with whomever he wanted.

"Boring." He shrugged. "Homework, eat, sleep, back to school."

She sighed and looked past him intently at something on the shore until he turned to see what it was.

"What?"

"Thought I saw something. Heron." She dipped her fingers and flicked water at him. "What else?"

"What else what?"

She shook her head.

"I don't know Ma. I'm not like you guys, always with your serious plans for everything. Your violins all day, every day. I'm pretty much just a normal kid. Pretty much just a normal nobody at school."

"I doubt that very much. In fact, I completely doubt it."

Now he needed his best poker face—maybe she'd seen the file of images on his computer labeled *tutorial*; maybe the whole conversation had been an elaborate ruse to draw him to confess in accordance with some very post-Catholic scrupulousness which required fully voluntary admission.

"OK, I'm pretty good on the ropes and pegboard at gym. Actually, I set a school record the other day for time on the pegboard." This was a lie. He hadn't even tied the record, though for a confusing, thrilling few seconds, dropping to the ground and scrubbing his sore hands against his thighs as Coach Alban, before realizing he'd misread his ancient stopwatch by a full revolution, punched a fist in the air and declared him the fastest climber in school history, he sincerely thought that he had. "And I can do more sit-ups than anyone in the grade." This was not a lie, though he was pretty sure he'd already told her over dinner.

She leaned on her elbows and tilted her face toward the sun before lying back fully in the boat. "This is good, though, isn't it. This is what we came for, right? A little sun on our skin. Tell me there's anything better. Which is why, of course, we choose to live in one of the rainiest parts of the world. Hard to believe . . ." She shook her head. "Once upon a time, I could not have imagined a life for myself outside the church. Well, barely. When I was your age . . . maybe a little older." She smiled at this thought but didn't open her eyes, the prominence of her front teeth visible in outline under her lip. *Parental failure to prioritize orthodontia for me*, he knew, from another of her many set-piece recountings of her early life in religious severity. *Call me vain. I'll bear the label and the reminder of neglect proudly.* "Never mind. Let's just float to wherever."

All these years later, still he remembered that afternoon, like it was a frozen centerpoint in time marking *before* and *after*. What was divided from what, he couldn't say. Just another afternoon on the pond with his mother. He saw the reflective shards of sun on the water's surface and heard the water stuttering under them as he leaned forward and back, rowing—the *plonk* of his oars sinking through pond scum, weeds, light flashing on mica silt—again sunlight stinging in his eyes and transforming the surface of the water, and he remembered his mother's easy, confiding tone, her arms draped along the sides of the boat. *A lost last day from childhood*, the caption under the picture might read. *Somewhere back there still, an ordinary day to get back to . . .*

—

When it dawned on him that his time at home and on the island had a real end in sight—that in future years he might look back fondly on these hours after school listening to music or watching the wet spruce boughs move against the window outside, his parents' footsteps ringing in the beams overhead, NPR playing by his mom's loom and the arrhythmic thunk of her feet on the treadle; certainly, his summers on the Sound helping their part-time fishermen neighbor, Mel Hipson, with his annual take of Coho and Chinook, the crabs or iced fresh slabs of salmon he'd bring home to grill or to freeze, some his own catch, some from Mel to be traded to his mother for vocal lessons—recognizing all of this as *ending soon*, he first misunderstood the feelings of relief and clarity lifting in him like the horizon opening out at dawn as he ran along the beach, sneakers peeling away wet curls of sand; misattributed those feelings to having at last settled the questions of who he was and what he should do with his life. Forward was all that mattered. Move out, go to college in Seattle or Bellingham. He'd earned awards in Spanish, and another for a culminating project researching Tlingit phonemes his senior year of high school. Languages. He'd study languages.

His two years of intensive Chinese language study had ended the final weeks of spring quarter the previous year, not for want of interest or ability, but due to a lack of vision. What would he do with a degree in Chinese language? Of course, he knew some of the options—politics, diplomacy, business; interpreter, educator—he just couldn't see himself in any of these roles. More importantly, starting into the study of Chinese he'd somehow missed the fact that eventually he'd have to go to China. Live there or at least visit for extended periods of time. No, not *missed*. He'd known, but failed to register or envision the inevitability.

He'd been too absorbed with the brush marks on the page, the direction for each pen line, the sounds and tones, endless vocabulary, half-backwards grammar. As classmates and acquaintances from other drill sections disappeared for summers and quarters of study in China, he felt himself stranded, marked, and staring into an abyss—another nightmare tightrope walk over a chasm. He wouldn't go to China. He could never go. He knew this about himself. Why, was less clear, just . . . he wouldn't.

A month or two after dodging his second-year final oral exam, "postponing" what he knew would be a humiliation beyond the scale of anything he'd experienced in his academic life to that point—rapid-fire conversational Chinese incorporating idiomatic, formal, and informal constructs that could only have become second nature by travel abroad, time immersed in the language—coming out of the produce section at the Haggen's Market he was surprised by a familiar female voice addressing him with his adopted Chinese name, Shur Wei. For a confused moment, he didn't deduce that he was the one addressed until he looked twice, saw her and grasped the situation: Lin Xiǎojiě, his native-speaking language coach from second-year Chinese. She cuffed him on the arm and backed him into an end-cap display of chips and salsas, berating him in a mixture of Chinese and English, *pig face, brainless, méi yǒu nǎozi*, laughing, so at first he thought it might all be a joke, and then asking him why—"Why! Why! Shur Wei, I not think you hate Chinese so much! What do you do now? You lazy no-good! You not even *try*, Shur Wei! You never even care!"—her eyes brimming with tears, hands in fists on her hips. There was something she'd done for him toward the end, he remembered—a favor to facilitate his exit, skipping that final oral, taking a "W" rather than a failing grade, vouching for him on a signed form—something he'd considered insignificant at the time, a bureaucratic formality, and which he now had to realize had been anything but. Had been, in fact, entirely personal for her—a betrayal and failure to meet magnanimity with respect, insult to her culture, to her, and a reminder of the isolation she had so often described for them in class, the isolation of being Chinese in a west coast town of drunken *Wàiguórén, Měiguórén*, children (foreigners, Americans); reminder too, to him, of how that very isolation, her sweater sets and chapped lips and loneliness, bobbed hair, ferocious tenacity drilling them day after day, how all of this had probably lain somewhere close to the root of his inability to go to China in the first place: he knew he could not face what she faced every day, mixing up words (*concubine* for *cucumber*), alone and homesick, hungry for foods she couldn't find. He wished he could explain, but as quickly as she'd descended on him, she fled. "Lin Xiǎojiě!" he called after her, but he knew better—knew she'd never accept an apology. Apology wasn't the point. Yelling was the point. Yelling and then leaving him with his ears ringing and the stupid, happy, white-boy smile he'd presented her at first sight, hearing his Chinese name in the aisle of the Haggen's, as the edges of his vision blurred and stung with feeling. That was the point.

His most recent idea was to cobble together something interdisciplinary at the progressive college on campus, using a few of the literature and philosophy credits he'd aced earlier on: study of language as a form of music and a logical system with no meaning attached. This was harder to petition for on a piece of paper describing and outlining an academic objective and interdisciplinary curriculum, but he had until the end of fall term to submit a first draft. He knew some of the teachers. They were ready for something eccentric from him. Expecting and welcoming it, even. So a year more, maybe two, and he'd be done. Five—six years total. Not a complete and utter failure.

Currently, he had papers to write for his linguistics and poetry of surrealism classes. But staring at the corkboard of images from his childhood hanging by his desk—his parents at the shore closest to their house; a shot at sea; the house from years ago, before his dad relocated all violin operations to the studio, covered in gray clapboard, cedar shakes and without his mother's sun porch/greenhouse—eyes cycling from image to image and around again, falling back to scan the same three lines of text in his lap, the same fragment of poetry, he found it impossible to think or to get anything done. *May, May, May.* He was, stuck and wanted to get up, pace the room again, or find an action, anything to do with his hands. More pushups. A sketch. Go for a swim. How long had they stood necking in the kitchen? Possibly no more than ten minutes. Maybe twenty. Long enough for time to play tricks, the heat of confluent longing spinning them across the room and back again to a doorway where he leaned under the weight and wetness of her mouth. What was so different about kissing her?

Everything. Nothing he could pinpoint. *Oh my god. I'm late now. You made me late!* she said. *What are we doing?* But then she didn't stop or leave, only opened herself further . . . until finally, eyes on herself in the hallway mirror as she applied lip gloss—no goodbye—the front door closing with a decisive snick, she rushed out and down the porch stairs.

He tried writing some of what he felt on the back of an envelope but then scratched it out. *Must have . . . lost my . . .* Made his habitual scroll shaped doodle above that, crumpled and tossed it at the garbage. He needed to walk. But he couldn't. Both papers were due Monday and failure at either would force more reckoning about the entire direction of his life.

Downstairs he fixed a plate of scrambled eggs and tortillas with cheese and someone's salsa orphaned in the bottom shelf of the fridge door for weeks now, or months—untouched and half full, crusted tomato juice flaking from its inner rim as he unscrewed the lid and sniffed. Still good. Through their leanest years of too few orders and underbid repair jobs, he'd learned from his parents a pragmatic skepticism of all fears food-related—expiration dates, mold spots, the bruised and browning ends of fruits and vegetables. If it looked and smelled mostly edible, you could eat it. Though he'd hated them for this, growing up, he now found himself championing their ways to friends and house-mates— salvaging, scavenging, rescuing—*Perfectly good. Don't throw that out! Such a waste . . .* In return for which they often called him, *Our diner of last resort. Save it for Paul, he'll eat anything!*

He watched himself in the darkened, rain-streaked windows over the sink and by the table, coming and going, grating cheese, flipping tortillas on the burner, his reflection flickering like flames in the orange inside light. The scarf from his mom's loom, fringeless and black, and the navy blue sweatshirt, both of which he always wore for late nights of paper writing—something about the comforting plush of inner lining beyond the shredding cuffs, and the weight of that scarf around his neck. He was almost superstitious about this. The hair he had from his father—black, with a side-parted swoop like a bird's wing. And the jaw. *Like that guy from the new Battlestar . . . Adama, but more nerdy. Thicker glasses,* people might say, meeting him. True enough. Always clenching his teeth, talking through his jaw. The rest—eyes, mouth, nose, shoulders—more like his mother or someone further back on her side. Nordic or Celtic. It wasn't bad, he figured—a set of features that was mostly appealing and proportioned, neutral enough so he never had to think much about it or worry. *Normal*, he might have said at another time in his life. *Just kind of regular*, except for the deceit and failure and the lack of direction, occasional panic and everything else screwing him up inside. How long before she figured out all of that about him?

He ate his eggs and the sour, burning salsa. Tore off chunks of tortilla to mop his plate and shifted in his seat not to see himself in the window reflections, returning again and again to that name—*May, May*—just under the surface of all his thoughts, alongside the Bach partita she'd played, those opening chords falling through his memory and raking the feeling deeper into him.

—

For a time—ninth grade, some of tenth—he'd lost himself in music. Listening, playing along to songs on the stereo, he spent hours in the downstairs rocker, headphones clamped to his head. Clancy Brothers, Beatles, Leadbelly, Emmylou, Zappa, Patsy, Aretha, Hank, Linda Ronstadt, Hoyt Axton . . . everything in their sizable collection of music spanning the decades. The few instruments around the house not violin-related—a battered rosewood parlor guitar with one tuner that barely turned, a Stella tenor banjo, his mother's upright piano—were alluring and fascinating to him for their sounds, shapes, smells, but most of all for their promise of something beyond or inside the music . . . and yet magnetizing only up to the point at which his mother suggested lessons: "You like that style? You want to learn how they do that—those kind of Hawaiian chord voicings like what you're trying there? We could get you lessons. You know Rick, Denis's . . . your dad's friend from over on Vashon, he could show you next time he's visiting. Or Ed! Ed totally knows that idiom. You remember Ed, right? He's a beast on the slack key." Until finally he caved: guitar lessons with the local music store instructor, a semi-retired session guy and songwriter from Austin. And as soon as he'd caved, he knew he was done. Or, on his way to being done. Not that he didn't enjoy seeing those familiar sounds given names in the clusterings of notes comprising chord shapes—*C7, G7, Dm, Gm7*—fingers stretched pleasingly, painfully, stacked together or arching separately over and against each other to land fingerpad-first not to deaden sound, but if she said, "Paul, hey, what about practicing—just a half hour, even ten minutes. Put in the time," then he wouldn't do it. Didn't want to. More importantly, he'd also begun seeing that he had no real gift. Poor enough sense of timing (and only slightly better sense of pitch), there was no point in overcoming his automatic defiance of his mother. He saw the dread in his teacher's face, watching as he uncased at the start of each lesson and ran a thumbnail or pick over the strings—the pained headshake as his teacher listened and finally said, "That sounds right to you? Really? You can't hear that . . . play your b-string again. Listen. Flat or sharp?" Or, his teacher's jaw muscles clutching visibly against suppressed yawns, eyes popped disbelievingly, "You didn't notice? This whole part here," he'd point at the page of tablature hard enough to dent the paper, "you didn't play these measures at all?"

He loved music. Loved what he felt in its logic and pulsing understructure, its tonal and rhythmic variance, loved the feelings of melancholy and estrangement engendered in his longing to have more from a song, listening—loved all of this well enough to know he should stop before he ruined it for himself.

After less than a year, his teacher was ending most lessons with some form of implied ultimatum—*Can't do anything if you don't want to practice, man . . . it's all about muscle memory and getting those sounds in your ears, right? You wanna keep asking your mom to write me checks, that's cool by me, but I'll be honest with you. We're treading water here at best. You gotta show a little more motivation, buddy. More dedication.* Still, it caught him by surprise the day they finished. His teacher was in one of the beat-up desk chairs under the front awning of the music store outside, smoking. Often he'd meet Paul here, using pre-lesson time for a smoke break or to talk with one of the other teachers or the store owner. Usually he and Paul would exchange a few words before heading inside, or before the teacher said, *Go on in. Tune up . . . I'll be a second.*

This day his teacher was alone. "Have a seat, Paul," he said, patting the other ratty, orange desk chair beside him, ashing into the empty soup tin of gravel and cigarette butts between them. He had on one of his usual shirts of odd designer fabrics and cool retro detailing—dark blue, velvet lined placard, subtle embroidery on the cuffs—cowboy boots and patched, shredded jeans.

Paul sat. He pulled off his knit cap, stuffed it in a pocket and mopped a hand through his damp hair, the sweat along his hairline.

"So I'll tell you a little thing I learned back when I was on the road with Lyle Lovett's band, before signing on with the Graceland tour . . ."

Rain splashed from the gutter-edge of the awning in a jagged stream, causing a curtain of sound and atomized droplets of cold water to enclose them, erasing most of the traffic noise from the street fronting the store.

"Ah, fuck it. I'm not going to tell you that story. Look, man, the truth of the matter . . ." He shook his head.

"What?"

"We gotta be done with this . . . these lessons. It's gotta mean more to you— playing the guitar—more than just something you do to please your mom. You know what I mean? She's a nice enough lady but, seriously, you gotta learn to do things for yourself. That's the key. Especially in music. If you can't . . . if you're just always about what other people tell you and what other people say you should do, punching the clock, then you get to the end of your life and you look around and you pretty much say, fuck man, what was that all about anyway? And then you die. The wisdom here, Paul . . . I don't know. You figure your shit out, but I can't be teaching you anymore. OK?"

Surprisingly, what hurt most, hearing this, was realizing that he'd never really wanted to learn guitar in the first place. What he wanted . . . he'd wanted to sit around like this behind the curtain of rain, talking. He wanted to hang out smelling his teacher's cigarette smoke, hearing his stories, watching him smoke, admiring the blunt tips of his fingers so gnarled and calloused from daily prac- tice, his hair crazed almost to quills by teasing and hair dye, and then he wanted to go inside and say, *Hey, speaking of Lyle Lovett, play me that song from . . .* Wanted to watch as a corner of his teacher's mouth tipped up and he said, *Naw, naw, not now, man—can't take up valuable lesson time with that old shit.* And then unable to help himself anyway . . . how his teacher's knee would jog up and down, the pick suddenly gluing itself to some inner life, some force of rhythm and exuber- ance extending from his wrist and forearm, pushing its way through the strings, vibrating the wood to sound, sound to the inner bones of Paul's ears, animating his teacher too, until they were both singing.

The surprising thing, the impossible thing, was realizing that he didn't want to be done after all. He just wanted to be done playing and practicing.

"All right, then? You'll tell your mom for me? I don't wanna have to be the one to break it." He dragged a final time and stubbed out his cigarette. Stood and jerked his pants higher. Held out his hand. "We're cool?"

Walking away, Paul was glad for the rain soaking his hat and hair, wetting his whole face and keeping him from knowing how hard he was crying or even if he was crying. Why? He couldn't have said. At home he saw smoke curling from the chimney in his father's workshop, the heat with it warping the air in a sheet so what lay beyond—trees, pale sky—appeared distorted as in a mirage, and he almost went as far as knocking on his father's door. Telling him the whole stupid, sad story and asking what it meant. Why he felt so much, and what was he supposed to do. He veered toward the cedar-chip walkway and across the grass. Smelled smoke from the workshop chimney and felt a band of heat move across his shoulders as the sun slid from behind the clouds; still the cold drizzle touching his wrists, the wet grass slicking the tops of his shoes with water. Heard the sound of a saw starting inside, the phone back in the house ringing, and thought better of it. He'd never find the right words anyway, and his father.... Another time. When he was ready. He'd throw himself at his feet and ask for help, say, *Make me more like you,* and ask to be guided into the trade. Not today.

—

"I have to let you in on a secret."

One thirty in the morning. Same dress, different shawl, hard-soled shoes he'd heard first clattering up the stairs fast and then kicked off in the hallway beside her door before the pounding of her bare heels came closer. Her knock. Less than five minutes she'd been in his room, the first few of which had passed standing awkwardly in the middle of the floor, as he registered the smell of alcohol permeating the air around her until it seemed not to have a source anywhere in the room but to emanate from everywhere within it; taking this in, alongside evidence of her drunkenness (a slight waver in her stance, slow blinks, words sliding toward their central vowel sounds—not so drunk she didn't know what she was doing and saying, but nowhere near sober enough to be trusted in anything she said or asked of him). He was trying to gauge the moral margins wherein he could or should formulate any response to her, while she recounted the evening's events. Dinner with friends, a party at the house on Balboa Street, back to the Shakedown Bar. *You totally should have been there it was the bomb, everyone was there . . . I said I had to be back early . . . didn't wait for last call . . .* And the last few minutes of which had passed lying face to face on his bed, a pillow shoved under his ear and forming a partial barrier between them, his hand on her hip to hold her where she was. And now this secret she was offering to tell.

"Are you sure?" he asked.

"Sure what?"

"About telling me your secret."

"Psshh." She waved a hand between them. "Shmecret." Here she paused to swallow and adjust her position, lick her lips.

He looked away at the curtains in the window behind her, their hideous floral pattern, the folds home to cobwebs and countless dead and living spiders. This was the kind of provocation for which there was no good response and possibly no good outcome. Miles from the way he'd envisioned the night ending. Light years.

She poked a finger at his nose. "Secrets give *power.*" The word exploded in his face with a faintly alcoholic mist. "Having one. Giving it away. *Power.*" She pursed her mouth and fluttered her eyes shut.

"Now you . . . you're waiting for me to kiss you?"

She stayed still, eyes closed. "In my dreams I don't ask. It just . . ."

Her mouth didn't taste like anything—toothpaste mainly, faint undertones of beer or vodka. Lips slid numb and compliant around his, the same as earlier but more fully open. Less give and take. Her breath blew across his cheek. When her arms came around his neck too hard, drawing him to her in a way that felt too rote, like she might not remember who he was or what she was doing, he pushed back gently with his hand at her hip. "Hey. May. I think you're too drunk. We can wait."

"I am, in fact." She laughed. *"Wasted."*

"We can wait," he repeated, nodding, though her eyes were still closed.

"You're so good. Where did you get so good?"

He laughed and sighed and turned onto his back. "Please. That's funny. I'm about as good . . ." He couldn't think of a comparison. "Whatever."

Seconds later when he turned back to her she was out cold, breath slipping evenly in and out, eyes flickering under shut eyelids. "May?" He pulled her shoulder back and forth. "Hey." He watched her eyebrows tighten together, a half-scowl. "May?" And when it was clear she wouldn't be roused, he sat up with his back to her a while, wondering. The right thing. What do you do. He could stay up working, but he'd hit a wall hours ago now—a snag or deficiency in his thinking that kept making everything spiral uselessly. Maybe he'd get another twenty words down. Maybe a hundred. Or maybe he'd rip it all up. And later . . . the fog in his head tomorrow. No. He could go downstairs to sleep on the couch, but last he checked another of their housemates had taken over the living room with friends gathered around candles and some kind of role-playing card game. Her room? Finally he toed away his shoes and lay back. Reached a hand for the light. Remembering the cautionary tale from his mother of a family friend who fell asleep drunk and died from aspirated vomit—*always sleep on your side if you're intoxicated, and never EVER mix pills and booze*—he stood again to pull the blanket around her and roll her away from him onto her side, then lay back again beside her, wrapped around her for warmth and still fully clothed, his nose in her hair which smelled of cigarettes and booze and under that the scents from earlier in the day—her, her sweat and the vaguely citrus perfume she'd put on for their visit to the violin shop. The Bach partita swirling through that, drawing him down, reminding him of the room full of violins, the plaster medallion on the ceiling and the table covered in violins on their backs and sides, and his deceit—the candled, red-striped light inside her instrument—and lastly his father's violin. The dark brown finish and the face inside looking out, waiting to be claimed.

——

"You've got an eye," his father said. This was early in his senior year, his last fall at home. Just back from school, he leaned at the front door, prying away his shoes, toe to heel, and kicked them under the shoe rack by the door. Both of his parents were in the kitchen, beside a violin case laid open on the table. It looked to him as if his mother had been crying, her eyelids outlined in pink and darkened through the lashes. He noticed, as he always noticed after any time away, that between meals and meal preparations the house smelled most like itself—damp old lumber and sheetrock mingled with laundry and dishwashing detergent—an austere, not unpleasant smell.

"What's up?" he asked.

"What would you say this is? What does it look like to you?"

He dropped his knapsack and went to stand beside them at the kitchen table, looking down at the violin in its case—a gold varnished instrument with double-inset purfling.

"I don't know, Dad. It looks like a violin. Is this a joke?"

"Come on. You've been around these things all your life. Just say. What does this violin look like to you?"

He lifted it out of the case and held it at arm's length, then closer. Sniffed the varnish and studied the grain. Tilted it to read the label inside and turned it to view the back. Two-piece, broad flames. Bulbous scroll. A certain looseness in the construction he couldn't place.

"Nothing much. Label says Niccolo Amati, but ..."

"I know what the label says. What does the violin say?"

"Well, it's probably not an Amati. Judging by the . . . I don't know. Pretty much everything? Arching, scroll, style of the f-holes. None of it looks like what I've seen . . . what I remember anyway. I mean, it's been a while. Probably it's something old, maybe really old? But not an Amati. My best guess, anyway. What, is there, like a question? Some kind of problem?"

His father sighed. "It needs the bass bar replaced."

"Sounds about right . . ."

"And your father has to decide now whether or not to tell the owner the truth. This violin was supposed to have been her life savings and retirement. Last valued . . ."

"Oh, it doesn't matter what it was valued at, Gwen!"

"Oh, I think it does. I think it matters very much. Six-hundred and seventy-thousand dollars. And so the question now is, do we say something, or let them go ahead and put it up for sale, and trust that no one notices?" His mother turned to his father and Paul began appreciating the parameters of the disagreement between them—a familiar one he'd heard off and on through the years, both of them taking different sides at different times. "She hasn't asked you. She hasn't asked an opinion, and that's been . . . that's our line. We don't play the hero. We aren't whistle-blowers. If the customer asks, we say. We tell them the truth because you're only ever as good as your word. But if they don't ask we just . . ." She zipped fingers across her lips. "So you put in that new bass bar, and you let it go. Keep the truth to yourself. Who's going to question papers from . . .?"

His father was already shaking his head, talking over her. "The buyer, the person she consigns with to sell it for her. Anyone with eyes, and even the most rudimentary sense of what's what." Here he gestured at Paul. "I mean, no offense. But if they're honest, if anyone can dare to be honest in this cartel of smoke-and-mirrors bullshit. Mark my words. Eventually, or even very quickly, it's going to come back around that I had this violin on my bench and I didn't say."

"What did they pay for it?"

"Never mind, Paul. You're free now. Go do whatever . . ."

"But who's vouching, Dad?"

"Oh, only some guys in Chicago you might have heard of . . ."

"The last time your father went out on a limb like this? You want to know about some very strange, very unfriendly calls in the middle of the night?" She looked back and forth between them as she spoke, so Paul understood the words were not for him; they were an appeal to reason, in his presence, which he was supposed to validate or underscore by witnessing. He felt sure he'd take her side if he understood how best to do so. "All about how unfortunate it would be, wouldn't it, should the woods behind our house happen to catch fire—all that nice dry wood in your father's supply, how fast it would go up in flames. You'd play games with these people, Denis? Put us all at risk?"

"You know what?" His father held up his hands, blinking. "I'm done. You win, Gwen." And looking back at Paul, "Sorry to have involved you. You can go now. Forget I asked."

"Asked what?"

"About . . ."

"I was joking." Avoiding his father's look of puzzled hurt resolving into irritation, a glimpse of something beyond that more like rage or despair, he went to retrieve his iPod from his knapsack, and then to heat himself some soup for a snack. He didn't want to hear any more words exchanged between them. Maybe he'd go for a run. Or ask to take the car, swim at the Y. See who was at the pizza place later. In sideways glances he watched as his father said a few words, shut the case, lifted and took it through the back door to his workshop. And later, bouncing at the stove and stirring a spoon through his chicken noodle soup in time with the beats on his iPod, he was startled when his mother came up suddenly, pulled one of the buds from his ear—he was now a full head taller—and leaned in quickly to peck him on the cheek. "Thanks," she said, breath mint-smelling and too close.

"What for?" In his other ear the music went on at half volume. He wondered about that: Like looking into the dark surrounding a movie screen and seeing only flickering, colored light and dust motes, no image; like folding down a pop-up card so it became a bunch of cut paper shapes. How did having the music in two ears more than double your experience of it? Now the mix sounded tinny and insubstantial, where seconds ago it had all but made him feel as if he were about to break out of his skin.

She shrugged. "It's hard to take a side in anything where your parents are . . . where differences between your parents are involved."

He wanted to ask how anything he'd said or done had seemed to her like taking a side, but thought better. "Any time." He smiled in a way he hoped was neutral enough to put an end to the conversation. Plugged in his earbud again and sang a few notes deliberately off-key.

But later in bed, waiting for sleep, her words returned in his memory: *All that nice dry wood in your father's supply, how fast it would go up in flames* . . . He remembered the period of months, two or three years past, following his grandfather's death—his father's father, a man he'd barely known, who'd lived somewhere in south central Oregon and whose few visits were surrounded by such an air of ostentatiously restrained calamity, his father's face shut behind a mask of hurt and of polite unconcern, all booze in the house locked in the cellar or the workshop, it had been hard to understand why he'd come. In the months of bereavement, his father had dedicated himself solely to carving scrolls. "Something I always meant to do anyway," he'd insisted. "Make a good stockpile. Sixty-eight to be exact. I don't know if I'll actually get there, but what the heck, it's something to shoot for right? One for every miserable year of his life. No. Not really miserable, just . . . Hey, if I carve enough of them, maybe I'll never have to do another one? Or maybe I could take up smoking a pack a day in Grampa Pat's honor and never finish half enough fiddles to go with them, in which case . . ." Here he'd grinned and kicked a foot at Paul, nearly connecting—slick soled, square-looking loafers he hadn't worn in ages, to go with the black shirts and slacks, Paul supposed, or somehow otherwise to keep him in mind of mourning. "It'd be up to you to do what you can with them."

"Nah."

"*Nah.* What do you mean, *nah?*"

For this, still he'd had no answer but a shrug. *Too easy. Too obvious. Plus, fuck you.*

"Well, we'll see," his father said. "Number twenty-two right here." He angled the neck and scroll in his hand to see something about it. "Not bad, not bad." Shook his head. "Anyway, you'd have to find *something* to do with them," he said. He seemed satisfied enough with this. "For now, it's a tribute. A way to focus and keep the hands steady. Cause no harm and live another few days. That's the best we can do, right? This one," he turned to lift one from the shelf beside him, "I'll be hard pressed to match. Just look at that! Sculptural. But that," he motioned with his chin at a half-formed thing on the floor. "Bad run-out. Make a good doorstop maybe. Wall decoration. Baseball bat for a midget."

"Do you think about anything else in the world, ever?"

His father sighed and didn't answer right away. "It's a fair question," he said. He nodded his head and continued with his work.

All that nice dry wood . . . He wondered if they were there still in the store room, the unused portion of those sixty-eight or not quite sixty-eight unvarnished heads and necks, all similar, none identical, each seeming to say the same things over and over about grief and loss and parting, and saying nothing at all—a curl, a wave, the perfect spire and furl of fluting from chin to earpoints. *I love you*, or maybe *I miss you*. Or, *Who were you? Was there something else I should have done?* Words his father wouldn't say to anyone, he was sure, and would never have said to his grandfather.

If the storeroom burned, the molds, those scrolls, his bench, his whole history . . . everything would burn with it. Everything but the few items in his father's fireproof gun safe—old bows and violins he'd saved aside from his years in the city buying and trading, and which Paul had seldom enough seen that he only vaguely recollected any of their details: pegless, hairless, missing tailpieces.

This was not something to think about.

He rolled hard onto his stomach and willed himself to forget.

The rest of his time at home, he stayed out of the shop. There were no fires or death threats that he was aware of. The "Amati" went out, with no comment and no backlash, and continued to make its way in the world unharmed and misidentified, so far as he knew, but with papers to prove otherwise for everyone who wanted to believe. On his second or third visit home from college, he realized that his mother too might be in the process of moving out—weavings in the living room sold or boxed away, her spinning wheel gone—but to keep up appearances, keep alive the picture of a happy home life for him, she was still returning if he were around. "No, it's not like that—not what you think," she said, when he finally asked. "A little air, a little better balance. Change in focus. It's good. We were too much on top of each other, your dad and me." He remembered seeing them out his dorm window the day they dropped him off—his last view of them together, as they cut across the parking lot jammed with other parents and new students unloading boxes from tailgates, morning sun cool and bright in a haze from the ocean; his mom's colorful blouse and the light on her hair easy to pick out of the crowd; his dad's walk, almost a swagger, the shoulders rolling—his dad suddenly drawing her nearer, her head to his shoulder as they walked on. How heartsick he'd felt, seeing that. So what happened? Was this his fault? "Don't worry," she said. "Really. You've got enough on your plate as is! We're fine."

—

The chin's eager elegance rising through sleep like a fish breaking against a current; beside that, like a face within a face, the subtler curvature angling her jaw slightly rightward, the right eye sloping almost imperceptibly, flattened or downcast; eyebrows blacker than shadow. What more could be known of a person's face anyway, observing it asleep and not expressive of any intended feeling, no emotion concealed or deliberately conveyed, or conveyed in order to conceal and deflect? He traced a finger from the corner of her eye to the light down of hair closest to her ear, wondering—the curlicue shape and channel of her ear where sound accumulated; its tonal discernment and ability to translate pitch and note value into feeling, the feeling then transmitted along neural pathways to fingers, arms, wood and bowhair striking the string into sound . . . how did that work? A miracle of sorts. All night, he kept falling in and out of sleep, seeing her in the streetlight through his curtains.

Waking, she seemed not to know where she was or anything that had happened the night before. "Oh my god!" she said. She sat up straight beside him, clutching at the blanket and then tearing it away, squeezing her arms together around her knees. His mom's blanket, spun and woven from her favorite blues and yellows, a gift to him days before he left home: *May it cover you and keep you warm, good times, bad times, and times I don't want to know about.* "Oh my god!" She yanked the hem of her dress to her ankles. "What happened? Tell me what happened. We didn't fuck."

"No. We did nothing. You passed out. I . . ."

"Oh my god, you have no idea. I cannot be doing this."

"It's OK we . . ."

"It is not OK! Move!"

He drew his legs to one side so she could clamber past him, upright. Hands on her knees, hair wild around her face, she spun to face him. "Where are my shoes? Paul! Where are the shoes I . . ."

"You didn't have any."

"Christ."

"Would you mind telling me . . ."

"I'm going to throw up now." And with that she lunged out of his room, down the hall, leaving his door open so he heard her in the bathroom—water running, faint coughing sounds followed by a toilet flushing, more water, and next her key in the door to her room, fumbling, scratching, catching, turning. The door opening. Slamming shut. And minutes later, her tuning up. Vengefully adjusting pitches and launching midway into the piece he'd been hearing her work up most recently. One he didn't recognize or like much—brooding, showy, German or Russian. With no warm up. He lay back, listening, wondering. The notes slid one over the other, towering runs of spiccato bowing, clumsy leaps from high to low, up and down, stopping, starting, nothing new in any of it—no new information pertaining to the night before or their afternoon together, her drunkenness, nothing beyond the reflexive need to assert muscle memory over failure—a nasal catch in the D string; too ringing brightness and plain thinness in the A and E, especially, but really in all the strings: the limits beyond which she would never push that crappy violin. And as suddenly as she'd started playing, she stopped. Penance done, he guessed. Maybe. For what, though? Or maybe she was throwing up again. He rolled onto his side for any last whiffs of her in the pillowcase, thinking, *Impossible that I should know her less now, that she should make even less sense to me now than twenty-four hours ago, but . . . Five minutes, I'll get up and back at it. Just five minutes more . . .*

Two

Around noon, he knocked, and hearing her muffled reply from within, "It's open," pushed her door open. For a few seconds he stood, unsure what to do next, how to proceed, what to say. Her open closet door was a seafloor vent disgorging its contents—jackets, dresses, belts, pants pulled inside out, socks, sweatshirts, stockings, leotards, a bathrobe, tennis shoes, racket, leather boots—a stop-motion picture of a clothing-volcano mid-eruption, some articles caught and tangled together at the closet threshold and overflowing a blue plastic clothesbasket, the rest strewn outward across the floor. If not for the laws of gravity, he supposed clothes would cover the walls and ceilings too, but aside from the few items draped on hooks and doorknobs, these were notably bare. A lone poster of Van Gogh's Starry Night. Cracks in the paint and plaster, the same as in his room. Tall, drafty windows covered in cobwebbed floral-patterned drapes. His first impulse, quickly considered and pushed aside, was to ask what had happened—the usual joking remarks *(looks like a bomb went off in here; do you need a map to find the door? Red Cross assistance?)* had never seemed as concretely applicable, nor as completely off-limits; to be avoided at all costs. Act like it's normal, he told himself. Don't even notice. She was on her bed, which was a mattress on the floor at the far side of the room, pillows pushed up behind her for a back rest, open notebooks and textbooks beside her and on her lap.

"Hey," he said. "Brought you this." He held up the mug of steaming tea he carried, chamomile-raspberry with chunks of fresh-cut ginger floating on its surface, a slick of gradually dissolving honey at the bottom. His mother's cure-all for upset stomach. "Thought you'd like it," he added.

She tapped a pencil in the notebook open in her lap and pushed her reading glasses back up the bridge of her nose. Then raised her hands, stretching, and beckoned him closer. "Thanks."

"Totally welcome." Socks, pencils, towels, slips, shoes, candy wrappers, note-books, blankets, an empty Oreo box, packaging for mail-ordered items . . . he picked his way toward her, stopping at the side of her bed. "Should I . . .?"

"Just set it there."

He bent to push aside the junk on her nightstand and set down the mug. "It's pretty hot now. Probably want to let it cool and steep a bit."

"That's really nice of you." No irony this time, but an undertow of despair in her gaze which was hard to distinguish from rage or hatred.

Again, he found himself unable to look away, staring back with pseudo-sincerity, pretend dispassion until his eyes stung and cheeks ached. "Totally welcome," he said again, this time nodding dumbly. And because nothing else came to mind, "You were sounding really great. Earlier. This morning."

"The Wieniawski Polonaise?"

He shrugged. "I guess. I didn't recognize it by . . ."

"Are you fucking kidding me? That piece . . . it's so retarded. It's sick. The only reason it *exists* is to remind violinists everywhere just how much they suck. No one can play it right, except genius prodigies and kids who started when they were, like, I don't know, in utero. I can get about a tenth of what it's supposed to sound like. Maybe a tenth of a tenth. And three weeks from now—no, less . . . *nineteen days*—because I've put it off since forever, I get to play it for my senior master class with the visiting soloist from . . ." She shook her head. "Never mind. You wouldn't get it."

"Try me. Anyway, I thought it sounded all right."

"Please! Enough with the false praise, Paul! Seriously. It won't get you anywhere." Her eyes no longer menaced hatred but blackened with it entirely. "Just don't. I suck. Period. And with a hangover I suck even worse."

Again he shrugged. "I'm not a music critic. I only know about violins. Like a car mechanic? That's how I hear. Just sounds. Like, qualities of sound."

She blinked and said nothing.

"I don't really hear music."

"The hell you don't."

"I mean, I hear music, but . . ."

"You've got ears like nobody's business, Paul! You hear *everything*. That's what . . . Jesus Christ, why do you think we went to the violin shop together yesterday? You think I asked you to go with me because I *like* you or some stupid shit? Just give me a break."

He should be angry. His pulse thrummed in his ears, vision constricting. Completely irrational, these swings and contradictions. He should leave now. "But it's only technical and mechanical, how I hear. That's all I'm saying. Not musical."

"Just shut up, please, shut up! You're so full of shit."

"Anyway, whatever that piece—Vinkowski or whatever it is—who cares?"

Again, the black look. Hard to say if the rage was against his attempted kindness in particular, or some way *any* kindness could only register with her as a reminder of failures and shortcomings . . . or against his total ignorance of classical violin training. "Everyone has to play Wieniawski. OK? That's how it works. It's part of the repertoire because he's like the greatest violinist of all time. Period. *Everyone* plays it, everyone destroys it. Except for a few people who are like really, actually *good*, it's so goddamned hard. You shouldn't criticize a process you don't understand."

"Criticize? What the? From what I hear anyway, the problem—at least half the problem—is your instrument, which is just kind of lame, and the rest is probably due to the fact that you don't really like the piece, cause it's stupid. To listen to anyway. So . . . so what. There's a whole world of music. That piece is corny crap. Play something else. Like the Bach yesterday. That was so beautiful. I mean really."

She rolled her eyes. Removed her glasses and sat forward, hands on her ankles, groaning and shaking her head. Downstairs someone was laughing and the stereo came on too loud and was immediately turned down and back up again halfway. Thelonius Monk—the opening measures of "You Needn't." More laughter and chairs scraping back.

"Paul." Her eyes met his and held. She shook her head. "If you're here because you think you're going to save me from my demons or whatever? You should know right now that's a losing proposition. I like you, all right? I do like you. I'm telling you this because I like you. I am a disaster area. I'm not a nice person."

He knew he'd have no explanation later, for friends, family, for himself, for anyone he knew. Quite possibly there was no explanation. He went back, picking the same path through her discarded clothing and detritus to the doorway, closed it and returned to her bedside. Monk softened through the floorboards with a clink of glassware. He waited till she held out her hands and finally sank beside her on the bed, crumpling books and notepads, drawing her to him, saying, *It's all right, it's all right,* though what he meant by it, he couldn't have said. He felt her nails on his shoulder blades, the fierceness of her mouth on his neck, the scrape of her teeth on his skin. He could leave, still. He could get up and walk away. Her arms cut hard around his ribcage. The scent of her hair and skin distilled in his brain like a potion. He couldn't move.

—

His father was losing his eyesight. Pressure behind his eyes had built to a point, and over a long enough period of time that the optic nerve was permanently damaged—crushed: peripheral vision gone and some central spots fading too, irreversibly. *Why?* he wanted to ask. *How? How could we not know? What are you saying?* His mother would not be interrupted. "I don't know that I'd have ever noticed, or I should say when I'd have noticed if he hadn't taken a little tumble the other day coming down the stairs." Her breath fluttered into the phone. "He's all right! I mean, apart from the vision loss. Some bruises. So . . . but I mean, you know your father. When's the last time he's been to a doctor for anything? When's the last time he changed his glasses prescription? What decade was that? Try asking about it. You just get a lecture on the failing American health care system and rising costs of insurance and, *Just take me out back and shoot me in the head when my time's up,* blah, blah, blah. So, he finally bangs himself up good enough that we have to go in and ask some relevant questions and luckily enough I guess, despite the fall, which had us expecting the worst, it's only chronic, not acute or likely as not he'd be fully blind by now."

He looked at his hands in his lap as she went on, voice rising and falling—the backs of his hands vanishing into the cuffs of his paper-writing sweatshirt. Wound the cable of the one earbud not stuck into his ear around and around a fingertip. Unwound it. Neat half-moons in the nails and veins visible through the unblemished skin of his wrists, soft finger ends so unlike the callus-edged tips of his father's fingers; his father's palms and thumbs smoothed and squared from handling wood and tools, the few scars from slip-ups of years gone by—the edge of one pinky tip truncated by a long ago misapplied gouge, his left forefinger tip permanently angled down and to the side from a severed tendon. All in contrast with Paul's own scarless, tender fingers. So was this his fault? If he'd stayed home, learned the trade, stayed by his father side—what then? What difference? He opened and closed his hands to distance himself from the dizzy wooziness rising in him, picturing any of it—and from the unexpected, accompanying rushes of cold, self-protective joy, realizing: *Not me. I still see. Still have an eye. Both eyes. The world of sight is mine.* Wrong feelings, but he couldn't stop himself.

" . . . like poking a hole in Jell-O, I think were his exact words. Clearing the trabecular channel. We might get some temporary relief from swelling, increased drainage, but nothing lasting and the damage anyway is done. Nerves don't regenerate. At this point it's too late and our only option is controlling further damage."

"I'm sorry, but who said that? About the Jell-O?"

"The surgeons! Laser surgeon." Her hand rubbed the mouthpiece as she went on, her voice more distant at first and then closer again. "He's not a really . . . your father's not a viable candidate for it at this point, and so our options will be mostly just targeting reduction of pain and inflammation. Just slowing the degradation. That's it. So eye drops, and not that he'd want it, but medical marijuana."

When he'd seen her incoming call he'd had to make a quick calculation: time spent talking, papers still not finished, versus guilt for blowing her off and rapid-fire redials from her later if he didn't call back soon enough. Well, he'd thought. He'd be quick. Maybe he could learn a little more from her about Jacoby's shop—Peter Jacoby, in particular—and hint at whatever was happening with May while he was at it. Set up an intrigue. Leave her wondering. Instead there was this news, eclipsing any other topic of conversation. He sniffed the backs of his fingers and caught whiffs of May's perfume in his cuffs and the neck of his sweatshirt. From down the hall, he heard her hitting the same run again and again, a shower of ascending octave double-stops followed by downward spiraling arpeggios and a final leap back to some ear-splitting harmonic precipice at the very top of the fingerboard, until finally, in something like a flat-affect mockery of her own playing, she went through again dead slowly, *détachée* bow strokes, like speaking to a child in a monotone, but hatefully, and then stopped altogether. Phone silence whistled in his other ear.

"The strange thing," his mother said, her voice lighter now, not as rushed or close to tears as it had been, "the really strange thing when they came back with the diagnosis? He seemed, I don't know, kind of relieved. Like this was a weight he'd been carrying around in private? I'm not sure I can explain. But what he said when I asked—he said, *Well now I know why I couldn't plane a straight edge anymore. That damn buzz I was chasing around forever last week, trying to figure out where the bump in the fingerboard was? I thought I was losing my mind or had completely lost my touch. But it's just the peripheral vision—the open field of vision! Logical enough. So I can work with that. Or not. But you'll have to help me."*

"How?" Paul asked.

"How what?"

"How can I help."

"No," she laughed, "not you. Me. Although I'm sure if you put your mind to it you might think of ways to help as well."

Now would come the turn in the conversation. He was sure of it. She'd ask him about himself. How were his classes? Any new developments with the inter-disciplinary degree option. Anything else new and exciting in his life? He braced himself, but the questions didn't come. Only her breathing on the other end of the line. The sound of a pot stirring or maybe a pen scratching on a piece of paper.

"Glaucoma. They don't call it the silent vision killer for nothing," she said. "Regular checkups—and that means you especially, mister. Now we know it's in your genes. *Super* regular eye checkups is the only remedy. It's one hundred percent treatable if you catch it early. But that's just it. *If.*"

He nodded and said nothing. Tilted back in his desk chair and looked into a corner of the ceiling where shadows and light converged. He didn't need his eyes checked. He was fine. *May*, he thought. He couldn't ask about Jacoby's violin shop now anyway. Fell forward in his chair again and stood. "Of course," he said and a few minutes later, as soon as he could, signed off with promises to visit soon, next weekend, maybe the week after.

Back in May's room he slid beside her and lifted the cord extending from the oversized headphones clamped around her head like Mickey Mouse ears to raise one of the cups. "Hey," he said, and she held a finger to her lips, tapping with a pencil, following the score in her lap, then lowered the finger to push him away, poking with a nail between his eyes and smiling. He rolled onto his back, waiting, watching the light fade across the ceiling. How many years since he'd watched his father at any phase of violin construction? Still he pictured it all vividly enough to wonder how he might have known—what would the signs have looked like? What might he have done to help? He pictured him from behind, knife in the kid-ney of a bridge paring open the arc. Cutting from under a bridge foot to match the top plate arching and back again to open the kidneys more, open the heart, bevel the wings. He saw purfling rolled flat and inlaid in the channel, sticking up, and again his father's hands, his knife steadily cutting along the excess, slicing it away. *You hone and polish the knife edge,* he'd informed Paul more than once, *until it's so mirror smooth you can read the fine print in the label of a light bulb reflected in it. That sharp. Because only a dull knife is dangerous.* Dulled knife, dulled vision. But how and when? And what had been his part in this? Surely he'd had a part. "My dad," he began, when May turned to him, hair touching his cheeks as she lowered herself, enclosing him in the smell he could not seem to get enough of. She shook her head and pressed a metal-tasting finger to his lips to silence him. String metal and ebony from her violin—her lame, crap, Strad-copy violin, against which she'd abrade herself tirelessly, colliding with her limits and imperfections until nothing but rage could stand out of the music. How anything he'd learned from his mother just now should translate into a wish for more sex this soon did not make sense. But it was all he wanted. He wanted her face and skin to fill his field of vision . . . to follow the curve of her collarbone . . .

—

As the last light of day struck her violin in its open case at the foot of the bed he woke, panicked momentarily at his still unfinished school work—and then let himself be absorbed in the way the sun lit her violin's varnish orange-red, showing the grooves and ruts in the fingerboard. Wear from her hours of practice dimpled the ebony like fossilized imprints of some prehistoric creature. Rosin dust and dirt sparkled under the bridge. A filmy suds of finger marks and smudges shrouded the shoulders. Was there anything, he wondered, as uncompromisingly beautiful and severe as this sight of silver, steel, and nickel-wound strings down the ebony black of a fingerboard? The contrast, the lines of tension from nut to bridge, the colored tail silks—anything as clear and promising as many hours of focus . . . pure distillate of determination, disappointment, reward?

He slid to the edge of her mattress and lifted her violin from its case, laid it across his bare shins and pressed with one finger along the length of each string, sliding from the nut to the end of the fingerboard and back again. From the finger-polished top to the sticky rosin-sleeved endpoint, there was a slight, cutting pressure against his fingertip. The ruts and grooves, so visible in the sudden last light of day, were nowhere near as evident to the touch as he'd anticipated. He felt them, but not like he'd thought—not like riding down the washboard road from the end of their drive to the main road at home. And picturing that, the trees wheeling by, the speed at which the bumps became least noticeable, he remembered. His father's failing eyesight. What was he doing here? He should be at home.

"Hey," she said, kicking lightly at his back. "Hey. What are you doing?"

He replaced the violin in its case and crawled back to her on the other side of the mattress. Lay beside her. "You need a new fingerboard," he said, falling beside her. "I just noticed. The light made it super obvious."

"Psshh. Says you. Expert."

"It's not a big thing. Maybe a couple hundred bucks. Take it back to Jacoby. Maybe he'll give you a sweet deal. Or hey, I know, maybe he'll let you take that violin of my dad's home on approval while he does the work . . ."

"Or maybe *you* could do it for me for free, or for, like, sexual *favors*." Each of these phrases was punctuated at the end by her playfully pinching at his arms and chest. "How about *that?*"

He laughed, swatting at her pinching fingers. "Right. So I get to permanently destroy your violin *and* have the time of my life, and you . . . what exactly was in it for you? Maybe we could skip the whole violin-ruining part and . . ."

She slapped his hand away. "Quit! Quit it."

Parts of her face surfaced through the shadows—pale nose, eyelid, eyebrow, half of her mouth—and moved back into darkness. Minus the usual visual filters, he felt close to her in a way he hadn't previously, and better able to register some essential thing in her—some core of sweetness, rage and melancholy vibrating there. "Come on," he said. "Show me."

"Show you what?"

"I don't know. How to play."

She puffed air through her nose. "In five minutes or less."

"Just the basics. Like, what's the first thing? What do you do?"

"What are you talking about? You expect me to believe you've never played a violin? Even once?"

He held up two fingers. "Word of honor."

"I find that hard to buy, but . . . whatever. Here." She sat up and motioned him to the end of the bed. "Like this. Stand." She fit the violin against his collarbone, the butt end of its shoulder rest digging into his breastbone and the cool concavity of the chin rest slipping forward under his jaw so she had to keep tugging the violin back up for him, pushing it harder against him. It smelled like her, but also like some other unplaceable austerity of wood and rosin dust and case glue. "No. Like *this*. Press down with your jaw. It'd work better if you had a shirt on, maybe. What is wrong here? Let's see." She squinted at him and stood back a second in the fading light, surveying, hands on her knees. "Maybe your neck's just too long. That must be the problem. There's just, like, no good contact! Did anyone ever tell you, you have a really long neck? It's nice, actually. But this is just so not working. The idea, really . . . what should be happening anyway," she said, coming around to loop her arms under his armpits from behind, hands on the backs of his hands, "it should lie flat like this, so you don't even have to think about it, like your jaw is this hinge holding it in place so the violin hangs there and your hands can kind of float around?" She sang some notes in his ear and tried to make his hands move. "But this . . . It shouldn't be so tense. Can you relax a little? It should be more like flying. Effortless. That's better."

In the end he was able to draw a few rasping notes unassisted. To press with his fingers and thereby increase the shrillness, and finally with her help, her hand on his, drawing the bow down and back in a straight line, able to feel the violin open with sound momentarily—to be struck through the chin and breastbone with sonic vibrations. With that came a metallic shimmering smell that seemed to dissipate the instant it had penetrated his senses, and a feeling like the ground rushing up at the bottom of a sharp downhill on his bike. And a pain at the base of his neck to correlate with the ones in his wrists and through his hands. If he relaxed into the heat of her arms under and over his, the weight of her against him, he could almost feel how it worked—could almost imagine it working without her—and yet as soon as she released him and stood back . . .

"Give it," she said, laughing. "You are truly hopeless. Here. Trade. I'll play and you . . ."

He handed her the violin but did not come around to stand behind her as she'd done.

"Come on!"

He shook his head and went to sit in her desk chair. "You play," he said.

She flicked at the strings and drew a few notes. "Maybe it's not so bad, this violin. What do you think?"

"In my hands all violins are equally terrible."

She stamped her foot. "Seriously!"

He tried to make out her face through the half-light as she continued flicking at the strings and fine-tuning, tossing aside her hair and then drawing a breath, widening her stance. "OK, OK," she said. "Here's something, since you asked. Don't judge!" And through the music that followed—a simple, slow piece of cumulative gravity—he watched the planes of her arms outlined in the shadow. The heart-shaped opening and closing of the circle made by her arms, playing; the shadows framing her face, indistinguishable from the black of her hair. He tried to know what caused her wish to play and its twin fear of being judged. Why this piece? Its scalar pattern moving around a core of tones, pedaling weepily between minor and major felt too predictable to him to like really, too familiar, until something in it or in her playing broke through the sentimentality and crested toward an unexpected serenity and grief. What new thing was he supposed to know or not know about her, from this? *It's unfathomable, what's in a human heart,* his father always said. *Not what the doctors tell us, though it's all of that too. Muscle walls, valves, chambers, aortas, veins, arteries, ventricles. Sure. But that isn't half of it. They're very good on the morbidity part, the doctors and scientists, telling us why and how we're dying. Not so much at explaining why we're alive. Except to procreate, which can't possibly be the whole story.* This was in the time immediately after the death of Paul's grandfather, when the details of his autopsy kept occurring to his father at dinner and randomly throughout the day, causing him to drift off or to make sudden pronouncements. *The best we know, the clearest we really get . . .* he'd stop mid-sentence, looking up and shaking his head, seemingly unable to complete the thought, or struck wordless at the obviousness of it. *We get pictures. Like afterimages, mirrored through music or words or paintings, whatever we can do with our hands if we really let ourselves, all these activities rooted somewhere in the mind or the heart, in feeling. They give us an idea of what might be in there. It's why we do anything. Not just because time is wasting, but because of something,* he thumped at his chest, *trying to get out. It's got to be. It's why I do what I do, anyway. Why*

I love violins. Because they can be a mirror for so much feeling.

She finished playing and it was some time before he remembered to say anything, or what to say. Rain slid along the glass in her window with a faint ticking noise, droplets thinning and glistening in the streetlight. Wind buffeted the side of the house causing one of the blinds in her window to stir, the string at the end of it swinging like a pendulum. *My father is losing his eyesight. After all these years . . .* No.

"That was amazing," he said. "Really, really sweet . . ."

"It's better with accompaniment."

"I loved it." *Wǒ ài nǐ.* The Chinese words surfaced in his mind reflexively. But wrong. Not *I love you,* but *I loved it.* Only, there was no exact Chinese equivalent for "it," no generic, catch-all pronoun, and probably you needed a different form for the verb to differentiate romantic from non-romantic love. Regardless, you had to say out the thing you loved. No vagueness. *I loved the just-now-played-by-you musical piece.*

"I've been playing that since I was like in early middle school? It just feels so good in your hands. Like, it lines up perfectly. For a while it was all you could get me to play . . ." She set her violin back in its case. "Drove everyone nuts." She bent to retrieve clothing from the floor, jerked her arms through the armholes of a T-shirt. Whipped her hair around again. Shook out a pair of jeans and stepped through the leg holes, snapped and zipped. This was one advantage of leaving clothes strewn everywhere, he decided. Assembling an outfit was a snap. With each article of clothing put on, he had the sense of her transforming, removing and reformulating herself in ways that would make her both more and less available to him. "But it's *Vivaldi!* Right? And past a certain, I don't know, age or so-called sophistication in your playing? You're not supposed to like it. But sometimes . . . Who cares? It just feels so *good* to play something that rhymes and fits so you can actually *play* it and get somewhere with it. So whatever. Fuck sophistication."

"Fuck it completely."

"And fuck pretention. You want to know what really bugs me? Never mind. *Here* it is," she said, brandishing a hairbrush at him and sitting at the edge of her desk to tear at the ends of her hair with it. "Would you mind, please, hitting those lights? So now that awkward moment. Were you thinking of asking me out for dinner ever? Say, like a normal date instead of creeping into my room at all hours of the day for sex and free violin lessons?"

He laughed. "Free concert, too. You forgot that part."

She blinked at him and said nothing, eyes flickering and blackening with something like the old contempt, now mixed with ironic scorn or humor.

"That's the real reason I creeped. If you must know. Free music."

"Then you have exceptionally bad taste and even worse luck, is all I can say."

He shook his head. "Can I buy you dinner anyway?" He had no money. This would go on his father's credit card. What time was it, anyway? Regardless, he'd be up all night writing, or he'd ask for an extension or just do a rushed job so he had anything at all to turn in, or ...

"What are we doing! We're housemates, for crying out loud! You do realize that. Never date a roommate! Rule number one! What does everyone say about dating your roomie?"

That it's super convenient? He shrugged. "I don't know. What do they say?"

"Oh, go put something on your naked ass."

—

Through the awful dinner at the brewpub of her choosing, where most of the waitstaff seemed to know or recognize her, and to whom he was introduced as her friend and roommate—*not like that, not my boyfriend*—he tore at his fingertips and tried not to tally up the cost of items ordered in advance, cost of tax and tip . . . thirty dollars, forty dollars, forty-five if she ordered another pint. He tried to hear over the racket of voices and music, to really focus, and to ignore the number of times her phone came out, its glow in her palms, her smirks at whatever was communicated to her by it—*That's my friend from choir, give me a break . . . oh there's a thing later tonight . . . look at this silly picture, can you believe it?* And then she'd change the screen to reply before she could show him. He tried not to track the passage of time too closely and to keep his worry about unfinished schoolwork at a minimum. Rebuffed from touching hands with her across the table or from brushing a lock of hair behind her ear, he consoled himself with the pressure of their feet together under the table; with the movement of her shins between his to the beat of the too-loud music (a new band she seemed to like but which he didn't know at all) and the subtler movement of her head connecting them invisibly via sound vibration.

"But it's hardly a date if you don't let me act like your date. Right? So what's with that?"

She leaned toward him over the table, hand cupped to her ear.

"I said . . ."

She shook her head, getting her shoulders into the beat now. "No, I heard you, Paul." She shrugged. "Nothing personal, I guess. Just habit. From this time I was having an affair with a married guy and . . . I, like, I don't know. It just, all the secrecy and sneaking around and bullshit with him, really makes me *hate* any super overt public displays of affection. Like, it's all some creepy demonstration of ownership, display of property rights, membership to the special elite club of committed people-who-fuck or something? See the pretty girl on the dude's arm, now no one's allowed to touch her or look at her because . . . ick. I just . . . whatever. Too many constraints! Why do you need it?"

"I don't. Personally. Just sometimes it's nice." He shrugged. "If you like the person. So what happened?"

"Nothing *happened*. What are you talking about?"

What happened to the married guy, he wanted to ask. He shook his head. "Seriously though. You were the one who wanted to go out on a date. Remember? So . . ."

She smiled and blinked. *"Do I contradict myself?"* She bobbled her head mockingly in time with the words. *"Very well then . . ."*

"Walt Whitman!" he said. "You had that class?" Briefly he remembered—Survey of American Lit., freshman year, his early morning walk through pines and manzanita, daily taking the back trail from his dorm room to class, fog lifting through the boughs and pine needles deadening his footsteps as he went, the roots threatening to trip him, coffee burning in his throat . . . and the questions always at the back of his mind: Could he do this at all? Should he be here? What was he doing? Why?

"What, you mean in high school?"

"High school! Get out. You did *not* read Walt Whitman in high school. Where was that?"

"Portland. Suburbs thereof." She drained her pint and set it on the table between them, close enough to the edge to invite a request for another, foam and suds sliding along the inside of the glass. "I already told you."

He tried to remember. Had she? He focused away from her on a reflection in one of the windows, lights from the rafters glowing like unmoving twin suns. Touched his drink but didn't raise it to his mouth. "No, I don't think you did, actually. I don't think you've told me anything."

She smiled, head tilted, eyes flashing scorn. "You want my background? Century High, class of 2008—*Go Jags!*" She punched a fist in the air. "That's in Hillsboro, just west of Portland, famous for Intel microchips and dairy farming. Two tenths of a point off valedictorian status, which, if you're not Asian or half-Asian, as in my case, maybe you wouldn't understand the specific gravity of such a failing. Suffice to say, I don't talk much to my dad anymore. Or my crazy ass mom, really. First chair in the chamber orchestra eleventh and twelfth grade, All-State two out of four years. All-District three out of four. Should I keep going?"

He shrugged. "If you want."

She pushed back in her seat. "People get way hung up evaluating everything based on past fuckups and successes, I think. Why be beholden to past bullshit that has nothing to do with who you are anymore and who you want to be anyway? Like who I am now has anything to do with who I was three years ago or five or even last year? No way. Right here, right now," she poked a finger at the tabletop, "it's all that matters. Fuck I need to go home and *practice*." She waved the waitress over for another round.

"OK, but . . ."

Before her drink arrived, their food was on the table. Heavy red plates of fries and sandwiches dripping sauce and melted cheese. "Man," she said. "I was dizzy-hungry. I did not even realize how hungry I was! *Destroyed* by hunger. Oh my god."

"Yeah."

"I always forget how famished sex makes you."

"Huh. I don't think I ever knew that."

She kicked him under the table. "Oh, Pinnochio! Your nose is getting longer."

"*And* my dick is sprained."

"Your . . . *what?*"

"Nothing."

Walking home, she kept a step ahead of him, hands in the pockets of her peacoat, chin tucked to its collar, and eyes focused forward, blocking conversation. "I used to think," he said, stopped at an intersection and then sidestepping parked cars, jumping a puddle to keep apace, "that if you walked fast enough you might dodge the rain drops."

Sideways glance. Nothing more.

And finally, the broken moments he would have to will himself to think past or disregard in the coming days—outside the door to her room, facing him, a hand on the latch. "So I need to hit the practice rooms a while now, Paul. Focused practice. I've got that thing in two weeks and I'm so unprepared. There's what, like an hour and a half before close?"

He shrugged. "I wouldn't know. But no worries. I'm up late. Two papers . . ."

"But that's just it Paul. This can't become a . . ." She moved her hand in a circle. "A habit or a thing or whatever. A *relationship*. Don't look at me like that!"

"Like what?"

She sighed and sagged against the wall. Pulled off her hat—handknit, from her Norwegian grandmother she'd told him earlier, as she'd tucked her hair under the earflaps, smiling in a deliberately silly way, one of her few concessions to a past beyond the general information about having grown up in and around Portland. "I don't know if I'll be sleeping here tonight. I mean, I think I probably won't be. It all depends."

"Oh. On—? You mean . . ."

"I don't mean anything! Jesus. I mean, I might not be here tonight, might stay with a friend, might not, I don't know, so please don't wait up or come looking for me." She raked a hand through her hair and looked at something over his shoulder. Exhaled once deeply enough that he saw the flush creeping from her chest to her neckline, the quiver of fabric at her collarbone betraying whatever feeling she had about what she was saying. "And *this* is exactly why they say dating a roommate is such an incredibly stupid and unintelligent thing . . . because of that . . . that look you're giving me right now, like *I'm* supposed to feel bad because all of a sudden it's *your* business to know whatever the hell I might be up to."

As his circulation cooled and shifted from his extremities to his core he became oddly aware of his surroundings—the unshaded lightbulb hanging by its electrical cord from an outlet in the ceiling above throwing double and triple shadows of them to walls and floors, cracks in the surrounding ceiling plaster, the narrowness of the passageway where they stood, more like a chute really or chute-shaped interrogation room, cold drafts from the window closer to his end of the hall hitting him in the backs of the legs, mixing smells of rain and earth with powder, mildew and soap from the bathroom at the other end of the hall, warped floorboards creaking underfoot as he shifted his weight and moved a half-step away from her. Was this what she'd meant when she said she was not a nice person? Or was this her best effort to conform to that self-diagnosis, live up to it, and push back from him because she'd promised she would?

"But thanks for a lovely dinner." She tilted her chin toward him. "Goodnight kiss?"

"I don't think so, May." He turned from her and headed for his room. "You know where to find me. Obviously."

Later with the snick of her lock turning, tumble of her feet going down, the outside door crashing open and shut again, he stood abruptly from his desk chair. Two steps across the room to his doorway he froze, hand on the doorknob, ready to tear it open and rush out after her to . . . do what exactly? Say what? *Who is he?* Did he really want to know? Did he have a right? Except that she might have looked back to catch him at it, his next impulse was to tear aside a window blind to see out and watch her on her way up the street toward campus. See if she carried anything beyond a violin with her, if she had a violin at all. Why care so much? What was it about her? *No,* he told himself. *It's a blessing. This isn't for you. A disaster. Not a nice person. Remember that. Not nice at all. Back to work . . .* He stood at his desk. *Miro, Soupault, Duchamp, Rimbaud . . . what am I trying to say about these guys?* The house ticked and creaked as heat came on and wind buffeted the west-facing wall, the west-facing windows in the alcove where his bed lay still unmade from the night before, blanket folded to one side where she'd lain and where she'd bolted upright out of sleep. Where the cold air would seep over him all night making his joints ache and his throat sore.

What was he even doing here?

Hours later, he barely remembered saving out his documents and shutting down; barely remembered his phone chiming and buzzing with texts and emails, social media updates, mooing vibrations into the top of his dresser—not May; they hadn't even exchanged phone numbers yet because obviously—then curling onto his side, surrealism paper done. One last attempt at the section in his linguistics book he hadn't yet surmounted, words doubling, inverting and shimmering back into his field of vision, some of the letters wearing hats and crowns or seeming to blur with other words unrelated to the text . . . until finally, lights out. Sometime toward dawn she must have found her way to him. This he knew first from the change in temperature—cooler air from the window alcove rushing in with his door opening and staying open, the window shade slapping out and back against the casement, and from her cheek, cold and wet against his. Not a dream. Her clothes awkwardly tangled with the blanket, knees in his back, icy hands under his arms. "Oh my god," she said. "It's so cold, Paul. Warm me up. See, I was good and came back. Like you wanted." Until his alarm sounded, the rest of the night he drifted in and out of sleep. He was underwater with some half-land half-sea creature stuck onto his back with its fins and fingers, its weight of hair and cool flesh, like the Da-Daist image he'd ended up copying and pasting into his last page of half-constructed argument—an example of anti-argument via anti-art imagery—a fish or a heart with some kind of vacuum hose extending from its neck or maybe its nose; its baleful, jealously watchful eyes merging with May's, blackening with contempt for him, sucking him in—and then he was awake again, feeling her breath on his neck.

—

In the days that followed—*nineteen . . . no, SIXTEEN days now, and counting!* she'd occasionally remind him, adjusting the number as days flew—he felt his life pulling from its centerline, like the way his father always explained geometrical eccentricities in the modeling of Guarneri del Gesù: skewed shoulders, bouts, f-hole placements, all of it pulling uniformly, rotationally from a vanished center line around which Guarneri must have set his necks, and further enhancing other idiosyncrasies built into his corner blocks and edges—all the construction-based background to Guarneri's work that now, centuries later, had vanished or become unreadable, making him appear as if he was some kind of mystic guru. Or else crazy, lazy, sloppy, drunk. Or confused—carving violins on his knee in a donkey stable. *When in fact, his father always asserted, he was just an artist, plain and simple. Nothing unrational about it. He had a process and what you see is a result of that process. Simple. Choices he made, based on a methodology and set of intuitions we can't study anymore except by looking back through the finished results. What you get, the message in all of it is actually pretty straightforward: proportion matters more than neatness and symmetricality. Period. Get that right, and you don't have to measure all the time.* But if there were a clearer, straighter centerline in his own life, Paul thought, he'd stay caught up on his reading. He'd run every day. Miss no classes, finish papers on time, take better notes that actually helped him prepare for midterms and finals. He'd be the guy who bought groceries regularly and cooked healthier, fresher food at home instead of dashing out to the co-op for soup dregs and day-old bread just before closing, or cheap bean, cheese, and rice burritos at Burrito Express. He'd get to sleep at a reasonable hour and leave time for friends who kept texting and calling—*Sup? No game this Wednesday? How do we level up AGAIN without you? Building characters now, are you in or not?* Instead, he slept late. Ran to class half-prepared or not at all, or rolled over and rationalized another skip, a little more catch-up for later, borrowed notes from someone. He re-heated leftover coffee or chugged it cold and listened for her coming and going—her key at the front door, the sound of her feet clattering up and down the stairs, her door-catch opening, closing, the wall of his room shuddering with the force sometimes, strains of music from her room, stopping, starting, over and over the same Wieniawski Polonaise Brillante. He became enlivened again only as time with her approached or just after it had passed. The skewed centerline wasn't *her*, he knew. Not at all. It was in himself. It was some foundational weakness or built-in structurelessness, built-in crookedness, fucked-up internal modeling that allowed her influence to pull him so hard. That, or a grayer more general need not to conform to whatever plan seemed laid out for him currently—*Millennial malaise*, as his mother called it—but rather to focus outside any plan and priori-tize time with her, thereby avoiding . . . what exactly? He didn't know. And as long as he let her pull him off center, he didn't have to know.

Walking with her, some rainy afternoons at her favorite beach cove close to school—a pebbled stretch sheltered by spruce and long-armed manzanita they'd occasionally escape to and where they were alone enough she was mostly free touching him, allowing him to touch her, a hand in his back pocket as they walked by the water or on foot trails threading through branches and under- brush, past long-dead fire rings, ends of driftwood logs blackened and tapered, the water a dimpled reflective surface shining back at the sky the same ever- shifting mix of silver tones, flat, gray-black swells, the tops rippling as if taut, waves lapping the shoreline—the talk between them always circled back to mu- sic. Violins. What she wanted, what she hoped for: Not a secondary education teaching gig, not a third-rate orchestra in some underpopulated corner of the country playing pops, movie scores, and bombast for the local old folks to fall asleep to in their soft-seat theater after a heavy dinner and bad wine. A combi- nation of private studio teaching and a playing situation that would satisfy and challenge her without wrecking her nerves. *That's all. Is it so much to ask? Somewhere in Seattle, maybe, or Portland if I could ever stand to go back there.* Pictures of herself from an imagined future, none very real or revealing, none hard to envision or to help embellish with details from a previous day's conversation or from his own life. Never the past. Like she didn't have a past, he thought sometimes, but always too late to ask, watching as she pulled on clothes at the edge of his bed, her back to him, light flashing in her hair, then she'd softly close the door behind her in case he was still asleep.

When he could, he told her some of the stories he'd been saving for years without realizing—the Amati that wasn't an Amati; the totaled Obici his fa- ther had built back from splinters, because with or without papers to verify, it would always be apparent to anyone with eyes (and ears) that this was an old Italian violin once much loved and given the utmost attention. Or stories of similarly re-worked violins that had crossed his father's bench over the years, unverifiable in provenance, but each with such care given in construction and repair, there could be no question of presumed value to someone, somewhere. *He's got a safe of these violins at home, you know. A hoard. His high grade orphans. Because he loves a mystery and can't help himself. But also because someday they'll all be worth a mint. So he says . . .* All of which inevitably—like another centerline pulling everything to its measure and proportion, its predetermined parameters—led them back to the violin of his father's she'd played and which had subsequently ruined her for any other instrument. *When I was little I dreamed there was like a magic wall you could walk through and on the other side of it everything would be perfect. Notes wouldn't fight you. No squeaks, nothing out of tune. Put your fingers where they want to go and presto! Bam. Perfect. Everything in tune. Now, I have that dream and it's not a dream anymore it's real, because that IS what it felt like playing that violin. Can you talk to him? Maybe he has another one like it. Probably someone's already bought that one anyway. Don't you think? How could anyone with the money NOT want to buy it? I mean really. What better violins are there? What's it doing sitting there, not being played! It should be played every DAY, by ME. It's my DESTINY. What the fuck.* He didn't tell her what he knew about this: that a player's attachment to any given instrument was always a mixture of hyperbole, faith, delusion, psycho-acoustics and some objective truth; that it could change overnight, and that in her case she might well be halo-izing his father's violin because of its cost and unavailability. Belief was synonymous with truth, or indistinguishable from it, where instruments were concerned—where anything of meaning was concerned. Love, faith, value . . . And for his part, so long as she believed he had some necessary attachment to her playing, maybe his hold on her would last—maybe their mutual, temporary hold on each other would last long enough to turn into something more.

Later, lying in her room and trying to read while she played, he'd come back to it: The skewing centerline. The nutty hollowed devil's box built around that line, carapace founded on flaws, crooked witchy thing covered in stain and satiny finish as fucked-up and irregular as his life, but with its centerline still crossing straight down the middle, into her dreams . . . alchemically, mystically, somehow crossing straight to a sound she dreamed of (and which was hers), but which she couldn't have or articulate without a better violin. He fell in and out of sleep. Rode the waves of her music down, past notes and tones and centerlines and his own disassembled worries about phonemes, poetics, deadlines, disappointments, Chinese words and phrases, landing at last in his father's workshop again—the neck blanks, broken violins in pieces, new violins, molds, clamps, tools . . .

—

As the day of her master class approached, the piece she'd chosen and auditioned with—the Wieniawski Polonaise Brillante—invaded his waking life. Its jokey, angular rhythms and showy bursts of sentiment tangled with his thoughts as he crossed the campus, breath coming and going in a rhythm with it, melodies and counter-melodies surging in him like he might be about to break into song. Reading, it bumped along under the surface of whatever he was trying to understand, pushing aside words so he had to go back over and over passages to comprehend; and talking to friends in passing, small talk on pathways, at the coffee shop, before class, he was always conscious of his abstracted state—the pulse of music under everything distracting and distancing him from what was at hand. His two shifts a week at the snack bar—dunking baskets of fries in fryer oil, flipping burgers, the backs of his knuckles chilly and gummed from scooping ice cream, milky handprints all around the metal container for making shakes—he was constantly distracted and screwing up orders. *Pickles no relish, sorry . . . Hot fudge and blackberry, my bad . . . Hold the mayo, totally forgot . . . That was a gluten-free bun you wanted, really?* If he kept it up, he'd be out of a job and his forty-odd dollars a week for grocery money. And hearing her play from down the hall, the notes acquired a more active life in his imagination—a set of graphics and cartoon images to go with the crazy skittering up and down passages, mostly cat-and-mouse chase scenes, old-time cops and bandits, sometimes on bicycles, edges tinged and funked like an old sketch or daguerreotype wherever the notes broke through, tone bottomed out, the reel skipping and starting over again with her stops and starts. Only in lecture classes did his brain finally quiet, the music draining away so he might re-focus—hear again the scratching sound of his pen over a sheet of blank paper; the professor's voice, and the chocking of chalk on a blackboard, or air from an overhead vent stirring in the hair of the kid seated ahead of him.

The day of her master class, he bolted from his final afternoon lecture missing the closing five minutes and still arrived late, having become lost in the maze of classrooms, auditoriums, and practice rooms that was the music annex—a blaring of wind instruments, cymbals, and timpani from beyond closed and partially closed doors to correlate with his anxiety circling around again and again, up and down half-flights of stairs, doorways with crash-bars that didn't open behind him if he needed to retrace his way, emergency exits, bulletin corkboards of event announcements and advertisements, until suddenly he was there. The basement auditorium, a low-ceilinged, amber-lit room like a vault, the closeness of air within deadening the sound, semi-circular apron of theater-style seats with retractable desks surrounding a stage area, piano, and single music stand. Just in time, he caught the door behind himself not to let it crash shut and stood a moment, sweating, breathing too hard, allowing his eyes to adjust. She was at the front of the room, one of six students on folding chairs beside the piano, all marked under the jaw with the same ruddy, tongue-toned badge of sloughing skin from hours of violin practice, all with their instruments in hand. *Lambs to the slaughter,* she'd told him, describing the process. *Not that it has to be, but these classes can be brutal. Come if you want. If you dare. Don't feel as if you have to.* He felt his way to the closest open row of seating and folded one down, lowered himself into it, bag on the floor beside him, all as quietly as possible—not quietly enough that a few heads didn't turn his way. May's eyes lifted toward him probing the back of the room, but evidently not seeing through the glare of stage lights. She'd said that the class was open to the public; was in a real sense simultaneously a performance, practice-performance, public class and an audition of sorts *(these are notable instructors . . . a letter from one, referral, assist of any kind, it's not unheard of—they want their little protégés out there spreading the good word . . . their little prodigies, which I emphatically am not).* His instinct, all the same, was to blend in—to look the part of a music student and avoid notice. He lifted the desk from the side of his seat, extracted pencil and notebook and tried to appear studious. Ready for whatever. The person at the podium speaking as he'd entered, a mild-voiced, reed-thin man in a blazer, also marked under the jaw as a violinist, was evidently not the visiting soloist—a name Paul didn't catch; Russian or Polish, a sequence of sounds he'd have to hear again to grasp—another man who'd stood briefly to wave and smile at the auditorium as his name was said, before reseating himself with a clang. "We are so fortunate to have him with us today for a few hours out of his busy schedule." Paul doodled in his notebook, a surge of well-wishes for May with a passage of minor secondary melody from her piece bubbling up in his thoughts so emphatically he almost felt he knew how to play it himself, almost felt certain of her ability to wring every last note out of the air, through the neck of that lousy violin, lay it all down finger by finger and stroke by stroke, perfectly metered and in tune. She could do this. He was sure.

" . . . And please remember to silence all devices. These sessions are informal but do require the utmost concentration. Oh, and remember too, please save your applause until the conclusion of each lesson and performance. No distractions, no flash photography or filming. This is for the students. And a last note—try to remember: Music is fun!"

By the time her turn came, he knew the drill and had a fair idea what to expect: With or without piano accompaniment students came forward from the group of six. They introduced themselves, waved or smiled nervously, made a few remarks about the piece they'd chosen, its time and place in the violin literature, and then they tuned. Drew a breath to focus. Played. The soloist might allow them to make it through their selection entirely—orchestral excerpt, concerto, sonata, whatever the case was. He might not. He might break in singing along and waving his arms like a conductor to emphasize dynamic instructions written in the score or other interpretations having to do with phrasing; he might do so from his seat in the front row, speaking in a deep, adenoidal, Eastern-European inflected gravel, or approaching the stage area to point at the score and clarify his instruction and quiz the student on his or her choices, gently at first but building toward an insistence on particulars. "What is this here, with the movement from major to minor! Is not always the same all the time, beautiful, like the way you play it—*dya dee dee, dya dee dee*—always same, same, same. Beautiful, yes. But no! Here in measure twenty is catastrophe! Here, right here at rehearsal letter C, chandeliers fall on dancers, something terrible anyway, and we are reminded of everything sad in the world. Dead loved ones, bombs, dead kittens, whatever it is you think of to be sad. So here, light and playful. And here, yes! Hard. Hard like you mean it with the downstrokes if you prefer that way, and then here," he sniffed once dramatically, *"dya dee dee,"* waving his arms again, singing and sliding a tip-toe waltz step in his loafers across the linoleum, the silky cloth of his dress shirt displaying overdeveloped pecs and a seemingly hairless or shaven chest, fitted slacks hugging to dancer-muscled thighs, "and now *here*, like you have lost everything. You see the difference? Now again, from rehearsal letter D to end. Please!" None of the pieces preceding May's sounded to Paul's ears anywhere near as challenging or complex, as technically impossible. Consequently, the soloist only occasionally took up his own violin to play through passages illustrating differences in technique—mainly bowing choices, fingering choices, choices of articulation and emphasis. Notes out of tune, notes missed, muffed, squawked or choked might earn a shrug. A laugh or head shake, "Yes, is difficult. The violin. Is the devil's box. Please to try again." *Eess*, Paul wrote in his notebook, phoneticizing the soloist's accent. *Dzee debhil's bux*. The presumption, he realized, was that issues and concerns relating to technique were mostly beneath the level of today's discussion. The soloist wanted to talk to them about *musicality*—about the art of interpreting marks on the page to match whatever the composer prescribed and intended, the *je ne sais quoi*, to make meaning from that and connect with a listener. Everyone played most *bee-youteeful notes;* faults and deficiencies in feeling, however, redounded to the player as faults of character. Deficiencies in experience or sensibility. "No, no, no! You have not lost enough. Here! Try again, harder. Feel please how he's saying something here about the little optimism he offered at the beginning of this phrase with these notes. Is plaintive, yes? Optimistic? Maybe things will work out? Here, not so much. And here you must lose *everything*! Lose! Lose, lose! Not dark enough. No!"

Bow dangling from one finger and violin under an elbow, May faced the glaring stage lights. "The Brillante Polonaise," she began, "is an important showpiece, like most of Wieniawski's compositions. I've been playing it for, oh, the better part of three months now and still I don't think I understand it. So, that's also why I chose it. Partly. To understand better because it's such a complicated piece, I think. But mainly I chose it, I guess, because I wanted a challenge." The corners of her mouth tipped up as she said this, though Paul knew from experience this wasn't a smile to reflect any type of humorousness, it was a dare. It was her pleasure at accepting or declaring the prospect of a dare. "Because I guess you could say, I *like* a challenge?" And then she was playing. Feet planted firmly shoulder-width, hair in a perfect circle reflecting light in twinned crescents at either side of her head and partially shrouding her face. There was no nervousness or hesitancy in her attack, and as she forged ahead, bucking the accompanist wherever his fingers tangled and collided in knots of chords and right-hand over left-hand jumps that exceeded his ability, blasted on, never missing a beat, Paul fell back in his seat, mesmerized, forgetting even to breathe. Maybe it was the addition of accompaniment, however clumsy and irregular, but for the first time he felt the picture inside the music filled in somehow, made three-dimensional—felt beyond the calisthenics and virtuosic play-this-because-no-one-can pyrotechniques moving in the heart of the music something . . . something preachy, pompous and preening, yes, vain as hell, yes, but also despairing at its own vanity, at the futility of all vanity and attention-seeking activity, and finally arching past that to something more melancholy and earnest having to do with how beauty might still, despite the odds and despite constant failure and misunderstanding, despite its own longing for attention, might still stand a chance to say something lasting; to transcend time and place. He was transported, certain this was what had drawn her to the piece in the first place; rapt, all the way to the closing measures of harmonics whistling and ringing practically beyond the range of human hearing and spiraling off again hilariously to revisit a final time the main themes and melodies before banging down on the closing double stops with a flourish.

The soloist jumped from his seat, clapping—the palms of his hands popping aridly, heavily together, shivers of phase-shifted reverberance beating and ringing tinnily to the corners of the room. "Brava. Bravissima!" He faced the auditorium. "Please to join me. Is not amazing? Brava, brava!" And as the applause shivered through the room and died away, he continued, addressing May. "You have played how many thousands of notes just now? And how many did you miss? Ninety-nine point nine-nine percent of all notes, I think you played? Bravissima!" He went to stand beside her. Faced the auditorium. "This is most fantastic." Turned back to May. "Congratulations. Now. Simple question for you. What is Polonaise?" *Po-low-naiz.*

"A dance."

"Yes! Very good. But what kind of dance? What do you know about it?" *Eet.*

She shrugged. Shook her head and flicked at her strings. "I guess . . . not much?"

"Is a Polish dance! Very special kind of joyous Polish dance, not to be confused with polka. Now. I am going to ask you some more simple questions about dynamic interpretation. What is sforzando?"

May blinked and didn't respond.

"Please to tell me, what is mezzo-forte and what is sforzando-piano and also grazioso, in your opinion, or have you not learned? Maybe because you are so busy memorizing notes?"

"I know dynamic terminology. I mean . . ."

"Good! Very good. Then maybe we can start because you play as if there is no dynamic markings anywhere at all in score. All the same. Note, note, note, note. Is not music. Is machine. Remember—perfection is only the beginning! Now show me please, where is beginning and end of first phrase. Please, exactly, where does first statement begin and what it is saying . . ."

May pointed with her bow at the page.

"Yes," he said. "Maybe. Or maybe here . . . Yes? And what does it say."

"Honestly?"

"If you know this already, honesty is always good!" *Goot*.

She shrugged. "It says you'll be lucky if you can play this at all. It says, *I dare you to try.*"

The soloist spun and stepped offstage for his violin and returned flicking the strings. "I think you have misread."

"I don't understand this piece. It's true. It's why . . . I said that's why I chose it. And because it's an important piece of the literature, but . . ."

"Yes, I see now. You are very willful. Very funny. But the violin is not a chore. Must be more," he played the opening phrase, "playful, yes? And since marking here is grazioso but also with sforzandos right here and here must be—what? A little light and graceful as a dancer, but still building to . . ." (he played the next notes) "like you mean it! Yes? From here, in the belly. And since there's no structure in accompaniment yet . . . so you can be little more free. Play here almost rubato." He exaggerated this in his playing, dragging the notes comically, and then tightened it again, bearing down. "But playful, happy, too. Grazioso. Light. But hard. Have you had these feelings recently? Try to remember. Dancers are just arriving . . . everything is so much optimism still. Hope. Expectation. We see skirts spinning. Maybe some taffeta, some lace, bare leg . . . Please try?"

And as May played, he sang along, buzzing the notes in his nose and throat and waving with his bow.

"Again, again! Yes! But have fun with it. Many, many years I spent playing Mr. Wieniawski's own favorite violin. His Guarneri *lady*. Did you know this? We are, how do you say, intimately acquainted. To me, always a sense of humor with the fire and romance, the schmaltz, if you wish to understand him. Now . . ."

Again she played, and again he sang along, obscuring the notes comically and waving his bow at her.

"Good, good! And next phrase?"

As this continued, a phrase at a time, Paul sensed May going on autopilot and recoiling—that essential core of melancholy and rage which he'd glimpsed in her, in the music today and weeks ago in Jacoby's shop, every time he'd heard her playing really—he felt it withdrawing ever further under the surface of the music; in its place a brittle schmaltz and showiness, an over-emotive swagger to match the Wieniawksi and the soloist's singing. ". . . No, be more free! Entertain us! These showpiece are for people to enjoy. Even if they are not so much fun to play! Dramatic yes, but no problem for us. Make us feel at ease. Here you play all right notes, but overdoing, I think. Fortissimo, yes, because he wishes us to make it known, this idea here—but please not so much aggressive . . . Now, here, here, new problem: How do you make four notes collectively fortissimo? Not by playing all the same—bottom note is same, yes? Top notes change. Yes? No. Don't be so noisy, like you don't even know how to play. We want it to sound like music! Like music to our ears! Not so aggressive. Please, not so far away from strings. Closer, closer . . . play through the strings. More legato. Not so hard. Less pressure . . ." Occasionally, through the buzzing vocalizations and humming, the instructions to her and ongoing refinement of dynamic interpretation, waving his bow like a baton, jabbing at the page with a finger, it was back again—the thing in her Paul was certain must lie somewhere close to the heart of her desire to play.

"You wanted challenge?" he asked, at the end.

She nodded, shrugged. "Yes. I did say that. True story."

"The violin is always that. Always. But music is more than just challenge. This you must remember. It can be very difficult," he struggled over the word, mixing his *d* and *z* sounds, *i* and hard *ee* sounds. *Dzee-fee-colt*. Paul spelled it out in his notebook beside the other phoneticized words in his accent. "This is one of its functions. The showpiece especially. To show off violinistically. They are for this purpose, yes? To say you can do *this* and this and also *this*. But to make them into *music* is something else again. For that you must remember to feel pain. Feel something. Please, next time less notes. More pain. More *feeling*." He beat a fist at his chest and nodded at her, eyebrows lifted. "You are so young and lovely. You must not try so much to make sense of your pretty feelings, please. *Only* feel. OK? Now. Next?"

Paul didn't stay for the remainder of class. He got up quickly and quietly before the next student could start. Went across campus to their house where, in the fading light of afternoon, the music that had sucked them both up and drawn the past few weeks of their lives into its orbit no longer echoed with his footsteps or in every hollow between breaths. Done. He went up the stairs to look out of his window, trying to decide something, as surprised at the suddenness of his feeling as by the absence of that music. The last ferry went at nine o'clock. He glanced at his watch; four-thirty now. This was long overdue. Weeks overdue. If he left on public transit within the next hour he'd easily make it. Five or ten minutes to pack. Fifteen more to get to the bus depot. A note to May to follow after him if she wanted. Text? No something handwritten, not to be received or responded to instantaneously; just to say, if she felt up to it or was interested, she could follow. But she wouldn't. Probably. She'd want to drink herself through the bottom of whatever feeling the master class had left in her, to spin around there a while willing herself to forget and stay angry as long as possible before climbing back out.

His bag, the old, leather-handled canvas duffel from his mother's college days, folded at the back of the closet under shoes and covered in lint and dust—right where he'd left it. He gave it a shake to uncrease it, folded open the flaps and threw in his change of clothes. Toiletries and books. Computer. *Headed home to the island for the weekend,* he wrote her. *Dad's worse, as you know. Come if you want! Seriously! Play violins! Sure he's got a few good ones. Call me and I'll tell you how to go. PS You rocked it righteously. Whatever Russian dude said. Pretty feelings my ass. WTF? You nailed it. See you Sunday if not sooner."* Slid the note under her door and before her class had finished, he was on his way. Headed home.

Three

Dawn came cold and clear. Before he might allow himself time for making an excuse, he was out of bed, in sweats and running shoes from high school days and headed up the hill path, ducking wet branches, drops of cold tree water down his back. Ferns soaked him at the knees as he hopped and slipped over leaf-slicked and mossy hollows where the soil resounded underfoot, light and loamy with roots, bound for the ridge trail. The mist was always thicker there and as the sun went higher, burning it off, he'd get glimpses of coastline below; then he'd take the rocky trail down, two-three hundred feet, where he could run another mile or so in the wave-slick sand closest to the water, scaring up gulls and cormorants and jumping over dead jellyfish. Gull carcasses and picked-apart crabs, starfish, sand dollars. The slap of the surf constant in all of it, salt air and wind battering his side. He'd never clocked the distance. Had only relied on the internal cues of his plunging breath and the burning in this thighs and calves to know when was enough. Where to turn back. An hour total, maybe a little more. His nose stung from the cold, forehead prickled with sweat and in no time he'd stuffed his hat in the waistband of his sweats, a coppery taste at the back of his throat and surprising shortness of breath causing him to stumble. Break stride and walk. Lope on again. It had been a while. Too long.

May had surprised him wanting to talk on the phone until almost two a.m., voice close in his ear as he lay in his narrow childhood bed, unstrung and turning to find the familiar grooves and hollows in the mattress, smells of dust and a crinkling of old feathers under his head mixed with his mother's powder and soap. His boyhood stuff had been mostly boxed away on shelves in the closet but was still visible in the half-light from the sky light on that side of the room—the tail of a stuffed dragon, an old marionette set, Legos, posters rolled into tubes, old school projects and certificates of merit, certificates of completion for one activity or another—the wall closest to him repainted but still humped and scarred wherever his tacks and tape had torn away too much sheetrock.

"It's weird, being here. But good," he'd said. "You should come. For real." He thought at first she'd be drunk. *Raging*, as she'd put it. Angry with him for having fled town, or else angry at her overreliance on him and trying to conceal that, mask it in some semblance of indifference, which might also provoke her anger if it proved impossible to keep up, all of which would be difficult to gauge at this distance. He didn't say anything about the master class right away, except for acknowledging that he'd been there and that he thought she'd nailed it. "He was super harsh, I thought, especially considering how much harder your piece was than any of the others."

"But you didn't stay." Not drunk. Not angry.

"I left after yours. That was enough, really."

"You missed Benjamin."

"Who?"

"Benjamin Asahagian. The star . . . boy genius. He was last. I could have killed him. Total freaking love fest. I mean, no. I can't fault him. He's just so good. Really, really good, and super nice too, so whatever. He should, like, be at Julliard, I swear. But he's from this Armenian refugee family. He played the Mendelssohn, and . . . I mean, it's also a demanding piece. Not a showpiece, but . . . so maybe that was my big mistake. I shouldn't have tried to outdo everyone with such a hard selection. But whatever. So I'm overly competitive. So what. Anyway, he just played it really, really super sweet. Like, it moved me to tears a few times. No mistakes. Maybe a couple, but it didn't matter. Kushnarov said it reminded him of a young Milstein."

"A who?"

She laughed. "As long as you can maintain this level of ignorance, we're golden. Seriously? Nathan Milstein?"

"I feel like I've heard that name . . ."

The conversation ping-ponged to him again—his trip over, first impressions of things at home—how his mother seemed to have more or less abandoned the idea of leaving, maybe because of his father's condition, who could say; his father's oddly lighthearted attitude about the changes, the array of new pill bottles in the kitchen, vision charts in the bathroom, new handrail on the stairs inside and steps outside, new traction tread on the walkway up to the door. He hadn't seen inside the shop yet to know how his father's condition was affecting work. "Tomorrow he wants me to go through all the crap in his vault together. I don't know, maybe he's hoping to get me involved. So I said I would. And my mom wouldn't shut up about feeding me until I'd eaten like three pounds of this tortellini and pork casserole. God. I don't even know what it was. Fucking delicious but now I'm going to die."

"They sound so great. Nice parents who actually care about you and want to do things for you."

"Well . . ." He didn't tell her what he'd come to believe about this—that kindness was another kind of entrapment, impossible to oppose.

"OK, I'll quit feeling sorry for myself now because your parents sound so decent and sane, whereas mine are like some form of specially aggrieved seabeasts from hell. I think that's what Kushnarov was really getting at . . ."

"Master class guy?"

"Yes! David Kushnarov."

"Your *pretty feelings?*"

She puffed a breath into the phone. "That was kind of despicable. And probably sexist. Would he have said the same if I was a guy? Duh. But the thing is, he's also kinda right. I do try too hard to control my feelings. No. I try too hard to control how *other* people feel, how they feel about *me* particularly, and how they perceive me, which is kind of all part and parcel—like saying the same thing, where music is concerned. Vanity of vanities. I should just find a way to be more honest somehow and direct, be freer and get over myself. Just go to the *music* first. Go straight to the music. Make it all about *that.* Or just quit."

"But the Wieniawski . . . man. I mean, kudos to you for playing it, but it's really the most godawful piece. So maybe it's not all your fault you don't know how to . . . whatever. Inhabit it or give yourself over peacefully, surrender serenely to the force or whatever."

"Be one with your breath." She laughed. This was in reference to the yoga class she'd tried for a while, second year of school—an attempt to gain better control over her nerves before performance. It hadn't helped. *It's one thing back stage,* she'd told him, *but when you're playing, how exactly are you supposed be one with your breath if you're thinking so hard you don't even know whether you're breathing? I'll stick with the beta*

blockers, thanks. You know, if you eat a bunch of them at once your heart just stops? How cool is that? No more jitters at all!

In the end he kept drifting off, coming back to her, watching the square of light from the window reflected on the wall at his feet. Imagining himself transported through it to her, falling past swaying shadows of tree branches, and then spinning back out—again her voice in his ear. The old childhood stuff boxed in his closet. The lumps in the mattress that no longer quite fit him. The crinkling feather pillow.

"The thing is, you've only ever really known me when I was in crunch mode. What you probably think of as normal for me is more like freak-out time. Get ready for senior master class time. I can be nicer, I think. I'll try to be nicer. Note to self . . ." (she deepened her voice to sound like she was reading from a bulletin) *"be nicer to Paul.* Check."

Why was she using this tone? Almost like an actress on a sitcom. Another deflection or defense, or something closer to the truth for her? In the brief time they'd known each other they'd never actually spoken on the phone.

"I'm losing it here," he said. "Gotta sleep soon. If I can."

"Hell. That's fine. I'm not even the least bit tired. Totally wired. If I can't find a way to make my brain shut up I'm going to have to stick a fork in my eye."

"That's sure to help."

"Which ferry did you say it was?"

Now winding along the coast, feet peeling up sand as he swerved in and back with the waves, jumping froth, strings of seaweed popping underfoot, again the plunge and surge of his breath, he wondered if he should expect her. And thinking about this, he realized how much he'd like to expect her; like to show her everything—this trail, the uninhabited coastline, the deteriorating and moss-funked timbers of his parents' home with the sliding glass doors and cedar-chip walk leading to his father's shop. The woodsmoke curling from his stovepipe and the moss-covered roof. *It's not a bad life,* he'd tell her. *Not a bad way to have grown up. What do you think?* It was probably why he'd chosen to come so abruptly in the first place. And what did this say about him? Here he'd left home precisely to get away from his father and his father's work—his violins—and what was he preferring instead? Wishing he could show it all off to the one person in his life enthralled by the same little universe of sounds and superstitions? He stopped, hands on his knees, watching the sand swirl with water, darken and go sheenless, air bubbles escaping. Then turned and headed back at a walk.

—

The feeling persisted in his father's shop, standing with him over his latest work on the bench that afternoon—a top, a rib assembly still glued to the mold, and a back plate turned in its cradle on the carving vise to show a surface as chopped and swirling with gouge marks and shadows as wind-ruffled water. "So this is me now," his father said. "A little slower and worse for wear, but if I look at it just right in the light, take a little snapshot in my brain and kind of *go* . . . it works. Mostly. I mean how much do you really *see*, anyway, when you're hacking away at a piece of wood? So much is going by feel and cumulative knowledge anyway. So. I don't know."

Paul traced his fingers along the inner curve of the wood on the vise cradle and tried to imagine. He lifted the finished top from the bench and lightly twisted it laterally from end to end as he'd seen his father do so many times. Tapped it beside his ear and listened for the reverberant overtones through the grain—winter wood, summer wood: sap, soil, water, wind, sun—haloing the dull *bong* of his fingers as they struck the surface. Smooth and arched as a distant horizon, he thought, turning it again and running his fingers along the arching. Curved and taut. *May*, he thought. He became aware of his father silently watching, head tilted and a bemused, knowing smile tucked at the corner of his mouth.

"What?" he asked.

"It's just good seeing you again."

Paul wondered about that—the word *seeing* suddenly so heavy and double-meaning, triple-meaning in unfamiliar ways: meaning literally *sight*, as in *good seeing you standing here in my shop*, but also, *good because who knows how much longer I'll be able to see at all*, and, *why have you been gone*, and also, *good seeing you show an interest in this work after all these years*.

He decided to take him on the simplest terms. "Good being here," he said.

"The corners were the toughest. I'm not going to lie. That one . . . I only blew through one other top, one other piece of wood getting it done. But this is how it goes now."

"I imagine." He looked but couldn't discern anything out of the ordinary in the channel, purfling, or edgework. "It looks great."

"Really, it's almost impossible, but I still have pretty good vision if I hold the wood," he lifted a finger and held it off center of his right eye, "just so and kind of let the image resolve there. Phew."

"Right."

"And I get your mom to help, if she's around."

"She mentioned that." He nodded.

His father nodded back at him. "And there's a kid. Nesbitt kid from down the road. When he has time, he's here. Learning. He's *interested* . . . so it seems. Nice enough kid. So I have his eyes too, if need be."

Paul went to the woodstove, kicked open the lever for the draft and seized the leather glove, wrinkled and stained with ash and wood grime, cranked open the door and threw in two logs. Bumped it shut again, sweet-sour smells of smoke, cinders and heat, enveloping him. He crouched, hands outstretched to the glass in the stove door, watching flames lick around and ignite through birch bark, hearing the faint roar in the pipe as the burn accelerated. He was chilled from his long walk back along the beach, and from the rain that had come up suddenly; his imagined imperviousness to the cold because of his heated skin surface, heated circulation, until it was too late and the chill had gotten through almost to his core. Still, in his head, a riot of windswept waves, rain, the clamber up the rocks to the ridge trail back.

"Sorry," he said. "Went for a little run this morning. Forgetting how out of shape I am, of course, and how quick the weather can change. Man. I got soaked."

His father bumped open the vise to rotate the wood he was carving. Next came the sound of his gouge cutting and rasping. Paul stood and turned so the heat burned the backs of his legs, watching his father at work: the slight head tilt between cuts and the tension through his shoulders as he leaned into it. *Here, let me*, he thought. *I've got this.* Only, he didn't because he couldn't; he didn't know the first thing. Nesbitt, whoever that was. Nesbitt would help. Or his mother. Why? Why this gulf, he wondered. Why would his father never look back to notice, only ahead at the next unfinished instrument, next job to get done, next goal or problem?

"Who's that one for?" he asked, and took a few steps closer to watch.

"Guy in Los Angeles. JC Romero." His father laughed. "Actually it's a funny story. Funny connection." He cranked open the vise lock, turned the wood again, again locked and leaned into it, cutting. "His wife—ex-wife now, but no matter, they had a few kids together so for better and for worse as some people say—Karen. She's an old, old girlfriend of mine. Actually, one of the very earliest for me, and the one to get me interested in violins in the first place, way back in the day. Her and her whole family. All from Planet Violin, as it were. Her mom taught at the college there; dad played up in the Portland symphony from time to time; sisters, all of them, all about the violin, all day, every day. Nothing but violins. And until her, I couldn't tell you a violin from a sousaphone, but . . . that . . ." He puffed at his work, tilted his head, cut some more. "Once I met them . . . no looking back." He crouched by the ball vise, staring straight ahead, his back to Paul. "Nothing like getting your heart good and busted to figure out what's next for you and what you need most in your life."

If Paul had heard this story before, he'd never heard it in this much detail, or hadn't felt he needed the details and therefore didn't remember. "What happened?"

"Well. She was a lesbian, for starters. Though that wasn't entirely clear for a little while."

"Wait. I thought you said . . ."

"Yes. That part of the story, her and JC, I wouldn't pretend to have any idea about. Some people need to go back over the same mistakes a few times, I guess? Maybe that's it. All I know—they're still quite close despite her being with this other partner, I've forgotten her name already. And evidently JC's been aware of my violins for some time now. They both have been as it turns out, so he made this commission, as a surprise gift for her. Three violins, best of the best, give her the full palette, full range of whatever I can do. And whichever she likes best, she keeps. If need be, he'll buy them all. I think the other wife or girlfriend—I forget if they have marriage in that state—anyway, I think she may be in on it too. Contributing. Ha! So money's no problem. But I haven't decided yet if I'll go to the party, myself. Kind of depends. I think I'd like to, but . . ." He scratched his head. "It's all a little strange, I think. So there's this one, and a nice little Cannon copy, and one from my own pattern. We'll see."

"She plays still?"

"Oh yes. Somewhere around Los Angeles. Not sure where." Again he turned the wood, again he cut. "I imagine she's pretty good. She was always quite good."

"I have a friend coming later today, maybe," he said, before he could stop himself. He hadn't meant to say anything until he knew for sure. But his father's story had drawn him out. That, or his wish for May to be here had become concrete enough he'd forgotten it was only a wish.

"Oh?"

"She plays. Maybe we can get her to give you a test run on the others. If you want. If they're ready."

His father faced him. Again the odd smile. He nodded. "I'd like that very much. All done but some of the setup. Take us five minutes to finish. You know. You know the drill. They're back at the house in your mother's . . . in the study. I was trying to shoot some good pictures there the other day. You could do it yourself, if you wanted."

"What—take pictures?"

"Setup."

"The hell I could. Anyway," he stretched, "I'm not for sure if she's coming."

"Right." He nodded. Didn't ask for a name or any other detail. "Still. You're welcome to bring them over and have a look, if you want. You'll see them there on the desk or maybe the shelf above it. Bring them on over, we'll get you going, cut a bridge, set a post . . ."

Paul went back to the stove and turned down the vent. Shoved his hands in his pockets and scuffed a toe at the dead cinders and ash on the hearth and plywood flooring. *All that nice dry wood in his supply*, he remembered. *How quick it would go up in flames.* How many years ago? And here everything was still, safe and good. "Back in a sec," he said, and ducked out into the wind-tossed afternoon, chimney smoke blown down at him and away again, tarry, acrid, the tarp over the firewood pile heaving and rattling with wind, the weather vane on the roof of the house spinning like a fury. In his head the weepy opening phrases of May's favorite Vivaldi began, or maybe it'd been playing all along and only with the racket of wind and rain filtering away other sounds and distractions could he remember well enough to hear it. If she was on the one o'clock sailing . . . he glanced at his watch. Unlikely. She'd have texted. Probably the three. If at all. He became so absorbed picturing her below deck in her old Toyota—the chewed-up upholstery and sun-cracked dash, chin muffled in the scarf he'd lent her, hat pulled almost over her eyes, asleep in the damp chill or fitfully napping and watching through the openings along the sides of the deck as the boat swayed and chugged across the strait to its berth, floating dungeon, floating cavern, vomitorium—he didn't remember crossing the yard. Saw without really seeing everything in his path—hostas, mugwort, roses, lavender he'd helped his mother plant one early summer afternoon years ago—as he jumped the cedar-chip walk to the soggy lawn, side-stepping puddles, and rushed up the newly treaded stairs to the front door, his head ducked as if to dodge rain drops. Didn't remember what he was doing until, with the doorknob taking form in his hand, he returned to his senses and realized. *No*, he thought. *Can't do this*. Then, *Why not*.

"Sure," she said. His mother was by the fire, on the phone, a hand covering the mouthpiece as she answered his questions. Always this contradictory impression he had of her, since moving away, that she was both smaller and larger, and more indelible, more brilliant, than in his memories—a quality of fierce watchfulness about her which made him want to stop everything and go sit beside her to hear whatever she might say next in her phone conversation. He wondered if it had always been like that and he just hadn't noticed, seeing her day in, day out, or if she'd changed since he left. "I moved them from that shelf, though. They're in one of the middle drawers. You'll see." She blinked at him. "I think there's a couple old cases or a double case somewhere there you can put them in? So they don't get soaked . . ." She uncovered the phone for a second. "Sorry. Be right back with you." Then, eyebrows lifted questioningly, nodding once, "OK?"

He nodded back, already turning and heading up the stairs.

The violins were where she'd said—in the middle drawer of her old desk, head to heel on their backs. Even before taking them out for closer inspection, he knew they were different. The patterns were the same as ever, familiar enough anyway, built on favorite forms his father had used for at least three decades now, but everywhere else—arching, channels, varnish—was evidence of his having followed some other impulse slightly at odds with his usual esthetic. Touching around the sides and corners and back Paul had the sense he was reaching through a curtain to somewhere broken or breaking in his father—a clinging to authority in all his signature marks and lines which, as it slipped from him, brought out this other less-deliberative picture he must have also always followed without knowing. The differences were subtle: Slightly flat spots and matte patches of color that struck the eye or seemed to float just above the wood. He sniffed at the varnish and pressed lightly to feel how soft it was—how malleable. *Look, it's another violin*, his father would have said (a favorite remark based on an old cartoon he'd hung by his bench for years—cat doctor coming out of the cat maternity ward to an expecting cat father, with the caption: *Congratulations! It's kittens!*). And it was true. Every violin made by his father's hands was, in a sense, the same as every other. Another kitten. And yet, not at all. These new violins were more like death masks, he thought, hastily pushing the thought aside. Especially the Cannon model, with its loopy asymmetry and off-axis arching. A self-reflective farewell claim staked against eternity . . .

Stop, he told himself.

He found cases under the old dresses and coats his mother stored in the closet there, snapped the violins inside, and made his way back to the shop. *Cut a bridge*, he thought. *I'm going to cut a bridge. That's it. Nothing more. Nothing I couldn't screw up completely and still cause no damage to the end product. Not a big deal. I'm not trying to save him.*

He kept his phone on and out where he could see it, in case she wrote or called, and picked up a knife as he'd seen his father do so many times. Settled on a stool at the bench where he guessed mainly Nesbitt worked, flicked on the overhead light, moving and adjusting its position until he could see clearly the grain in the wood of the bridge blank, and began. Within seconds he became conscious of following a pattern in his brain dictating actions and movements almost beyond his own accord: flipping the bridge around, paring wood from its feet *like shaving peels off an apple*, his father had said so many years ago—*nothing to it . . . find the shape inside the shape, because no two violins are exactly the same and so every bridge blank wants to be fit exactly, cut to size . . . and because if there was an easier way, the work wouldn't be worth doing*—rocking the feet on the face of the violin to test-fit and trimming away more wood, glancing back and forth between the feet and the violin face to approximate the curvature and lifting the violin closer to scrutinize the shadow and light under each bridge foot. He could do this. Maybe, after all, aside from having an "eye" he also had a "touch." A knack, a natural gift. Why not? By osmosis or genetics or some form of magic, maybe the centuries of violin wisdom and practice he'd grown up surrounded by had soaked into him at a molecular level so he'd never even have to work at it to succeed. Just pick up some tools and go. As a kid, he remembered suddenly, he'd always pictured the bridge as a kind of medieval promontory, ornate and man-shaped, like a high-voltage transmission tower and cut all around with cryptic marks; a tower overlooking a fortress of sound; crazy brace to be scraped and fitted, held in a sea of music and color. Funny, he thought, because he'd been both right and wrong, seeing it those ways. *No ideas but in things.* Where had he heard that? He couldn't remember. Some class from ages ago. Intro to American Lit again. But what about a thing that changed as your ideas for it changed; a thing whose shape and essence had to be changed to match whatever subject it served, like a bridge? A thing . . .

He became aware that his father had stopped work and was now watching from his side of the room. No other sound in the shop but the tick of the woodstove cooling.

"Like you never took a day off, right?" his father asked.

Paul shrugged. "I would not say that. No."

"Well, this is nice anyway. You're giving it a try."

"You haven't seen the end result. Just wait. I aim to disappoint."

"Ha." He went back to carving. "You'll want some chalk for later. In the drawer to your right there? You remember that part? And the crowning template. Same drawer. Remember?"

He didn't remember any of it. Remembered only watching his father day after day, knowing and resisting simultaneously the innate impulse to ape his every move, and the feeling that all parts of his father's trade corresponded with some mutant gibberish at the back of his head. In this case: where to rub the chalk and how to see the high spots on his bridge feet, where to cut more, then re-chalking and going again.

"Just don't make it too thin." So he was watching again. "I think we want to start a little chunky. Leave room to cut more. For the Cannon copy anyway. Might be on the bright side. The hard side, tonally. That's a hunch."

"Good plan."

"More wood in the bridge should calm it down. If you screw up . . . forty bucks for the blank, my cost. You can make it back somehow. Big deal." Again the sound of the ball vise opening, closing, the gouge cutting. "So who's the girl, oh mysterious one? Someone you've known a while?"

Since starting to fit his bridge, he had not thought once about May. Now as her face filled the internal screen of his vision, her recollected smell, the slight weight of her against his chest, he had to stop. Hold the knife exactly where it was. "May Park," he said. "One of my housemates at school who . . ." He sat back and stopped work altogether. "We started I guess you'd say *dating* a few weeks ago now. Not quite three weeks ago. Probably a terrible idea, being roommates and all. But she's great. Music student. I really like her. Maybe a year older than me? I'm not sure. Anyway, it's nothing serious."

"Violin performance?"

He nodded. "Yes."

"Nice."

He could ask about Jacoby now. Mention the trip to his shop with May that had started everything, the violin of his father's May had fallen in love with, and the role his father had subsequently played in their courtship. But that would be giving away too much—involving him, asking too much, or inviting his influence and approval. "She's good, I think. Really pretty good."

"I bet."

"She tried a violin of yours in the city a few weeks ago." Like he couldn't stop himself.

"Yes."

"At a shop in the city, I forget which—I guess it's there on consignment or something. I didn't catch the story. And we were . . . she was trying out violins. She needs a new instrument."

"Yes?"

"It was amazing. Really, truly incredible. She liked it a lot. Best violin of the day by a long shot."

His father grunted and kept working. "I like her already."

"But definitely out of her price range."

"It's always the way, isn't it. We want what we can't have."

Not necessarily, Paul wanted to say. *Why do you have to be like that always with the all-knowing Jedi bullshit?* But his phone had begun buzzing and lighting up with messages. He poked the screen to life and read: *missed the sailing ☹ holy hell with this wind we'll be lucky if we make it alive. if the next one isn't canceled say a prayer for me and see you on the flip side xox*

"That's a message? That sound?" his father asked.

"Text. Yes. May. Looks like she'll be on the later sail."

"You'd better get cracking if you want her to play one of these."

He made no reply. Went back to cutting and fitting. The room cooled as the fire in the stove died down, and he became conscious of the temperature of his skin and the wood in his hands reaching equilibrium so he could no longer say where one began and the other ended. He blew to clear wood shavings, his breath on his fingers and whistling faintly around the openings in the bridge, and felt his father standing at his shoulder.

"Here," his father said. "You got a nice start on it, but you'll be here all day at this rate. Let me . . . if you don't mind," he held out his hand for the knife and then the bridge blank, "if I can just . . . I'll give you a little push. Since we're pressed for time." And as his father turned the bridge around between his fingers, holding it to the right and the left with one eye winked shut, then the other, it turned back into itself—no longer part of Paul's hand, medieval promontory, idea, symbol of anything connecting him with the past or with his father, just a flawed and fumbled first effort. A hacked-at bridge blank, most of its wood still intact, which his father would now rescue. "Do you mind? See, if I can . . . just for a second. More like this . . . and then a little more like this over here. We can save it." As he spoke, he lowered his hands and turned the bridge one way and the other, paring into the heart, skimming the feet, describing it all around with the edge of his knife, slivers and splinters of wood dropping to the bench and floor as he opened the lungs, beveled the wings. "See? And then a little more here . . . here . . . remember?" He lifted it again for a look under the light, head turned to see it from the corners of his eyes. "Not bad, not bad. Nice piece of wood. You did all right." He smiled, rubbing the bridge between his fingers and thumbs, head cocked in the way Paul knew suddenly had always repelled and irritated him. Too pleased with himself. Too cocky and self-enthralled and on the lookout for praise. "Just a bit more here . . ." Again the knife stabbed and flew into the outline of the bridge and then he was pressing it flat to the bench, slivering away excess on the facing side. "And like this, and like this," he said. "Remember? It all comes back now?"

Back from where, he might have said. *What comes back is that I kind of hate you and I will never be any good at this . . . I will never even halfway catch up. Why try.* "Sure," he said. He shrugged. "I guess." And stood back from the bench.

"Take it down just a little more, crown and score it. Baby. You're golden. You're done."

Paul waved a hand at him and headed for the reclining chair by the fire where he turned on his phone screen and scrolled to May's text.

"Paul?"

"You've got it," he said, "I'm too slow. Another time." He flung himself against the seat cushions wondering what he'd ever expected. "It's fine." *Keep a puke bag handy,* he wrote. *Sorry to make you come all this way hopefully it doesn't suck too much.*

She wrote back almost immediately. *snap! let the sucking begin please baby you know right where I live*

"Paul?"

Yes I do.

"Yes," he said, sitting forward. His father had transformed again—gaze lost in the middle-distance, features slack. As much as the wood his father worked was transformed and given shape by his hands, Paul realized, so too that shape and the work itself was constantly transforming his father. He'd always known this: the violin was like an enlargement of some *thing* in his father's brain or heart, some ideal which maybe didn't exist anywhere in reality and which, consequently, his father couldn't ever quite measure or get across to his satisfaction. What he hadn't realized was how the work, the act of trying over and over, altered and enlivened his father—turned him impish, jovial, ageless. A stranger. Unconcerned with worldly matters. But as soon as any one of the many rote woodworking processes or tasks surrounding the business of making a violin no longer had his full attention, you got this other guy again. The slump-shouldered, sucker-faced guy who wanted something from you but couldn't figure out how to say what it was, could only look at you with vague disappointment and concern and the expectation of defeat tucking the corners of his mouth . . . all forms of displeasure that were really only an anxiousness to get back to work. To forget himself and be transformed again in his work.

"Yes," he said again. "I'm sorry for quitting so fast. It had nothing to do with you. I'll try again. Promise. Now's probably not the best time."

The corners of his father's mouth hooked lower. He blinked, shrugged, and turned away. Opened the vise, rotated the piece of wood in its cradle and leaned into it.

"Oh, hell," Paul said, standing again, tossing his phone behind him on the chair cushions. "Crowning template. Where'd you say . . .?"

"Middle drawer on the right," his father said, still working, not looking up. "It can be discouraging, I realize. This business. Sorry for stepping on your toes. That's my fault. Probably a little less than cool. Definitely a little less than cool. I just get carried away sometimes. Truth be told, I'm not the world's greatest teacher. Never have been. As I'm sure you know."

"How would I know that?"

"Fair enough, but maybe if you thought about it a second . . ."

Paul flipped the template one way and the other against his bridge blank trying to understand how the overlay worked, how to align it.

"Match treble side to treble side," his father said, still not looking. "You can figure this out."

"Sometimes . . ." he began. But the thought forked and cornered in too many directions for him to say it aloud without falsifying some part or all of it.

"Yes?"

"I wish I'd never left, sometimes."

His father sniffed once and blew to clear the wood chips. Cut a few more strokes. "That's nice to say, but you do what you have to in this life. If there's one thing I know. No rules. No one's asking you to choose anything, only so long as you're happy."

The rest of the afternoon, they worked in silence. Only the sound of their tools on wood, wind in the top of the stove pipe, his father unlocking and relocking the vise, leaning in again with the gouge, the zip of his gouge going through wood, then the finger plane, breaths blown to clear surfaces. Soon the woodstove had stopped its creaking and no flames showed in the glass, only a glow of embers. He stood back, stretching. Went to the chair where he'd left his phone and as he lifted it to check the time, felt the notification arrive in his palm with a dull chime. Another text. *fuck*, he read. *sail delayed and now canceled for mechanical not weather* ☹ *waited almost two hours already*

He glanced out at the clearing sky, high clouds striping the upper atmosphere and lit by the last rays of sun, blue, orange, yellow. Like fire season, almost. He remembered a summer morning from years earlier, coming into the kitchen, his mom alone there at the table reading and eating fresh-picked berries from the colander, taking them by the handful and crossing and recrossing her legs, flipping the paper in front of her. "Fires all across the state," she said, chewing. "Looks like our favorite winery might have burned down." And glancing up, seeing it was him, not his father, she caught herself before whatever it was she would have said next. Her face reddened. "Hey," she said. "Sneaky. I thought you were your father." This was the main thing about visiting home he decided, this constant layering of experience: being in the present and the past simultaneously, and reminded of forgotten memories at every turn—the angle of light through a window, the rattling of a tarp on a woodpile—like each memory had its essence displaced into the substance of some physical object and was contained there until you returned to awaken it; no, in fact, more likely the act of stepping aside from the normal flow of daily life and allowing yourself back into this context that once had seemed like the whole world to you—so full of meaning—caused it to look like a stage set for . . . stage set . . . Here the thought ran out.

Before he could key back a reply, her next message arrived, and another after that. *next sail isn't till seven!? i give up* ☺*blech. will you bring me a new violin please pretty please???? driving now. ttyl xox*

"More messages?" his father asked. It wasn't a question, exactly; not a rebuke either, but almost.

"Yes," he said. *Easy! At least one*, he wrote. *We'll miss you. Call when you can.* "Sailing's canceled for mechanical. She's not coming after all. Boo-hoo."

His father grunted and leaned into his scraper for another few strokes. Turned the cradle in the vise and stood back. "Life on the island," he said, pushing up his glasses. "Your fate governed by the whims of the weather and vagaries of the Washington State ferry system, on the daily. Who knows what was coming for you on that boat? Maybe nothing. You'll never know. Same as anywhere, I guess, just a little more noticeable. I've done about all I can here for now anyway. Let's get your mom and have a damn drink."

Again, his phone chimed and buzzed. "Sounds great," Paul said.

"Tell her to visit another time." He surveyed his work a moment, hands on his hips. Shrugged and untied his apron. "It's coming. Anyway. Another day, gone. Boom." Hooked his apron on the nail by his bench. "Unplug that glue pot for me, would you?"

"Got it." Without looking he yanked the blue cord connecting the glue pot to the wall. Plug still held in one hand, stale fumes of animal hide and bone meal like distant flatulence wafting from its surface, he opened his phone in the other to read: *no need. free tonight after all! find me or i'll find you can hardly wait!!! xoxox* . . . and an emoticon smiley with oversized eyelashes and swelling hearts instead of eyes. May's number and name in the display, their conversation from earlier marching along above that in little bubbles. No mistaking it. Her number, her name, but words intended for someone she thought was not him. He laid the plug over the back of the bench seeing nothing, only the letters glowing in his screen, that emoticon, feeling his heartbeat in his throat.

Can't wait either, he wrote. *But who did you think this was?*

"You OK?"

"Uh," he answered, still staring at the display. "That's a very good question. Probably."

"Don't you people ever talk anymore, like face to face, or is it all messages and posts flying through the ether? That Nesbitt kid I was telling you about earlier. Can't hardly get him off his device sometimes. It's like a whole other world inside that thing for him. Like a goddam Palantir."

"Oh, I don't know." Again, his phone buzzed and lit up in his hand. "I guess. Sometimes it's . . ." He shook his head. "We *say* it's easier to communicate by text, but it sure can misfire, too."

"Like now?"

ooooops!!! sorry plan to meet up with girlfriend for drinks. dumb me!! not to worry keeping it sane

"Yes. Like now. Maybe. Hard to say."

"You're not *breaking up* with a girl by . . . Is it still text messages you're sending?"

"Yes. Texts. And no. Not breaking up. I'm pretty sure you have to be *dating* someone first in order to break up with them. Whatever." He scrolled through options until he found a good confused, ouchy emoticon with a bruise on its forehead, selected it and clicked send.

"Someday they'll have chips in our brains so we can communicate telepathically. I hear," his father said. "God save us then. That's something I *won't* be sorry not to live long enough to witness."

His father killed the lights and together they went out, down the steps to the blue-shadowed grass beyond where the lights above the studio door could reach, and across the yard, the pressure of his father's hand at his elbow so light and firm he barely noticed at first, until it struck him: *He can't see. I am now guiding him through blank space*, he thought. *Through the dark. How did this happen so fast?* "Almost there," he said. "Steps here."

"I see that." His father dropped his arm and grabbed the railing, pulling himself up. "Thanks for the assist. I'm not an invalid."

———

He left his phone unplugged in the dark on his old bedside table to die and shut itself off. He didn't want to know more—or, he did, but not this way. Not by phone. Face to face, as his father had said. For now, best to let it be; stay in the circle of light at the kitchen table where the three of them sat, a bottle of his father's favorite Islay scotch between them and plates of old favorites—tomatoes in pesto, candied salmon from their smoker, rosemary crackers, goat cheese and bleu cheese from a local artisan, salami, fresh greens from his mother's cold frames, and final remains of her tortellini from the night before. "You're sure it's enough?" she kept asking, getting up to check in the fridge, the pantry, the cupboard for more. "How about some honeyed chestnuts from France? We've got a package . . . must be expired by now. No! Look at that. Still good. All these gifts from clients. We never eat them in time."

"Speaking of," his father said, "I'd take some of that Baltic salmon. From Holz? *That* looked good. Worthy of a special occasion."

"Dieter Holz of the so-called Sartori bows and the fake Maggini?" his mother said. "Ha."

"The same." His father tossed back the last of his scotch and refilled his glass, gesturing to ask Paul if he wanted more. "Every year, this Holz, he sends *gifts* because I sold him a violin once, wholesale. Like he owes us anything. I will never, but I swear *never*, tell him that half the junk in his collection is not what he thinks it is. Gifts or no."

"Some of it's real. Nice Gemünder," his mother said. "Actually, some very fine American stuff and a few modern makers—present company included— but the rest of it . . ." She shook her head.

"They're another breed, aren't they. Collectors."

"Not a *breed*, honey, unless you count idiots as a *breed*. Just people with too much money who want to show off and act like they know anything when in fact they're . . . just idiots. Trophy hunters of the violin world. Not a breed." A smell of fish and spice followed the sound of a package pierced and peeled open. "But they do send you a nice fish sometimes! Look at that. We should open a champagne to go with it. One year—no joke . . . Was it last year?" She broke off laughing and Paul had to realize, from the pitch of the laughter and her somewhat askew stance at the kitchen counter, she was more than a little drunk. " . . . he sent these cheese balls the size of your head all encrusted with nuts and prunes. I mean, *awful*. Like hardened CheezWhiz in a ball! With health food bling! What are you supposed to do with that?"

"Fed it to the birds. They liked it a lot. Squirrels, too."

"And here's your fancy salmon," she said, sliding back into her chair at the table. "Bon appetit."

They each cut a piece and for a moment nothing more could be said. "Jesus," his father said, chewing. "Almost as good as ours."

"Better."

"Holy mother. There is a God." His father nodded. "What do you think?"

Paul let the flavors sit at the back of his mouth and fill his palate—smoke, fish, brine, lemon. "I don't know," he said. "Tastes like a smoked fish?"

As the evening wore on, watching the shadows on the wall or drifting through their voices to the reflections of them all in the sliding glass doors leading to the back porch, he'd occasionally remember: May's voice, her face, her touch and smell, the feel of her against him. He'd see a flicker in the reflection, face or hand, and think it was hers. Because she should be here. She'd been on her way. And then he'd push back against the urge to go upstairs, plug in his phone and let it update the record of missed calls and texts. See if she'd tried to reach him. What she might have to say. No, he thought. He'd invested too much already. Why so much? Let it go.

"Our boy's down," his father said.

"I thought I sensed a disturbance in the force."

"His lady friend . . ."

"Not my lady friend," Paul said. "I would not call her that. We're like house mates. Were." He was drunk, he realized. Tangling his words. "Still are. And a couple weeks ago, nineteen . . . no, twenty days ago, to be exact, we started, like, dating. I wouldn't even call it that though."

"A violinist," his father said.

His mother raised her eyebrows, tilted her head. "Wait, wait, one thing at a time. What do you call it then?"

"What do you call what?"

"Whatever it is that isn't dating."

He tilted his glass to see the half-crescent of amber left at the bottom, considering. Swirled it and drank anyway—the malted kick of fumes; the sweetness and numbness as it dissolved. "Probably, you call it a very bad idea."

"School isn't hard enough for you already?" She slapped herself in the forehead. "Jesus. God. Why?"

"She was on her way here," his father said.

"Wait, *here*, here. Like, to our *house*?"

"Yes. But the sailing was canceled," Paul said.

"And was anyone thinking to *tell* me about it at some point? Hello?"

He looked to his father whose eyes slid quickly away—*You're on your own, pal,* the look said—as he reached for another bite of salmon.

"My bad," Paul said. "We just got caught up, working."

"Well that's a good thing, anyway."

"She played a violin of mine," his father said in a higher register, more like musing aloud to himself. Smiled and again drained his glass. "You said she liked it."

"Loved it, actually. Best one of the day, by far. It kind of . . ." *Got us started? Got her to go to bed with me?* He shrugged. "It was a great fit."

"Does our boy know how to pick them?" He refilled their glasses all around and angled the bottle to see what was left. "Girl that likes a good violin? She can come another time. Any time. Tell her. Stay a while. Where did you say it was, where she played it?"

"I didn't. I think it was Peter Jacoby's? In town."

"Jacoby the *Jackal*," his father said. Too loud, too full of feeling. "Jack of all trades, master of one: How to fleece the good people and part them from their hard-earned cash-money . . ."

"Don't," his mother said. She shook her head.

"What do you mean, don't? Don't *don't* me," his father said. He cut another piece of fish and spread it deliberately over a cracker, the expression on his face like an invisible string had snapped open some shutter in the recesses of his eyes. "It's what we called him! To his face! Sometimes." He chewed noisily. "Not the most scrupulous character in the business, let's just say. Not the most savory. Not the worst either, by a long shot. Did he introduce you to Albertine? His sister?

Kind of a family-run business, last I knew . . . couple of brothers, sisters. The father would have passed on by now, I'm pretty sure. I'm pretty sure I read that somewhere."

Paul remembered Jacoby's quick, mincing walk; his trimmed beard and the deceptive stumbles in his speech which were really a way to draw you in, elicit trust and keep you off guard. *Jackal.* Sure, he could see that. He tried to remember if he'd been introduced to anyone else. "Not by name, no. Just Peter . . ."

"She's the one to really watch for. If she's there still," his mother said. "Should you have the good fortune of any further dealings."

His father nodded. "Peter's kind of a poofter. Sorry. Can be. Nothing you can't handle if you watch yourself. But watch yourself."

"What's the story?"

"No *story.*" His father chewed, swallowed. Folded his hands and focused his eyes upwards and to one side, considering his next words. "We worked with him a few years in the very beginning, Karl Marcowicz and I. This is before Marcowicz went back to his own little family atelier full-time—wife, twin boys, bunch of gold medals, the full-meal deal. Anyway, we did some restorations together there. A few setups, that kind of thing. And the stuff we saw going on there, at Jacoby's shop? It was pretty shady. Nothing huge. Nothing we cared that much about. Unpapered bows and violins that weren't what the consignor wanted Jacoby to sell them as. And I mean, *really* pretty obviously not, but . . ." He opened his hands, blinked, grinned. "There was one in particular, just a kind of nothing violin sent to us from Warden's shop in Chicago, so-called Goffriller that needed a new bar before he could sell it. And I looked at that thing at least a dozen times before I finally had to say something. Probably shouldn't have, but it just didn't sit right, charging whatever it was then, thirty-five thousand dollars for something that was probably worth closer to three *hundred.* You know," he gestured vaguely, "'What are you doing, Peter? This isn't a Goffriller. You know it isn't a Goffriller. Anyone can tell. It's some random German shit that looks maybe, *maybe* a little like a Goffriller. Doesn't even look Venetian. What are you doing here?' And he said . . . what Jacoby said, he just kind of gave me that look. The stare. You know he's blind in one eye so you never can tell which eye he's seeing you from—I never figured it out anyway. Always gave me the creeps, made me feel like at a disadvantage somehow. He says, 'Denis, there's such a thing as being too good for your own good.' Something like that. 'It won't get you very far in this business. Might even get you killed.'

"I mean, I already knew it's part of the game you have to play, if you want to sell violins and have any kind of reputation with the big dealers. They send you their b-list crap, no papers, and you have to sell it for their crazy prices and pretend not to have noticed. That or . . . I don't know. Like he said. Get killed. Get put out of business. Who wants to find out?" He sat back abruptly. "That little number though, with the Gofriller . . . it was too much. So we walked. Took our couple of tools and projects that weren't part of the shop and never looked back." He drank and seemed momentarily lost in memories. "Great Django-style rhythm guitar player, too, though. Both Peter and his dad. It was kind of their thing. They'd sit around the shop all day, playing jazz . . . So what happened with the violin?"

In the few pictures of his father as a young man that Paul had seen, he always had the impression of him as superimposed onto whatever was going on in the background. Like he was straining a little too hard to project a certain look for the photo, a certain indelibility; or never fully trusting the camera to capture his likeness. Stiff and posed, you might say, but it was more than that: One shot of him at his bench, with a grin as tight as the death grip he had on the violin neck (one of his first) in his hand; another of him tilting from a sailboat, water flashing by in the background; one with Paul's mother, the day they were married staring straight ahead, barely smiling while she hung on his arm, laughing, head thrown back. The disjunction between those images and the way his father tended to describe himself in stories and anecdotes—righteous, active, the voice of calm and reason—always left Paul a little heartsick and confused, wishing he might have known him as a young man and also very glad that he never would. "Which violin?"

"The one your not-girlfriend played?"

"Still there, so far as I know," he said. His voice sounded wrong to him, words coming from a distance (the scotch?) like a recitation, as he told them everything he remembered about it—the rusty brown pigment and finish of his father's violin, the beauty in the carving, tool marks in the f-holes and scroll. The sound.

Even just talking about it, he sounded like a fake and a poser. Someone pretending to know more than he did. "I don't know what you did," he said, "but the tone on that instrument . . ." He shook his head. Better not try to describe it, he thought, but he couldn't stop himself. "It was a perfect match anyway. One of those things. So much depth and warmth and fundamental. Like a rich caramel. Still plenty of articulation, though. It was hard to walk away. Very, very hard, actually. For a while she wouldn't stop talking about it. It's why she wants to meet you. And maybe also why she feels a little intimidated. Which . . ." He shook his head. "I don't know. But eighteen thousand dollars. It's way out of her range. I think she doesn't get along with her folks too well."

His father sighed. Picked chestnuts from the bowl on the table and popped them in his mouth, chewing noisily. "It's a fair price," he said. These words also had a little too much force, enough to make Paul tip his head to the side, wary of flying nut particles. "That's what I get for them now. Sorry." He scrubbed a hand at the table surface. "Bring her with next time so I can explain. Apologize in person. It's a living wage."

His mother snorted. "Living wage."

"It is! If I can keep up the pace, for however long, we're fine. We're fine!"

She shook her head. "I am not having this conversation with you right now."

"It's true."

But Paul knew from experience, once started, *this conversation* would not be put off. Or it might be, but temporarily. The weight and momentum of disagreement (an old and ongoing one) would continue in headshakes and glances, clipped double-meaning words, indirect jokes, eye-rolls, until it pushed its way back to the foreground—all of his father's usual justifications and assertions (*I work alone, I don't need to play that game, the who's who game, pleading around for favors and attention to jack up my prices; it's enough that I keep building and people love what I make, and besides, how much more money do we really need?*) to be countered by his mother's more practical sense and financial worries (*It's called marketing, it's called trying, Denis, get over yourself; you need a web presence at the very least*). Eventually they'd get back to it. It was nothing he wanted to hear again.

Paul pushed up and out of his seat.

"Back in a sec," he said, and headed for the bathroom, sure to turn on the switches for both the light and the overhead fan to drown out whatever they said next to each other. For a while he stood, hands dripping water, looking at his reflection in the mirror over the sink, wondering. Here was where he'd first encountered his drunk reflection, years ago, back from a night out with high school friends partying in the graveyard and trying to talk himself down, make the words line up sensibly in his head again before facing his parents or dodging them altogether: that giddy face, ridiculous and childish, slightly unfocused, beating in and out with his pulse. *Who am I*, he'd asked then, and seconds later found himself doubled over the toilet and throwing up noiselessly, with some surprise at the force of it—the ease with which it came. Also where he'd first shaved and laid open a patch of skin over his lip that wouldn't stop bleeding. And later, where he'd smoked up before school occasionally, blowing hits out the window and waiting, staring into his pupils in the reflection until the rest of his face vanished, pieces at a time. So what remained of any of that now, he wondered. Who was he after these years away? The same as ever, but older? Better at nothing? At staying away? He leaned closer. "Cretin," he said. "Faker." Stuck out his tongue and stepped back again, grinning. Hit the lights and went to join them.

They leaned together at the table over something his father was in the process of sketching onto a scrap of paper, their heads tilting to follow the development of lines, quietly exchanging words, and nodding—not arguing; not disagreeing, after all. He was surprised and pleased, enough so that he didn't want to intrude. Wanted just to stand back and savor the picture. "Your dad's new idea," his mom said, waving him closer. "Come have a look. It's a way to mount mirrors and magnification at the bench to enhance his peripheral vision and make work a little easier with the glaucoma. Is he a genius or what? Have a look."

But the jumble of lines on the page seen over his father's shoulder, without explanations leading into them could mean nothing, or very little to him. "Nice," he said. "That's great." His father hashed out a few more lines, rotated the paper and added what might have been shading. "Like this," he said, "and like this . . ." Paul pictured him at the bench surrounded by repeating images of himself and whatever he was working on, his hands in triplicate or quintuplicate pushing a tool over wood, the various work angles canceling each other or converging at some point in infinity where they folded over and vanished.

—

In the middle of the night he woke and didn't remember where he was. His legs ached and as he kicked his way onto his back again, seeing the square of light on the wall at his feet, the tree shadows moving in it, he remembered. His parents' house. Alone. The run along the beach that now burned through his calves and thighs. He reached for his phone and almost before he could stop himself, plugged it into the charger. "May," he said. The dream he'd been having must have involved her, but was fading too quickly to call back in much detail—something about a bat trapped in a room, and her leaping around in a shawl or a scarf, waving her arms like wings to mimic it. All those nights with her in his bed at school, her shoulders curled against his chest and the back of her head tucked at his chin—the ease with which she always leaned into him, let her head ride there in the hollow at the base of his throat and dropped straight into sleep, stayed there all night—he should have known better. He could have been anyone to her.

"What, don't you trust me?" she said, the one time he asked about this. "I trust you. You want to hold that against me now, that I trust you? It's a choice. Is there some reason I *shouldn't* trust you? What's going on here? Right here, right now, isn't it enough for you?"

He hadn't had answers for these questions because of course, there were none. "Never mind," he'd said. Slid a leg between hers and rolled tighter against her, timing his breath with hers until he was able to forget and sleep again.

free tonight after all! find me or i'll find you can hardly wait!!! xoxox

What was she doing, right now? With whom? Who was she?

No.

He leaned from his bed and yanked the charger from his phone again.

He didn't want to know. Didn't want to see or hear any more words from her until they were face to face.

—

Late next morning, before leaving, he followed his father back to the workshop. Watched him build up the fire in the woodstove and as he crouched there, feeding in strips of birch bark and kindling, the firelight on his face first more yellow than orange, Paul went to inspect his own work from the day before. It was no good. He saw that immediately. Clumsy. The few untouched lines from his father, those confident strokes opening and beveling the inside wings of the heart and kidneys, the smooth taper of the facing side, now appeared as if they'd been stranded in a hackery of cut marks and gibberish. Botched. The feet fit and that was about all you could say. Positioned against the gleaming gold belly of his father's new violin it would be an obscenity. An embarrassment or at best a non sequitur. His father had been humoring him all along. Suckering him, maybe, to get him back at the bench. A good bridge was a signature of sorts—he'd heard this a thousand times—a byline, a final flourish, and no violin of his father's would leave the shop with such a grotesque piece of work attached.

Hearing the woodstove door bump closed and his father's footsteps approaching, before he'd come close enough to see, comment, offer false praise or a critique, Paul winged the bridge at the black plastic waste bin beside the bench where it struck the plastic with a snap, bounced once inside, and stopped.

"Fail," he said.

"Hey, hey!" His father went to the trash and bent, fishing through wood chips and paper towels until he'd found Paul's discarded bridge. "You don't get to throw that out. Come on. You save it, or you learn something from it anyway." He held the bridge up, right eye, left eye, and then lowered it, continuing his examination. "Not the worst I've seen, by a long shot. But you can do better next time," he said finally, and placed it on his bench. "Your knife . . . that knife you were using anyway, might need sharpening. I'll show you another time." He motioned with his head for Paul to follow and as he looped the strings of his apron around his neck, tying off in the front, walked to the safe at the back of his shop. "Let's see," he said, and spun the dial. "I keep it real simple so I won't forget. In case you ever needed to get in here without me. Brain dead simple. Zero, one, two." The lock clicked home and he pulled back on the handle. "*Open says me,*" he said, as the door pulled away. "Now, what I wanted to show you . . .

where did I put it . . ." He removed some violins Paul remembered dimly from years ago, handing them off or placing them on the shelf beside him—one with square shoulders and exceedingly high, flat arching, and gold yellow finish; another, reddish in color, no fingerboard, and the unglued top plate making a slight rasping noise against the rib assembly as Paul took it, set it aside; one with a ringed grain in the back wood, maybe poplar he thought, no purfling in the top; another with no neck or scroll, just a body, the varnish worn away around the shoulders, dirt and rosin abraded into the finish alongside where the finger-board would have sat, and a crack straight down the face—each with its secret history, life story, failed wish to have been more, to have been loved . . . "Here we are," he said. "Most of the stuff here, I kept it for one reason or another. I don't know. Some of it goes way, way back. Some of it is straight-up junk. You probably remember. Even if I personally can't stand the thought of ever doing another goddamn restoration in my life." He shook his head. "This one, though, I'm particularly fond of. My crown jewel of the junk box. I don't believe you've seen it. Needs a new bar and those cracks cleaned up, re-cleated, new pegs . . . Probably a few other repairs. Bunch of other repairs. Nothing major."

Brilliant red pigment where it remained in the face and back, like it had been pushed up through the varnish, or had ebbed like a tide over the centuries to reveal the sandy gold ground and grain of wood in the bottom quarters of the back plate, the pale blush of old spruce in the shoulders of the front. Looking at it, Paul could almost hear and feel the imprint of notes through that un-even disbursement of colors—the layers and underlayers of tone, one gold and unadorned, another vibrant as vermillion; high and low, sweet and stern, and the breaking point between, where the color faded or tore aside like mist on a mountainside. "Stunning," he said. "I can't place it." He flipped it again to look at the front plate, the whiskers of dirt and blacking on the left side above where the chinrest would have sat. The scroll with its thick, sleek turns and a distinc-tive scribe down the center line, like a part in a girl's hair; a crack between the peg holes on the treble side; the flowing back of the scroll reminding him, as always, but somehow more strikingly, of a horse's neck or a rook. "He kind of chamfered these turns here on the scroll," he said, "and maybe added blacking there, which you can still see a little, and these little black marks on the face too, so I guess he was trying to antique it at the time. Which is really cool. So he was copying someone, but I can't say who. It's kind of like if Strad and Guarneri had a love-child. The pattern, the length and just how kind of big it looks . . . It's like on a Strad model. The measurements look normal enough, though. Nothing weird, eyeballing it, anyway. But then the arching and those corners, the f-holes . . ." He shook his head. "Totally Guarneri. It's kind of amazing. Not really Cremonese, not really French either, but kind of both. Is it like two hundred years old? What's the story?" Again he flipped the violin front to back and lost himself in the grain, the imagined tone imbued there, that gold-amber ground and the medullary rays of summer wood, winter wood so visible, light crossing into shadow and back again.

"Giovanni Pressenda," his father said. "My best guess. And for exactly all the things that stood out to you. You do have an eye. Can't cut a bridge yet, but you can see." And through his father's thumbnail history of the builder's life— *Farmer's kid, itinerant musician, started building in his mid-thirties, in Turin. Nothing but his books and a few tools left to nephews in his will, very modest lifestyle; maybe learned from Storioni, maybe not, probably not self-taught anyway, who knows . . . Sold some new violins to Tarisio and one to Paganini, so he had a decent following in his day, some notoriety, but not enough to get rich; three hundred violins total, give or take . . . Seemed to care about pretty much nothing but building violins, once he got going*—Paul barely removed his eyes from the instrument. Something in those lines and tool marks matched with a feeling just under the surface of feeling in his mind, closer to dreaming. The arching, the opacity of the varnish, the suggestion of a voice in every detail. Yes, he thought. Of course that's who you were. Of course that's your story. You can see it in every detail. You can feel it ringing right through the wood: A man with a face like his father's but with a different severity or sensuality outlined in the wrinkles around his jaw and forehead from a lifetime of words, expressions, and gestures in Italian, not English. Prouder and more hopeful maybe, but otherwise the same.

"Some of those repairs, you can see, were done very well. Very lovingly," his father continued. "Some are more of a hatchet job, who knows the circumstances there. I did what I could with the varnish already. Started on it anyway. Best guess is it made its way here after the Second World War. Somebody played the stink out of it anyway, that's for sure. And then by fate or chance it ends up in a hock shop. No papers, no identification. All I can tell you," he scratched at something on the back of his neck, "both Karl Marcowicz and I, the second we saw it? We knew. I said, 'Let's each write down what we think on a piece of paper, separately, see if we agree. Blind.' Sure enough . . . same identification, to within a year. Because you can't miss it, really. Like, it's straight out of the book, line by line, detail by detail. Take it to any of the houses that could paper it for you, though? They'll tell you it's junk and give you five dollars, maybe five hundred if you're lucky. Then they'd turn around and sell it for a quarter million or more. Try and sell it yourself? You can't. Not for what it's worth. Not without papers. Maybe I just have too many enemies in this business anymore, truth be told . . ."

None of this history or background connected the violin with Paul or predicated his guardianship of it in the next phase of its life, and yet he felt drawn, called upon to serve its preservation.

"I'd like to fix it up," he said. "Whatever it needs. I think I could do it."

His father blinked at him, beaming inscrutably, shaking his head, maybe seeing him, maybe seeing him as a shifting blur with missing patches, who could say. He laughed once like he was barking. "In your dreams," he said. "You touch that violin . . ." He shook his head. "Start with this," he reached and held out the yellow violin with high flat arching. "If you want to fix violins. I knew I saved it for a reason. Junk from an old girlfriend, way back when. From Spain. I got a few others like it kicking around. A few dozen others. Do that and about twenty-five more, maybe a hundred more, we'll see. Then we'll talk. That violin isn't going anywhere. One hundred and seventy-odd years already . . . it's not going anywhere. You want to work your way up to it? Fine." He was still beaming, eyes clouded with feeling, the ugly yellow violin held out like a scepter. "But if you touch that Pressenda before you're ready? I'll cut your hands off."

"What?" Paul asked.

"What *what*? That's the first time in a long time I've seen you care so much about anything. Good to know you're still alive in there. You'll be all right."

"You mean, because I care about something you understand. Part of your little world. Nice."

"Oh, fuck you. *Something I understand. My little world.* Sure, it's something I understand. Whatever." He turned and set down the yellow violin. "All I can tell you right now. I see the look on your face. I know what it means. And if you want to learn, you want me to show you any of this stuff? I'm glad to do it. But you'd better not waste a lot more time." And in a cooler, dismissive tone of voice, "Let's get you back inside so you and your mom make it out of here in time for your boat. Skedaddle to Seattle."

Four

On the top deck, protected on two sides from the weather, wind-whipped fog and rain, spray from three decks down creaming the bow and sides of the boat, he stared back at the island, watching it recede until soon enough it was indistinguishable from other humped and shrouded island shorelines and treed inlets resolving out of the mist and then, as they rounded a corner bound for open water, gone altogether. The ship's horn blasted once and again from just overhead, reverberant and jarring even with the advance-warning announcement—*Ship's captain has asked to advise passengers that there will two short blasts of the horn*—grating through all his senses as always, and the silence after, the distant crash of water below, wind whistling over every part of the ship as they picked up speed, starker, plainer somehow. Emptier. *Finish out the quarter,* he thought—his mother's parting advice. *Finish it out, do the best you can with all remaining work, and see where things land. That's it. Evaluate once you're done. No decisions now.* In his pocket was the bridge he'd swiped from his father's bench—his bridge: the smooth wood surfaces and curlicue shapes cut into it around which he ran his fingers, jamming his fingertips in the heart and kidneys and flipping it again in his pocket to press the slightly crescent-shaped feet in the joints of his first and second fingers. Why he'd taken it, he couldn't say. He just knew, passing on his way back out, seeing it there on his dad's bench and waiting as his dad closed down the woodstove before following him out, he couldn't leave it. A mark of his failure. Sign of having tried again and failed. Couldn't leave it for his father to fix or throw away or archive. As soon as his back was turned, he slipped it into his pocket.

Finish the quarter out, he thought again, like a mantra, again feeling his way around the bridge in his pocket, the crown and feet, the sides with their cutaway openings. The few smokers who'd come on deck with him immediately after boarding had long since finished their cigarettes and gone back in to get warm, but he couldn't tear himself away just yet. He wanted to see out into the open strait for a few minutes, as far to the horizon as possible, the water almost the same steel gray as the sky but harder, wind-ruffled—to let whatever he saw there match with the feeling just under the surface of feeling he hadn't found a name for yet but which seemed to him badly in need of some corresponding shape or containing perspective. If possible.

Finish the quarter, he thought again. *Make no decision till it's done and then see what's what.*

"Because whatever it is you're considering here," his mother had said, her hands on his shoulders so they stood squared off to each other. "Whatever it is, you owe it to yourself to finish first." Water had misted in her eyebrows like frost, and along her hairline. Her forehead shone with it. "OK?" She shook him lightly and attempted a smile. "Are you listening? I know you're weighing a lot right now, a lot of decisions, and your dad's health . . . It's important. There's some urgency. But you're more important than any of it. Your future. So take your time. Are you listening?"

He'd nodded. "Why do you keep asking?"

"I can't tell always."

Wǒ bù zhīdào. Wǒ tīng-le. "I'm listening . . ." *Tīng-le.*

Like that part of his brain had been shut off—the need to deflect whatever he was thinking about into phoneticized word sounds, words in other languages—since arriving on the island, at their house, he hadn't thought once about Chinese or linguistics, word sounds given shape by the various parts of the mouth, breath pushing over teeth and tongue, vocalized, unvocalized . . . none of it. Like he'd forgotten. Why? He had no idea, but an answer of sorts was in his mother's eyes, the film of tears as she hugged him to her and pushed him back, sending him away: All the feeling in her and between them that he needed to deflect or attenuate. And because he had nothing more for her than the usual, in response. *See you when I see you next. Hang in there. Love you too* . . . And this time, the extra words, "I will. I'll finish out and decide later. Promise."

He flipped the bridge crosswise and squeezed hard enough to snap it in two, but it wouldn't break. Flipped it the other way and squeezed. Still, it wouldn't snap.

Some kids who looked vaguely familiar—maybe a class or two younger at his high school, one with gauged ears and spritely, elven features, the other black-haired, thin-bearded, both in dark hoodies and skinny-jeans—had come out to smoke. "Got a light, man?" one asked, somehow too seriously. He wanted to laugh at them but shook his head instead, and shortly after, with the familiar smell of cigarette smoke on salt air blown at him and away and suddenly back again, he turned his back from the weather and headed inside. He caught once at the door, missed, and as the floor swayed, grabbed again and pulled it open, stepping over the threshold, inside. *May,* he thought, and only then, feeling in his jacket pockets, inside, outside, pants pockets, realized he must have forgotten his phone entirely. Still sitting right there on his old childhood nightstand. One glance at his duffel bag on the bench where he'd left it before going out on deck, and he knew. He remembered the rush to pack and get out the door. The quick tumble of his feet going down the stairs. The rush back up for his toothbrush and razor. It wouldn't be in there; hell, he thought, unzipping and rummaging through all the same, to be sure—books, change of clothes, snacks from his mom. It would be a long afternoon with no diversion and no chance of reaching May or anyone until closer to evening. Until he was back on campus, back at the house.

Just make it through the quarter, he thought again. *No decisions till then. Calm. Calm. Lĕngjìng.*

But the words had lost any placating effect they'd had for him.

—

Approaching the house from the alley side, the overgrown hawthorn and Oregon grape covering the east facing wall, burying it in foliage, kitchen and dining room lights glowing inside and the big window giving him glimpses of the table where he'd eaten so many bad meals alone and where he and May had first sat talking, the music came back on in his head. The skittering cat-and-mouse-chase music of her Polonaise and the reel of black-and-white scenes that had looped with it. That manic cheerfulness mirroring the hopefulness in their talks about her future and about violins, and then the anxious feeling of always living toward those moments when he'd hear her feet pounding up the stairs, her key in the lock. Something hidden just under the surface of feeling there as well. She was . . . Who was she? Their days together had been so few and condensed, anything he knew about her, he realized, had always been distorted by the intensity of his own feelings for her, because of . . . well, everything. Her fingers, her voice, her hair, the smell of her skin, the ridiculous volume of her footsteps, the feeling of her mouth on his, her music. He couldn't think and be in the same room with her. But how else were you supposed to know someone?

He'd never imagined he'd miss that piece of music but hearing it in his head, he wished he could go back to everything he hadn't known about her then in exchange for what he didn't know now.

On the sidewalk, outside the fence running around the property, looking up at the "tower" room that was his, the bay of windows where his bed was, he stood a while wondering—letting the rain soak his hair and cut cold lines along the seams of his jacket and the gaps in his shoes. Nothing but drafty and cold in there too, he knew, however welcoming and rundown Victorian-chic it looked from the outside; full of spider webs, everywhere cluttered with old furniture and junk items left by the owner or previous renters. Well, he thought, and lifted the latch to the front gate, catching faint strains of violin music from her side of the upstairs as he went through and headed up the walk, up the porch stairs— nothing he recognized immediately; a new piece for her maybe, late Baroque or classical—maybe it would be all right. Maybe nothing had happened while he was gone, or whatever had happened wouldn't matter and they'd take right up where they'd left off with their non-relationship. His half-hearted attempts at finishing out his degree; her terminal self-hatred and the bad violin she seemed stuck with for any foreseeable future. More phrases caught his ears and vanished and in the intervening silence, checking the phrases against anything he could remember, he recognized the piece—another Bach partita. And here it came again. Not the one she'd played for him at Jacoby's. Slower, denser. Full of chorded passages that felt, in their dissonance and harmony, like they meant to break the violin apart, splinter or lay it bare. The Chaconne. The ultimate in solo violin music. He waited, listening, wanting more now that he knew what he was listening for, but heard only the tat-tat-tat of what sounded like a metronome gradually resolving to the sound of water falling from the eaves onto the rhododendron beside the porch. Rain through tree leaves. No more music, if there had been any to start with. Was he dreaming?

Later he'd wonder if he'd turned back, never slid in his key to open that front door with its sidelight stained-glass windows giving a false sense of cheer and prosperity, never stepped over the threshold and gone in, up those stairs and into his room to dawdle ten minutes running a towel around his wet hair and changing out of his wet clothes, sitting at his desk for a second and waiting for the music to start up again, waiting for a signal in it telling him what he should do next, how to proceed, if he'd done none of that—stayed away, never come back or never left, charged his phone and kept it on all the time, not left his phone on the island, anything different—maybe he would have averted the course of fate; changed the outcome of all his various actions and inactions. He tapped the eraser end of his pencil on the textbook left open on his desk, seeing the words there, not registering any of them. There should be music, he thought. Finally he pushed up and away from his desk, unable to wait any longer. Stood in the hall outside her door for a moment, still listening—a cough, a throat clearing, her voice on the phone, anything to give him a cue, let him know she was inside; the bright interrogation-style lighting of the hallway bouncing upon every dirty surface and windowsill—and finally knocking. Reached up for the key he knew she hid at the top of the doorframe because of so many previous lockouts, unlocked and pushed open her door.

Twilight-dark inside. The room, as always, thick with her clutter of discarded clothes and books and random junk, the smell of her blown at him by the portable heater as it kicked on with his entrance—that sweet combination of her sweat and soap and hair in every item she owned and which he could never have enough of, never have close enough somehow—and as he picked his way to her, eyes still adjusting to the semi-dark, in the wedge of light thrown from the hallway, he caught sight of her foot at the end of the mattress and knew. Something in how she lay turned on her side, like a still-life pirouette, arms outstretched around nothing, hair strewn behind her, rays of varying darkness. Not right. He drew a breath and didn't let it out. The music he'd heard must have . . . Where had it come from? "May!" he said. "May? Jesus." He rolled her onto her back. No response. Cleared her mouth as he'd been taught however long ago in life-guarding class, parted the lips and blew in. Cool skin, no pulse. Breathed more with her in and out, in and out. Tasted alcohol. Garlic. Something like dead leaves. Tobacco. Slapped her cheeks lightly and tried again, chest compressions, mouth to mouth, lifted her shoulders and dropped them against the mattress. "Jesus, God, no, come on! May!" She was supposed to be laughing at him for having forgotten his phone and for being so paranoid about her text from last night. She was supposed to be putting away her violin, loosening the hair on her bow, telling him something about the piece or how much her playing of it sucked and then they'd have walked out together for cheap food. Maybe he'd have shown her the bridge in his pocket and said, *Down payment on the future. You want the rest, you'll have to wait. Might be a few years, might not be anything close to as good as my dad's, but I'm working on it. It's coming . . . Promise! You're sounding great by the way. As always* . . . Their shadows stretching ahead of them, splitting and falling behind them again with each buzzing streetlight, the rain persistent as mist, they'd have walked on until he found the courage to ask, *So, who is it*, or maybe, *Who was it*, and then, *So, are you in or are you out? Is this a thing or isn't it?* Again he leaned over her chest, pumping, air he'd blown into her wheezing out suddenly like a sigh and giving him enough false hope he laughed out loud, lunging at her mouth to breathe with her again, in-out, in-out, until he knew it was no use. She must have been gone for hours already. He lay across her and then beside her and tried to lift one of her arms around him, to draw her to him and see into her face one last time.

—

Of the first people to arrive at the house, once he'd found the code to open her phone screen—*Keep it brain dead simple*, he thought, like his dad probably, re-membering the pattern he'd seen her fingers trace over the keypad innumerable times, and after a few tries landing on it: 1-2-3-1—after the EMTs and police had come and gone, one was the reed-thin violin instructor from her master class. The one who'd been at the podium speaking when Paul first entered the class, now in a Yale sweatshirt and faded jeans, wet pink crescent imprints from his glasses in the corners of his eyes and indentations along the side of his face from the glasses' arms visible each time he lifted them away to sniff and wipe his eyes, changing his face from older to younger and back again, until he had enough composure to ask Paul what had happened. *Why? How?* The married man, Paul thought. Top of the list of her "favorite" numbers. Her instructor, yes, but more than that—the one whose house she'd been headed to the night she came back to him? Jeremy Hagen. Whatever had been between them was not finished, either; had not been finished when May and he first hooked up, probably. Hair more black than silver, a lanky austere appeal in every angle, the light touch of his fingers under his chin to wipe away tears, again lifting aside the glasses to dry his eyes—Paul understood with a certainty that felt to him as if it came from the recollected touch of May's cool skin and her mouth which had lain open without speaking. This was more than a teacher to her. Had to be.

"What do you mean, you don't know? How can this *be*? It's impossible!"

Paul had no words of comfort, no information. "I was gone. I'm so sorry."

Eventually they decided Hagen would contact the parents and the rest of the musical community, the school authorities. And with this determination and a subsequent series of actions, people arriving, voices filling the hall outside her room, the downstairs, other roommates, friends with no better place in mind to convene, another piece of the puzzle fell in place for him: shaped like himself in silhouette, small, and not near the center of networked, interconnecting pieces that had been her life. Not the boyfriend. *Roommate—not like that!* He was her bounce-back attempt at creating friction and distancing herself from an overbearing teacher's attentions at a crisis point in her schoolwork. Necessary, but not. Someone outside the circle of music majors and known faces and therefore safer, more distant and distance-making. *I'm a heart surgeon too*, he'd heard his father say once, joking and not-joking, shaking hands with professionals at a dinner party for orchestra patrons, donors, and friends. *But I do my operations from the outside and my tools never touch anyone. That gives me the right, too, I suppose. No bypasses, no stitches—I go right*, he smacked his hands together, *for it. I save a lot of people. Probably not as many as you. A lot.* Whatever had been awakened in May by his father's violin—his own connectedness with those feelings an inherited and unearned affection—he'd mistaken it for something else. Something more lasting and significant in her life. In his own life. No, he'd allowed her to mean as much to him as she had, because she *had* mattered that much for him. Casing her violin a final time after Hagen had gone, he pressed around the shoulders and held it close for a last whiff of her, anything left in the wood from her years of playing—all the desire and self-loathing poured through it. Spun it at arm's length and plucked a string. Heard in the sound as it faded across her room, that maddening sameness, the same cheery brightness. Her voice and not her voice still in the sound. Her voice, but missing anything essential that was her.

Though he had dragged his thumb shakily over the icons for her call log, missed calls, incoming, outgoing, and text messages, he never clicked through to any details and never read anything. That felt too . . . invasive, and anyway, he didn't want to know. She had called him once, late the night before. Not her last call but close to it. No further texts. This was enough to know. When the police arrived he handed the phone over, with her code, otherwise untouched, and the explanation that he'd used it to call out a few times because his own phone was lost—911, Hagen, his parents, a few other of May's contacts under "favorites." "Good god," they each said, coming into her room and looking around, or if they didn't say it, shook their heads to communicate as much. "What happened here? Can you tell us . . . is this how she lived, generally?" He shrugged. Said nothing. Did it matter? "A music student?" Until the toxicology report, there would be no known cause of death. For now they ruled it possible suicide, possible overdose, bad combination of recreational drugs—alcohol, MDMA, pain killers, Spice. Who could say. Later would come the clearer picture: May, alone, drunk but not blacked-out drunk, swallowing one of the blue methadone pills from someone's stash (another left in her purse still) to help herself sleep it off; to really go deep—shut her brain up and stop the racing in her heart from too many Red Bulls; the jittery, over-nerved sensation from the last few weeks of constantly practicing—calm it all and just sleep. A few last calls and texts, and down . . . Not suicide. Though for now, they had only guesses. "She liked to drink, you say?"

"I didn't say that. I didn't actually know. If she was drinking, she seemed to drink a lot. But I really don't know."

The self he was left with at the end of this, burned through, sleepless, unmoored, felt at once truer and more familiar—who he'd meant to be all along—and a total stranger. A shell or remnant. Starved stick figure haunting the house where his parents lived, poking the embers in their woodstove, bringing in loads of firewood when he could remember to, washing dishes, wandering up and down stairs at night and standing for hours at the front window looking out. Wind and rain through tree limbs. Sky clouding and clearing. Sun, no sun. Fog. Waiting for something. The final word about May, he supposed. What she'd died from. And after that, still waiting, for what he didn't know. Until then, until he was able to divert his attention long enough to recognize the feelings rooting in his solar plexus and radiating from there to his hands and wrists—the urge to make or save or touch anything, turn it to a shape worthy of its final outline—the days burned and flew. He stood aside and watched them burn, let them burn.

— ■ —

Years later, Pressenda in hand, strung and restored to his father's satisfaction, he returned to Jacoby's alone. The day was cool and rainless, the sky ribbed with high-flying cumulonimbus and lower, faster-moving clouds in shreds and wisps just below that, intermittently blocking the sun and magnifying its light—what his mother called a cheater sky. A loose, half-grounded feeling in his head to match the meteorological distortion, as if he'd slipped aside from time again—like a hangover, but different. The same bell jingling overhead with his entrance, the same smells of violin varnish, polish, Sacconi, rosin. Same thickly padded carpeting underfoot and ostentatiously resplendent presentation of violins on shelves and racks, ribs out, lit by overhead track lighting and floor-to-ceiling windows hung with thick drapes to block outside noise. Gold, brown, rust, red, and every color between. Jacoby at the counter, leaning on an elbow and talking with a customer. The same stuttering capitulation and head nods and tight strut as he went to get a violin and another and another from the rack by the window. "I'll be with you in a just a sec," he said, not quite facing Paul, and ducking around a corner with the customer to set him up in a test room. Paul had called ahead to make sure of their hours and that Jacoby himself would be in, but he hadn't set an appointment. No reason Jacoby should recognize him or think anything out of the ordinary about his being here.

"Now," Jacoby said, returning behind the counter, hands folded on it, leaning toward Paul grinning. Again the faintly ravaged mouth concealed by facial hair. "What c-c-can I help you with today."

"I have this violin," Paul said.

"You have a violin. I see that. Any idea . . ."

Paul had lifted the case onto the leather-topped counter and now paused in unzipping it. "I know what it is and I know what it's worth, roughly. It's pretty hard to mistake it. But . . ."

"There's always a *but*. Isn't there?" Jacoby cocked his head to one side, still grinning falsely.

Paul flipped open the top and removed the cover inside, turning the case so Jacoby would be able to see. "We guess about 1842. Maybe '41."

"And whose fine work would *we* guess it is?"

"There's no guess. You'll see."

"I'll see?" He leaned closer. "May I?" he asked, and before Paul could answer he'd lifted it from the case and now stood admiring it in the window light, raising and lowering his glasses. The right eye, he realized, was the one he could see from. Not the left. The brown eye, not the green one. "You say you did this repair yourself?"

"I didn't say. But yes. With some help. That's my work."

He flipped it to look at the back. "I should know you, I think. This is very fine. Very nicely done."

The back, to Paul, was still a dead girl's black hair streaming sideways; always would be, regardless of any color in the grain or added pigment. "Well," he said. "You do, actually."

"I do?"

"We met . . ."

"This is all a bit too much of a game for me. I'm sorry." He returned the violin to its case. "Very nice. Bravo to you for fixing it up so nicely. Do you have papers?"

"No." He breathed evenly in and out. "That's the *but* part. No papers . . ."

"Ah, well, there . . ."

"And that's where you come into the picture, because we know you sell some violins from Warden's shop in Chicago occasionally and we figured, given that relationship, maybe you could partner with us to sell it—call in a favor there with Warden to have him paper it, do a three-way split, something like that, minus the cost for my restoration and his fees. We could use the money. And regardless, this is a violin that should be *played*. Such a gem. Don't you think?"

"Do you always speak in the royal *we*, mysterious-one-who-I-should-know, or are there other pari ties involved? Other parties to be met?" He winked the blind eye and stood back, beaming.

"Just my father and I."

"Oh for fuck's sake. You're Denis LeFault's kid. Listen to you, talking like some kind of violin Mafioso. Some little hood." He smacked himself in the forehead. "Jesus. I knew that. I recognized . . ."

"I told you . . ."

"Like, years ago now, you came here with that beautiful girl, what was her name, and then I read about her in the paper! I did. I saw that and I recognized her. I thought so, anyway. What the hell was the story there?"

"I'll tell you," he said. "First tell me what you think."

Jacoby pressed his hands to the countertop. Puffed his cheeks full of breath and contorted his mouth inward, the ravaged shape of it more visible through his facial hair, the scar across his upper lip. He wouldn't resist, Paul thought. He couldn't resist. Jacoby blew the breath out slowly, shaking his head, adjusting his glasses again. "It's an awful lot of money, if it is what I think. Even split three ways. But if it isn't . . . you know, and without papers. Who knows. Your father burned a lot of bridges around here. Not just around here, actually." He crossed his arms. "This is a tough one."

"I'm aware. That's why I'm here and he's not."

Again he grimaced, blew his cheeks full of air and exhaled with a sputtering noise, shaking his head. "God. I'm going to regret this. Albertine will kill me. I could give you a few thousand—say, five thousand for it—right now. But that's about the b-b-best . . ."

Paul drew the case toward himself, covered the violin inside and closed it. "I'll keep it in mind," he said. "You're just the first shop I'm trying, because my dad's still kind of fond of you despite everything. But whatever. We'll keep trying."

"Who . . ."

"I've got a list."

"Smart kid."

Paul lifted his eyebrows. Waited. *Is that a change in heart?* "Thanks."

"Maybe next time we can work out more ag-g-greeable terms."

Next month, or sooner, he thought. "Sure," he said. "Next time." *Begin with the best,* his father had said. *Lay the bait. Next time, you bring him some crap he can't resist because he's got that missed chance he didn't take in the back of his mind. Tell him you got half a million for the Pressenda. You want a little less for this one. Trade high if you have to. Sell low. Keep at it.*

"That time I was here, all those years ago," Paul said. He lifted the case from the counter and stood it on its end, between his feet. "You had a violin of my father's. The one my friend at the time, May, played. It was exceptional, if I remember right."

Jacoby shrugged. "I wish I could remember that far back. There's a lot of violins in the world . . ." Then he snapped his fingers. "Oh, in fact, I do remember that violin! By golly. Sold it shortly thereafter. Must have been a few months later? I don't know. Young kid with a bright future. Very talented. High school student. Parents refinanced the house to buy it. N-n-nothing I could say to talk them out of it. Th-th-that thing was a hoss. I said so at the time."

"You did."

"You wait long enough, you know . . . eventually everything sells. But sometimes you wait a little too long and buh-bye. Missed that boat. Most fiddles though, if they're good enough, they sell themselves. Half the time, I have to remind myself I have a job here at all." He slapped his hands on the counter.

"Well, I'm glad to hear that—glad at least someone's playing that violin."

"Last I knew anyway."

And as he went back out through the door with its bells jingling overhead, into the bright overcast light, waving a final time over his shoulder and stepping down to the street—hearing traffic noise and voices of passersby, heels on pavement, an ambulance siren wailing in the distance and police siren much closer yelping-chirping once sharply before going silent again, plane floating along overhead, the delayed sound of jet-engine noise thudding to the ground around him, momentarily blocking everything else . . . all worldly sounds easily supplanting the airy padded quiet of the shop interior—through it all, came the plaintive sounds of a violin tuning up somewhere back in Jacoby's shop. Playing. The whole time he hadn't noticed. Or he had noticed, but in his constricted focus on Jacoby he'd somehow never registered any effect of hearing. No, he thought; he had. He'd heard it. Scales and arpeggios. Quick comparisons between instruments. Back and forth. And now, as the player warmed into it, that same music—Bach partita number one. Not his father's violin and not May playing, but the same music—those opening chords and the dilation of time and feeling to surround them. *The beginning of the end of the best violin music ever to be written,* as his father always said. *The most perfect music ever written for a solo violin. Maybe the most perfect music, period.* Those notes he would always associate with May and the afternoon he'd sat with her, listening, seeing the bare points of her shoulders in that dress, the light in her hair; her smells intermingled with all the smells of the violin shop; her wrist cocked over the strings and pulling down, the sweet discord of wire and wood resolving to perfect fifths, to music, and feeling in what she played that his life was about to shift on its axis and go out of balance in ways he couldn't anticipate but already half-welcomed . . . This was the same feeling, he realized . . . the one he returned to now day after day, with each violin he opened up and laid bare in pieces on the bench, looking for the way inside. Looking for what had gone wrong. Where it had broken. What could remain. What to replace. What could be saved. What couldn't.

His foot caught against the pavement. He looked up abruptly, her name in his mouth—thought he saw her, a girl like her anyway, flitting across the street ahead, violin case slung by its strap over a shoulder, laughing too loud, the bright cadence of light reflected in her hair . . . gone, almost as soon as he'd seen her. Not her. Couldn't be.

He focused his eyes forward and went on his way.

WE
UNLOVELY,
UNLOVED

You had a dream of playing the violin, or maybe it wasn't your dream. Maybe it was the dream of a parent or dead grandparent channeled through you, displaced onto you. Or the long-forgotten dream of your childhood . . . walking home from school and hearing through open windows, from the house recently vacated and occupied now by strangers in weird hats and dark clothing, where your best friend had always lived and where you still slowed in passing, half disbelieving her absence, hoping to catch a glimpse of her through a window or outside on the lawn sunbathing—those soaring, unmistakable tones. Lush, prissy, preening, unforgiving. Too full of feeling. Something from another world, another time and place, familiar and drenched in sentiment in a way you knew at once was a bridge to and an abridgment of all real feeling—suffering meant to signify and transcend its own expression simultaneously, too dignified to be called by any one name. Instantly you'd wanted it for yourself, the sound and all associated feelings, or wished that both might one day lay claim to you, lie down beside you and pour sweetness through your ear like honey, though you were only seven or eight years old at the time and couldn't possibly know anything about this, or suffering, or the rest of your life, or what you might want out of it. Higher, higher the notes went, circling raptors on a thermal, arrows arching against gravity, leaves spinning in a breeze. A prickling along the back of your neck: announcement to your soul from itself, salute from intellect to intuition, from genetic information to cognition. *That sound is me.* Though it would be years and years, more than forty, before you remembered long enough to find one of us, join the local community orchestra—school, life, law school or medical degree, work, family, insurance and mortgage payments, deaths, boats and cars and family trips, more deaths, tennis games, golf, a surgery or two, divorce, fake teeth, sunsets, boredom and finally, there it was again: the violin. Time to take up that old dream of playing the violin.

Or you never dreamed it. You simply chose, the day in fifth grade everyone had to pick: band or orchestra. Winds or strings. Chose because the boy ahead of you with his long-handled comb in his back pocket, the pockets of a darker color and fabric than the pants themselves, and constantly drawing your eyes, reminding you of the fullness implied above the rolled-up cuffs of his shirt, too, the hints of coming manliness in the sinews of his forearms and shoulders, because you heard him say it first, *violin*, and wanted in every regard either to *be* him, to grow up sooner, to have his affection and attention, or to mug him in a dark alley (or to be mugged by him) and have him all to yourself. You chose, too. The violin.

Or, you woke from a sleep so profound and restful—brilliant, early summer light dusted with pine pollen outside your window, dazzling with possibility— your only evidence that you'd lain here all night, unconscious, the dents and wrinkles left in your sheets and pillow . . . and that sound in your head. The sound of something vestigially connected with dreaming. No, you'd heard it the night before, too. In your grandfather's study or maybe it was outside on deck chairs with him, listening together, watching him take in the last light of day from behind the crooked shield of his beloved newspaper, the smell of his Scotch, humming and bobbing his head as he read and crinkled and drank and took in the fading light without ever really looking at it, growing noticeably more excited as the violins amassed toward some feudal proposition involving cavalry, horns, bursts of timpani, until suddenly the soloist peeled off ahead of them all, alone on his war horse, standard weepily waving in the wind, armor gleaming. And here it was still, that sound in your head, as if you were with him again, listening, and you knew. Whatever it was—it was you. You had to have it closer, not as a thing separate from or outside of experience, but as an angle of selfhood you'd always known about without exactly knowing, like last year when they took out your appendix, or your sister's tonsils the year before that. Invisible parts and pieces that had been there all along and doing their job but which you couldn't know about until someone cut them out.

Whichever way, you found us. We found you: we unloveliest, unlovable legions of unnamed cheap violins in sizes incremental to full, never meant to be

loved or kept by anyone. Meant to get you started, nothing more. Hatched in
batches and carved by machines and on assembly lines, no one of us exactly
the same, but no one of us really any different from or better than the others.
Bodies scarred by neglect or abuse, the student who dropped us, the one who
kicked us, the one who banged with his tuning fork on the outer edges of our c-
bouts because he was lazy or stupid or harbored an unexamined resentment for
all that we stood for and all that we could not help but constantly remind him
of—his clumsy fingers, tone-deafness, lack of focus, deficient small-motor skills,
his mother's disappointment—despite his teacher's and parents' reminders: *Are
you paying the deposit on that piece-of-crap violin? Are you going to fix it? Is that how you'd
treat a Strad?* Our bellies gouged by an ill-fitting array of mismatched fine-tuners
wound to the ends of their threading, the gouges filled with brown shoe polish
or wax and food coloring, coated in super glue or epoxy, left to oxidize. Heads
stuffed with a mishmash of pegs, mostly not our own, some refusing to turn,
wrongly wound and threatening to split us at the cheeks, in our cheap plastic
cases smelling of other children's fingers or of bubblegum or that bubblegum-
like unwholesome burnt-eraser smell of classrooms worldwide, or of pine tar
from a melted cake of cheapest rosin. Banged against your leg as you ran for
the bus, thrown under a bed for the summer, tossed in the back of a car and
left there overnight to freeze, then left many nights, wood fibers shrinking inside
varnish, so days later when you finally remembered, brought us in, threw open
the case by the heater or the woodstove, you might watch in dismay and amuse-
ment as our varnish checked and crazed with cracks. A pointless, meaningless
litany of lines signifying nothing. *Piece of crap, look what just happened to it! Like rock
candy!* If we were horses you'd put us down. Call the slaughterhouse, salvage
whatever meat might go unlabeled into dog food and render the rest into glue
for more violins. More and more violins.

Here we sit. A crate of us, whole and busted into parts, cracked tops, stringless
heads and necks, stoved ribs, dusty shoulders, earless scrolls, peeling tops, all in
a jumbled pile. We, representatives of your forgotten dreams, left in the base-
ment when the store owner went bankrupt and no one—checking inventory
and selling off stock, store fixtures, cash registers, etc., to make good on back
debts—shined a flashlight far enough down the stairs to see us here or thought
to make note of our very negligible value. Or maybe they did see and chose to

leave us exactly as we are. Not worth anyone's trouble. Alone, in the dark. Not a note or lick among us. Where the crate sits, the drip from an overflowed toilet or backed-up sink, a busted water pipe of years gone by, has warped some of us and coated others in a brackish, mineralized deposit of hard water and floor seepage and dirt.

Lifelong service toward an unglorified end . . .

Once, we were loved. Not all of us. Some. Sorted through for salvage and resurrection occasionally by the balding young apprentice-luthier, his apron pockets weighted with files, eyes huge behind glasses, who probed and measured until he quit, moved north to Seattle to open his own shop, and no one took his place. But love for us is not the alchemical solvent, Philosophers' Stone, by which better violins may be transformed from wood, varnish and glue into the musical, metaphysical equivalent of gold. Of perfection. Of God or some deified set of geometric, tonal ideals, auctioned for millions upon millions and bearing a title ostentatiously connected with an imperial, transcendent past— the Lady Blunt, the Cannon, the Messiah . . .

Take Martha, whose husband in his mid-fifties drifted off in his easy chair after a heavy dinner of sausage lasagna and his favorite Caesar salad from the market across the street following a hard day's work, a final smoke and sips of bourbon as he slipped into a stroke-induced coma and never woke . . . The last years of Martha's life were enlivened solely by one of us—a dark, square-shouldered German, slightly undersized and so a good match for Martha's crooked, slow-moving, smallish fingers (quicker at disassembling munitions and cleaning sidearms at the base where she'd spent most of her life), the shorter reach of her arms accommodated by the imperfect, too-small German's mensur. Crooked neck, varnish the color of a dirty cigarette soaked in walnut stain, ugly wide-grained top, too much shine in the yellow-gray burl of the back, artless unslotted f-holes . . . but who can measure the value of those years following the husband's death, liberated at last from his snores and his habits of picking his nose immediately after sex and flossing his teeth at the dinner table, burping without a hand over his mouth, but also his general good-natured companionability and kindness, tenderness with cats, and the nights they'd sat outside watching the sunset over the backs of other identical houses across the alley in the fading Sacramento heat, inversion purpling the dome of the sky from horizon to apex—who can say what those years would have been without the ugly, undersized violin from Germany? Who can set a value on that? The nights sitting across from his empty easy chair, covered now in music books, sheets of music, cheat sheets, and simple scores of tunes and songs from her childhood, practicing scales and finger exercises assigned by her teacher at the store where she'd bought the violin—where she'd picked it out with a feeling like love-at-first-sight from the lineup of them hanging by their scrolls on a pegboard display, each as dim and ugly and flawed as the next? *That one.* Those nights and the other nights, once she was ready, with new friends from the same music store working up a head of steam on some of those old-time favorites, all of them together in a unison, losing themselves to the sweep and rhythm of melody indicated by the black marks on the page, its lunge and soar to someplace better, someplace sweeter, freer, together blurring past any missed notes, out-of-tune bits and muffed phrases . . . Good nights, many of them. Some of the best of her life. At the store or sometimes at Martha's house. Son deployed by Bush senior to the Middle East, her pension still paying out enough to keep her in beer and chips and beef jerky. New music and strings for her violin.

Or Marvin Fong: second-generation immigrant, heir to the family grocery; his lack of interest in all things commercial or store-related—placing orders, stocking shelves, greeting customers with a smile, working longer hours to get ahead—as puzzling and alienating to his parents as his ease with the backward, treacherous English language and his ludicrous dedication to "sessions" with the local button accordionist at the corner pub or anywhere else they could find to play with the other pipers and balladeers, whistlers, fiddlers, banjoists, players of the stick-drum shaped like an enormous tambourine, sometimes step dancers, arms straight at their sides, legs kicking and flying . . . Every night but Sunday, the songs and jigs and reels of a culture more incomprehensible to them and remote from China even than California. What was wrong with him? He barely drank and never made a nickel playing—worse, he seemed content eternally stalled out in bachelor brotherhood with the accordionist, as indifferent to the effects of that as he was to the lack of any commercial value for his endeavors. *Why do you not want a son? A wife? Why you do this to us?* Marvin's violin—an overbuilt Suzuki, machine-sawed f-holes shedding splinters of wood fiber, bridge like a sink plug, distant, wiry tone—had been a gift from his parents early in high school (and one they ever after berated themselves for having given) to help him fit in and solidify his place at the back of the first violin section in the school orchestra. Theirs too then, they decided finally, to insist upon having back in return for the store and all of their savings, the day they announced their retirement plans and asked him please to step up. Abandon the shenanigans and take over. What else could he do? Years after their deaths he found it again, the old Suzuki still strung and mostly in tune, sleeved in rosin dust from his years of sessions, at the back of his mother's closet and hidden under a stash of unworn, black shoes she must have bought decades earlier at a bargain, so she'd never have to shoe shop again. But it wasn't the same. Without that button accordionist who'd long since moved on—without the buzz and wheeze of his reeds, every phrase of Marvin's stamped over by the braying, joyous fractiousness of the accordion's push and pull, his always starting and ending the tunes, calling through the ruckus—*One more! Ho!*—no joy in it. The violin sounded like it always had, by itself: empty. What he'd really wanted . . . something good to fill his spare time. Little enough pleasure in his solitary life anyway, who needed the reminder that once it had been different? That once he'd cared? Anyway, he could hardly remember the first thing about how to play, or any of the tunes on his old tune list. He traded the violin at the shop in partial exchange for a new Casio keyboard with some decent rhythm presets and early 90s-era looping capabilities so he could play by himself without sounding quite so alone, if he wanted. If he ever felt like it . . .

The celebrities among us: one, a Czech or possibly Hungarian Strad copy and notorious spinner of tall tales. Cracking, over-thinned back, sunburst-patterned finish mostly blasted away and weathered by time, top freckled with ancient drops of blood. Sold or traded first to a Depression-era brothel in Lovelock by a traveling salesman—one of a quartet of cheap instruments painted white to suit the madame's preferred virginal string-quartet parlor staging—and played indifferently by a rotating cast of whores in lingerie and garters who did not love it or dream of playing it or wish for anything much beyond sleep or escape; some older, some teenaged, some in makeup thickened with lead, one with a bow arm driving like a water pump, another who never played, only hid it under a damp bare arm (prop, shield, foreign object) that stripped away some of the white paint and caused its surface to smell faintly of lilac, soap, talcum, and days-old sweat. Until the night it was stolen by one of the girls, Hispanic and of indeterminate age, in the middle of a police raid, carried by her over deserts, valleys, mountains and fields, on trains and later horseback, farther west and south, not because of love or dreams or any dedication to its well-being, but as her sole collateral against future harm. Hocked at a shop in San Diego, and weeks later stripped of paint, back plate thinned to an inch of its life, Czech label gone, and strung up in fresh Black Diamond strings—sold again at three times what the shop owner had paid out, to a leather-capped, red-whiskered troubadour, years younger than the age given in any of his questionable documents and on a desperate one-way quest out of town, as far from his jewelry-store-owning parents and all their disappointment in him as he might ever get: Fiddlin' Will Slim (né William Eric Goldman). Up and down the California coast—on stages and in bars and play-houses, calling square dances and country dances; in a hammock under the stars beside Slim, weather permitting, witness to any number of drunken young ladies charmed out of their clothing by Slim's singing and playing and his way with words; rained on in the open back of Slim's flatbed and once left in a parking lot for hours before Slim, chagrined and somewhat panicked, returned for it; later, when musical styles changed, stuffed with foam and plugged into a Fender amp and distorted through wah-wah pedals for psychedelic effect, and when the styles changed back again, the foam replaced with the rattles of two rattlesnakes and the pink garter of a girl he claimed to have loved—year after year, the Czech went with Fiddlin' Slim. Once, to the doors of Carnegie Hall on a trip east. Another time loaned to a notorious big-eared fiddler from Bill Monroe's band for a sold-out grange hall show in Crescent City, and nearly not returned; instead, Slim and the big-eared fiddler sat up all night drinking cases of cheap beer and smoking cigarettes, playing everything they could think of in common to play. Benediction given at the end of that night: *Damn good to know you, Slim, and good to play this old box. Lucky thing for you I don't just shoot you and keep it for myself, like I say. You take good care of it.*

On it went, until the night Fiddlin' Slim, in vintage wedding lace, work boots and fedora—part of the shtick for his latest set-ending, stunt-fiddle number—

tripped on the dress train and fell headfirst from the stage and was not caught by any of his adoring fans, the Czech baptized in his blood but otherwise miraculously unscathed. Slim's last words, caught in a froth of blood and broken teeth and mostly inaudible above the volume of the rest of the band who peered down at him from the edge of the stage but did not stop playing right away—*All my life, this violin*—the Czech raised like a scepter at one of his fans, the only one to grasp the enormity of what was passing and what had been bestowed upon her. Thereafter enshrined at her home with other Fiddlin' Will Slim (and Elvis and Kitty Wells) memorabilia in an alcove-like corner of her living room lit with Christmas lights and candles. Surrounded by posters and cassette inserts, set lists, guitar picks, signed pictures, souvenirs, coffee mugs and dried flowers, the Czech spent its last worldly years gathering dust, slowly splitting its sides from its top and back, glue joins everywhere giving way, fingerboard as sunken and shrunken as an old heel of cheese, so that the day the woman finally passed and her children came around with insurance assessors to clear out the place, see what might be worth keeping, selling or donating, the violin was declared worthless and donated to the shop where it was briefly inspected, plucked at, tapped around, and boxed into the basement, its near-celebrity past forgotten.

Another, stitched together from scraps and shards of Italian tone wood at a family-run German shop, mid-November 1938, by a shop owner who in anticipation of losing everything he owned had already broken apart the most valuable instruments from his personal collection into a handful of scattered parts and pieces, the value and provenance of each known only to him, in order to avoid seizure by the culture-hoarding, culture-whoring Nazis. As a final gift to his most promising client—a girl with baleful eyes the color of ferns in rain, quick, decisive fingers, and a head of unruly black curls inside which ticked a metronomic precision the rival of which he'd never witnessed; a passionate lyricism that always put him in mind of his own allegedly gypsy-blooded grandparents—to keep her playing and in good spirits through whatever might come, he went to work and painstakingly spliced together ribs of three different instruments; scroll from an unattributed Italian he felt certain was the work of Andrea Guarneri grafted to a neck from his own stock; neck block branded with his customary marking; top salvaged from a ruined Ruggieri, and the back from a Tononi, cracked and cleated and patched a half-dozen times. For weeks he sneaked back and hid in the rear room of his shop, working by candlelight at night and in shafts of moonlight or dim winter sun through a broken rear window to avoid notice, cold air mixed with snow and rain freezing his cramped, chapping fingers, careful to avoid any misstep. No time now for mistakes. Each shard must match the next exactly, no undoing anything, no leaving anything to chance—all the while thinking: what a ridiculous, pointless exercise, ridiculous final testament to his life's love and work, monument to a lifetime of skill and craft, an entire family lineage of trade skills and secrets, to be passed undocumented to a client with love, yes, and some real sense of urgency or hope for a better life for her somewhere else, someday, yes, but really with the utmost certainty of the futility of it all. The pointlessness. Why music in the face of war? Why music ever? Who cared about fine violins? *Because*, he told himself, filing, clamping, gluing. *Because, because, it is all that I have and all I have to know myself by. And anyway, what else would I do? Fight hatred with more hatred? Where does this end?*—until at last it was done. French-polished to mostly hide any irregularities (but not completely; he wanted his craftsmanship subtly on display) in the mismatched patchwork of colors and grains. His final work. Out of the shop and out of his hands, to be played by her wherever and whenever for the rest of her life, in England, Finland, Shanghai, and later America, until years later by a series of unexpected events and ill-considered bequeathals it wound up in the window of the hock shop in Sacramento, at first visited daily by the niece who'd hocked it and who continued to fight the addictions which had caused her need of fast cash, and later weekly, biweekly—visited and played until at last she fell off the wagon and was never seen or heard from again. Later misjudged by the young new owner of the shop—*Piece of junk. Look at all these messed-up repairs*— and thrown in the crate with us. Finito, the life of the patchwork violin.

The rest of us, fractionals, full-sizeds, a skein of busted bows, the same every-where and serving the same purposes, we claim no such history. Fingerboards marked with dots or stripes of paint or of tape—white, blue, fluorescent candy-colored "frets" to assist the more tone-deaf students with finger placement— only the shiny, hardened residue of adhesive left now, a chip or two of color . . .

Or maybe you dreamed of us, but for one reason and another never laid a hand on us or on any of our brothers and sisters the world around; never felt the pinch of our unaccommodating plastic chin rests, the sting of our end-pins and tailguts catching at your neck; never breathed the faintly bitter, beery acrid spirit-varnished wood-and-rosin smell of us, or felt the ache through your hands and fingers as you fought to pull a tone from us. Your last days on earth you lay attached to machines, one minute threaded to the next by heart-beats and inhalations timed, measured, and assisted by those machines, noth-ing musical in any of it, and dreaming whatever the dying dream. Random moments; nursery rhymes; times spent and obligations missed. In the back of your head somewhere, maybe, a sound like the one that first made you know of us. A picture with it: summer evening, light in the highest branches of the trees suggesting an earlier time of day, shadows covering the ground and lower leaves and branches, rainless clouds towering along the horizon and re-fracting too many colors changing too quickly to name, grass cool and slightly damp through your dress and against your bare calves, hint of dew hanging in the air, not yet fallen, as the orchestra came to order and tuned. All your adult life still ahead of you, that night. Patter of applause with the conductor's entrance, so like other things you loved—rain through tree leaves, butter siz-zling, brook water over stones, the rush of adrenaline before a kiss—stage-lights up full now as he raised his arms for silence. For the downbeat. And who knows? Maybe some part of that dream persisted, trapped around the bed where you slept alone the last years of your life, until the day your family came to clear the house, and entering the bedroom—transistor radio beside the open window left on, or suddenly switched on by an electrical impulse discharged through the air upon his entrance into the room, a change in radio frequencies caused by his presence—the child you'd always hoped might play for you (and who did, for a time in grade school, though grudgingly) stopped dead, hearing: the opening phrases of your favorite concerto spiraling up and up. A cry from beyond bursting out of the silence and static at a volume too loud to attribute entirely to chance or fate, and causing the hair on his neck and shoulders and the backs of his arms to prickle—the notes perfectly ordered and phrased in much the same ways they're always phrased, and saying the same things about life and death and love and triumph and hurt generally shared by players of that piece. So he called them to him, his remaining family. To see the curtains spinning full of spring air and emptying again. To listen and let the notes pass, and you with them. To hear in them everything you wished you might have said, but didn't.

THE
FIVE

Cat on a Hot Tin Roof, that was it. Twenty-some years since first seeing the play, and still Gary remembered: leading man Brick on his crutches, drinking, drinking, not speaking, not giving anything away, waiting for the click. *I drink till I hear the click in my head that makes things peaceful!* In his own case though, no wife to nag him, no football injury, no drama, and certainly no longer anywhere near the prime of his life. Just himself, by the little fish pond in his back yard, between the yew bushes and the gooseberries on the one uncovered lawn chair, the others in the fading light humped under their covers like wheeled beasts. Barely an inch into his cigar and two fingers of scotch gone, but he knew it would come. It had to. The click, the snap. And when it did, some surprise at the suddenness and potency—the total deliverance as reliable as everything else in his life that had become in recent years *not* so reliable: the passage into narcotized pleasure as the sun dropped a little lower, light thickening with refracted color along the horizon, and coolness eating at the edges of the blanket where it didn't completely cover his shoulders, his bad shoulder especially, and the marble stepping stones inset across the lawn, each a little oblong eaten around the edges with grass, leading to his back porch, glowing through the dark like a lit-up magic moonstone pathway to the indoors, a magical hop-scotch game. He lifted the cigar and held it close for the sweetness of the burning wrapper, the unplaceable toffee scorch warming his lip and fingers as traces of smoke burned his sinuses and made his eyes sting; another sip, another pull on the wet cigar end, another, waiting . . .

Part of his mind was on the case still. Diagrams for containment structures, pools and ponds, formulas for concrete and plasticized liners, and Polaroid images from the worksite: crumbling concrete; broken, damaged concrete; failed liners; concrete soaked through with chemicals leaching through the surrounding gravel drainage to the water table because so many years had passed since anyone bothered to check. Long enough that trace amounts had begun showing up in peoples' tap water. That was the inciting, triggering event. And now the plaintiff wanted a lot in restitution, understandably. A whole Washington state town had lost its water supply. Not a very big town, but still. And his job? Mitigating damages. Making sure that if anyone took took a hit, it was the construction company and crew whose formulary had gone awry or had perhaps been oversold or specious, based on faulty science, and not the water-treatment plant. *Mendacity! All mendacity! Nothing more powerful than the odor of mendacity. It's the smell of death!* Again, that play, though in this instance, more like the smell of raw sewage. Because if he was honest with himself . . . well, if he was honest with himself he wouldn't have taken the job. But he'd taken it, and he'd take others like it, because he'd long ago decided that caring didn't matter. Winning mattered, and not even so much; beyond that it was all garbage. A game where no one really stayed on top for long except maybe the people with money.

Better to savor these moments of fading sunlight and let the music from his stereo inside playing on repeat through the open window of his study work its spell. If it could. Once, it had been all that mattered to him—music. That Ravel string quartet, in particular. Enough so he'd imagined that when he died, some part of his soul might come back to adhere eternally in the space of his quartet's chairs pushed together in a square, their music stands angled together like headless angels back to back, wings thrown up to hold the score. And that music! Ravel. In their best moments he used to feel that the quartet had forgotten itself as individuals, as people, and that in doing so they'd conjoined to make a fifth member. A fifth player in the quartet. Ridiculous. Yet he'd felt this often enough that showing up for rehearsal sometimes and looking around at the other three members drinking coffee, uncasing and getting ready to play, he'd have the distinct impression someone hadn't arrived yet. Who was it? "I know what you mean!" the cellist said, the day he mentioned this feeling and all of them had agreed on the spot: it was something special, their little group. Their sonic outpost of not-quite-mediocrity and fun in a life of workaday professional routine. They even privately called themselves, The Fifth Person. Fifth Element. Or sometimes just, The Five.

The thing about the containment ponds and their failed liners . . . No. He pushed the thought away. Enough. He'd read enough, seen enough. He was ready for the witnesses. He'd destroy them with cross-examination. Questions that let no air in, no equivocation, explanation, or nuance. Just yes or no. *Answer the question with a simple yes or no, please.* The stenographer's fingers would be stroking the little keys on her machine and he'd lean forward across the conference room table to glare in a way transcripts couldn't show, punctuation and word choice couldn't convey. Again he drew on the cigar and sipped his scotch. Pictured his violin in its open case on the piano top, unplayed for how many years now because of his bum shoulder and some corollary apathy, despondency in his core, the last rays of light caught in hazy columns of dust and pollen around it. He'd opened the case before coming outside just to see the violin again. To touch it and feel through the ache in his shoulder the longing to draw notes.

It had been a gift—well, not quite a gift, really; a gift first, and later, as time passed, a way for them to part without blame or hard feelings and to make good on debts, money Gary had loaned Maurice and never expected back and yet which had, in its way, weighed on everything between them. For many years afterward, until he realized it was delusional on his part, self-aggrandizing maybe, he'd liked to imagine that that violin might provide a form of telepathic reconnection; that it might one day draw them together again. Each note stained with a residue of feeling from that time in his life—his earlier artistic, bohemian years with Maurice, his mid-twenties, early thirties, finishing law school, not yet a partner at the firm—and in turn permeating the fiber and geometry of the instrument. Another kind of containment pond, he supposed, only metaphysical. Metaphorical? Containment pond for lost feelings and impressions. Ridiculous. And in the accumulation of varnish in its corners and in the channel, too— what Maurice had called the builder's signature marks, along with the scribed line down the middle of the scroll, like the sharply creased part in Maurice's hair, only black—a corollary *something.* Something akin to lust or longing or the sounds those feelings would produce if they could be displaced into music. The promise of notes that would say some or all of what there was to say about that longing and lost opportunity, that vanished era of his life, and might cause time to slip its bounds so he could fly back there. He was sure it was possible. It had to be. If you could feel it in the music and in the euphoria about to trip him over into its embrace, was it not real? How much more real could it be? He tapped his fingers on the arm of the chaise lounge, drumming fast passages with the music from inside, and felt it had to be so. *One day, one day, when my shoulder's better, I'm going to. Play myself right back there again. That's it. Poussez, tirez.* Another draw. Another sip, his legs flung out over the footrest. Or did it matter? Maybe he was there already. "We were sweethearts," he said aloud. "That's all. Best time of my life." Was it? He nodded. "Best. Yes. To you, Maurice Valloger, wherever you are."

He raised his glass and drank.

Angling his head back as far as the chaise would allow, he saw the moon, yellow-red and huge through the lower branches of the trees. He held his eyes open for as long as he could, until he felt the light to have impregnated the retina, soothing him with a feeling like peace. Calm. Almost there, he thought. Long ago he'd imagined music would be his life. No, he'd never thought that. He didn't have the skill or the talent, the patience, will or discipline, and besides, he'd started too late in life. Maurice had fooled him for a while, he supposed. No, not fooled him. Given him false encouragement. No, not false. Genuine according to his own terms, but not based in reality. He'd given him the encouragement he would have *liked* to believe in order to keep them floating along together another year or two and wanting the same things from life.

And with that thought, somewhere between too *late in life . . . the same things from life*, came the click at last. The sudden lift, the threshold blown past, only this time with a catch at the back of it like plunging to the bottom of a deep pool. A breathless, punched-gut feeling and soreness behind the eyes. He sat up to understand better and see where it had all gone, his fish pond, the last light of day flashing its colors across his windowpanes and to hear that beloved music . . . the notes giving him a direction home, how to find his way back from this chilly outpost to where he belonged . . . with that music. *Too late . . .*

—

"Poor fuck," James said, resisting the urge to strike him, settling instead on adjusting the angle of his head back a little further against the chaise headrest, pushing the chin down so the mouth yawned open wider showing gold and silver and otherwise discolored teeth, a cavernous black beyond, where the tongue pooled against the soft palette. So he looked solemnly, supremely idiotic. "Your race is run," he said. "Dumb fuck." And resisting no more, struck him with two fingers on the chin. "What do you care anyway? Old fag. Old poofter." For a second he thought he saw the eyelids flicker and twitch, returned to life, but it was nothing. A trick of the light. Trick of the eye or the mind's eye. Enough to make him tip back on his heels though, dizzy suddenly and a chill like compressed air blowing up his arms and along the back of his neck. A feeling that would haunt him for days afterward.

He'd been at his parents' house, in the gazebo out back, waiting for them to return from wherever they'd been for the evening. He was ready to fess up and come clean, pledge sobriety, rehab, whatever it took and whatever they needed to hear in order to let him back in the door, because he had an inkling—an urge to show respect and say a better goodbye. Nice hot bath, food in his belly, a nip or two from his dad's hooch when no one was looking, a place to hide out and freshen his perspective for a minute. Give them a squeeze in the morning and then be gone, because that much was certain. Tomorrow he'd leave this piece of shit town again. And then that music playing over and over from next door—goddamn frilly old people music—when it hit him. Who left that kind of shit on repeat, that loud? Someone who wasn't there, that's who. Someone who wanted to give an appearance of being there when he wasn't, to keep intruders away. To protect his stuff.

So he'd scrambled through bushes and vaulted the fence. And there he was: the old man in the light of the motion-sensitive porch lights that suddenly came on and beamed across the yard and onto the motionless, transfixed face. Older and blotchier, more shrunken into himself than whenever it was James had last seen him. Ten years ago? Fifteen? His gleaming, dented white head, the plaid blanket slipping down one shoulder. Staring skyward and not blinking, not breathing. Faint smells of cigar and burning fibers. Dead? He'd gone closer to confirm.

Once, years ago now, early middle school, he'd gotten tutoring from him in

French, *pro bono* as his father had so often said, so regularly reminded him—generally as a kind of threat or new incentive to try harder, do more, improve his grades, care more about anything—never anticipating the associations and resistances it triggered in James with each repetition: *He's tutoring you pro bono! One of the greatest legal minds in Spokane! That's how much we care . . . we all care. Pro bono! Rate of zero dollars an hour! When are you gonna smarten up, huh?* "Yeah, *pro bono* all right," he said now, remembering. Not that it mattered and not that anything ever happened, really. James was always too stubborn, unwilling to please anyone. But the suggestions had irked him endlessly, seeming to present him an opportunity to leverage the situation to his advantage (but an advantage whose specifics he could never grasp or access fully enough to know how or why he'd want them), an aspect of his predilection to prey on people for pure fun which he couldn't somehow embrace yet: *It is so hot today! You mind if I take off my shirt? You can take yours off as well. Those pants must be so warm. Corduroy. Skin is always best in the open I think, breathing in the open air . . .* James never played along, never acted as if he heard or noticed anything. No articles of his own clothing removed, but the old man in his boxers and socks, white tank-top, the mounded semi-circle scoops of hairless skin not quite centered above each kneecap which he always forgot about until he saw them again, little white islands in a sea of black leg hair. French verbs conjugated. Masculine, feminine, plural, l*e*, *la, les*. Rolled r's. He'd studied the situation and tried to know how to turn it to his advantage or any advantage in it that he might want. And he never stopped thinking about ways of avenging himself whenever his father reminded him, *pro bono! It's pro bono!* "Nothing pro about it," James finally did say, just the once. "Pure straight up bono, more like, Dad. Hard homo boner if you really want to know." And then the look on his father's face. Like an elevator plunging down and down, the eyes quivering with what looked like a mockery of outrage and disgust; savagery or bloodlust. So predictable, so easily played. *You never said. Why didn't you say?* And then it was over, no more French from old Mister Frenchy. Bunch of idiots, all of them.

Inside, he clipped and lit his own cigar from the box of them left open on the sideboard. Blew smoke and inhaled deeply and coughed it back out. "Jesus H!" he said. Who would smoke such a thing? Who would even concoct such a thing to be smoked in the first place. He carried it with him as he toured the house all the same—the dusty knickknacks and cut-glass dishes of marbles and pennies; mirrored shelf-backing beyond giving him glimpses of his own stupid face, blond-red hair, scarecrow-thin, beard in need of a trim; and row upon row of books, framed degrees, framed pictures of the old man with friends and family and a Scots terrier. He kind of remembered that dog. A smell of cooked eggs and rotting fruit he also vaguely remembered. Cat swirling briefly around his shins, surprising him badly enough he dropped the cigar as he entered the kitchen with its greasy fixtures and slick floor and dim yellow light. He watched it roll to a dark corner under the cabinet where the old man's filthy silver coffee machine sat with its one arm upraised like some kind of warning or salute and a mess of coffee beans and ground coffee all around it. Box of cereal beside that with its folds open, plastic liner sticking out. "Corn Chex," he said. "The old man had Corn Chex for his breakfast. What the hell." And back out again to turn off the music, when he saw it there: the violin on its velvet-covered dais between the stereo and the piano, case lid flung open and silk blanket pulled back. "Well, hello," he said. "Now that, my friend, is what we came for. Pro bono!" He clapped his hands together and went closer. He didn't inspect his treasure beyond noting that it had strings and a bow with its hair all disheveled and turned loose somehow, not in a ribbon like what he thought he'd seen before. Touched the violin once on the shoulder with a feeling like familiarity or regret, and closed the case. Walked out with the music still blaring, for the third or maybe fifth time rollicking to some quaint outburst of sentiment he supposed once upon a time might have matched with feelings people had relating to fame and glory, victory with an underpinning of some long-lost sadness, and which therefore in a way felt to him like the exactly perfect soundtrack for his actions—imagining himself as some sneaky old-timey bandit in a smuggler's mask and striped tunic, top hat or fedora, slinking like a mime to the door and looking both ways before stepping out into the evening and thereafter immediately straightening his pose again. Just a musician. Just another violinist on his way to a show somewhere. He left the door open and went on his way up the street to the closest bus stop, muttering to himself, "Fuck all of you, but fuck *you* especially, and *you* and *you*, all of you, and you . . ." —each you punctuated with a heel strike on pavement and a picture in his head of the offending person, and those words, *pro bono*, echoing under the beats, violin case tipping up in his grip and flowing back again at his side.

—

A Review and Critical Essay Upon the Great Polish Violinist, Henri Wieniawski
Marcus Sanders, *Daily Alturan,* California, 1873

If the value of anything could be fairly estimated by its rarity, then great violin players could not be too highly prized: for among the countless musicians who have devoted themselves during centuries to the time-honored "fiddle," how few have reached the highest eminence? Indeed, if we were to say not one in ten thousand (taking all ages and countries into consideration), we should probably be speaking within bounds.

We state the fact without pretending to account for it. Were we called upon to do so, we should answer negatively, and simply suggest that it is not (as many suppose) because of the extreme technical difficulties which the most perfect of instruments presents; for there are many, and mere boys too, who can master these by dint of very hard work judiciously directed. If that were all, we should have plenty of great violinists. But there remains always the mysterious "I don't know what," the *Je ne sais quoi* in art of all kinds, which defies analysis and can no more be explained than the *fifth essence* of Plato. The *quintessence.* The very reason for being.

It is something that must be felt rather than comprehended. It is what we vaguely term "poetry," which, if it were susceptible of strictly reasonable interpretation, would be poetry no longer. Who would think by closely examining the rose to arrive at the secret of its fragrance or its beauty? Or by anatomizing the skylark to reach the source of those "profuse strains of unpremeditated art" poured like liquid gems from its full heart? Who wants to know the causes or meanings of those divine rhapsodies?

To state, therefore, that Henri Wieniawski can do everything manually or digitally possible upon the violin, would be to describe his splendid abilities very inadequately. When we inform our readers, *dilettanti* or professional, that the subject of this sketch is equally at his ease whether dealing with double notes, thirds, sixths, octaves, rapid pizzicato with fingers of either hand . . .

She tipped back in her chair, pen nib held inches above the page, poised to plunge on with more words, more and more insufficient words; and as the generalized feeling of misgiving that had stopped her expanded from the ache in her writing fingers to her wrist, elbow, and shoulder, her solar plexus, from there widening to a deeper spiritual malaise—one with which she was all too familiar, and from which she knew would spring a despicable (from her own perspective) level of preening and pomposity in the next words and sentences, if she didn't check it, and quickly—she considered again, as she had sitting down to write about Wieniawski, that this was all an exercise in futility. That no words, however carefully meted out and justified, backed by philosophical reason and claims of cultural pedigree, cultural exclusivity, hidden or half-hidden behind the too-permeable wall of her pen name, would ever fully explain or impart a sense of the man himself, and more ineffably, a sense of his effect on a listener. On her. Four curtain calls and encores and still, after it all, that transcendent radiance, so that standing beside him, you felt as if you'd been drawn into the orbit of a sun or star, some blinding fiery force, illuminating, burning up, creating ghosts and nimbuses of anything too near; capable *only* of radiation and never of a more human characteristic such as, say, returning her attentions. Of listening, or hearing. Seeing. Staying still long enough to be in any way receptive. Moments at a time, you had glimpses, of course, because surely somewhere back there was a heart and mind like a normal human heart and mind, at work behind the eyes and mouth, mustache and goatee, the pompadour, the full belly with its gold watch chain strung across. To take such a man as a lover . . . No, this was not the thought that had frozen her and which now caused her to lean back, an elbow in one hand and the Waterman safely capped not to dry out the nib, because evidently she was done writing for the moment. Though to be honest, the thought was inevitable, the sexual thought. You didn't stand near him very long after hearing him play and *not* become positively aware that the force of his genius, the pure energy and radiance, had a progenerative quality too (it had to) instantly making any woman near him another pagan Chrysogenee *pierst into the wombe by sunbeames brighte* (as in Spenser). But no, it wasn't the sex thought that stopped her. Because what he *didn't* know was how his fixation on music, on himself, on these flourishes of expression that were almost beyond human comprehension, barely executable by other violinists, what he didn't know was how this might make him vulnerable to the world and its less refined, less caring elements. Radiance, yes. Star, yes. Sun, yes. But also a kind of blind and helpless sun. A stupid, trusting sun prone to manipulation and therefore in need of guidance and protection. This was what had stopped her, because of what she'd overheard at the post-concert social and hadn't sufficiently reacted to or reflected upon until this moment, pen capped, elbow in hand, with the dawning awareness of her pale presence beside him and the ghostly insufficiency of her words to describe or measure or convey anything worthwhile about him and his music—the puffery and preening, the wish to contain or control, always falling short. Because Oleg Granoski, the symphony society's default concertmaster, a man she'd known for years from fundraisers, performances, socials—Oleg Granoski was not a man to be trusted and she had not intervened when she'd seen him from across the room talking rapid-fire at Monsieur Wieniawski, waving his bony fingers with more than the usual animation and flare. Oleg. Now she had an image of Oleg playing the violin—with his whiskery overgrowth of sideburns and his devilish, crooked curlicue physique, so much the inverse of M. Wieniawski's. The sheen of worn threads around his jacket cuffs and collars, the sweat stains in his shirts, the violin always like a question mark in his hands—a clumsy tool for a hack who'd once had better ambitions—cheap and mawkish, like a carnival barker, but a carnival barker with an earnest solemnity about the eyes and a desperate sincerity not easily dismissed, an aura of heartbreak worn casually but ostentatiously, serving both to underscore and negate any instantaneous distrust of him, any sense of his innate criminality. "Poor Oleg," someone almost invariably ended up saying. "Poor man . . ."

And so, though she'd seen them from across the room talking, she had not had time to intervene on Monsieur Wieniawski's behalf. To block and explain, or later, when Wieniawski speaking to a group of them gathered around him, launched into his own exposition on the subject, to insist that he rescind the arrangement: *But you see, this is not the violin of my dreams,* Wieniawski said, *this Pressenda . . . a very good violin, yes, but a mere shadow of the Guarneri which is the love of my life, second only to my wife. Like Paganini, yes? He too had one violin from Pressenda and another from the great Guarneri. But Guarneri, she does not travel. She is too picky. So here, on the shores of America I will leave Monsieur Pressenda for sale by your illustrious concertmaster, Oleg Granoski, who has offered. Only you must promise me to use all proceeds from the sale, after my cost for the instrument which is already almost nothing really, a donation more or less, you must use it to assist in the funding and establishment of your very own San Francisco Symphony Orchestra, please, so that next time, when I return again, and I will cherie, please do not look at me like that, so I can perform with them and know that this was all for the music! All for Wieniawski's music! A gift in the name of music! From this violin to the good people of San Francisco! From Monsieur Pressenda and myself to you!* Instead she'd stood there unable to think or to speak. Only nodding dumbly at him, laughing with the others at his beautifully Polish-inflected sing-song English, wondering at the luminosity of his presence, the greatest violinist of all time . . . and only too late catching at his sleeve. Long enough to hold his eye and stop him at the champagne bowl and to say ten words, maybe fifteen, winding up toward the warning that she never managed to say aloud . . . *Don't want to talk out of school,* she'd begun, *but, oh. Oleg . . . listen, people talk. He's not as secure as he once was, he's not the most respected.* But she didn't want to appear indiscreet. It was all rumors anyway. Rumors and impressions based on appearance. *Poor Oleg . . . poor man.* Wieniawski's eyebrows had gone up with this imprecation and, as the rim of his champagne glass touched his lip and vanished under his mustache, flattened again, the eyes shifting their focus to someone behind her, she lost her nerve. He was already preparing an exit from the conversation. With one finger he touched away the foam in the corners of his mouth. Swallowed and lifted his chin. *Yes? Yes? Such marvelous champagne,* he said. *From America! You are so much more fortunate here than in any other country of the world I have seen. Your Oleg will sort himself out, I am sure. We are made stronger this way. Always. And if not . . . plenty of good violinists, plenty of younger violinists ready to take up the helm. The reins? Ready to lead. Maybe I am not so worried. Now if you'll excuse me . . .*

What she'd meant to say, the warning she'd meant to give . . . diffracted and deflected in his radiance, because what did her worry matter? What did anything matter, face-to-face with such a man? But she was certain. For all his magnificence and magnanimity he would be fleeced: never be paid back for his violin; never see a penny from the sale of that violin accomplish anything he'd intended.

Now she pushed back her chair and stood.

She knew this as certainly as she'd known anything in her life. She had to see Wieniawski. She had to warn him. *Your violin . . . do not leave it here! Take it with you, please, or find someone else to sell it. Not here! It will disappear otherwise and this should never ever happen to a violin that has once soared to such heights and been so beloved. Oleg Granoski has no respect for this! He is nothing. A poseur. Don't leave your Pressenda with him!*

She rushed out and down the stairs, glancing at her watch and realizing it was probably too late—the train had gone and she'd never catch him, unless, God willing, something had intervened to cause a delay in his departure. Out she went into the brilliant day, the noise of the street welling up around her, clip clop of horse's hooves, a distant bell-buoy clanging, children at their games, and farther in the distance the hoo-hoo of the train pulling in. She'd never get there in time. The thing about fate, she realized—you might well see its pattern or design emerging plain as day, yet you could never intervene. She felt silly and small for trying. Also indignant on Wieniawski's behalf, and certain she was right: the fate of one of the world's great violins was about to be shifted from its course, ruined, and not a thing she could do to save it. No one cared. Her eyes filled with tears.

—

Ron hadn't seen her in almost a year. Seen her once, that is, but on the other side of the street, pushing a stroller in the same direction he was headed so he only glimpsed her in his mirrors—side-view, then rearview, amid cars and pedestrians. A motorcyclist hovering on his bumper. Joggers. A couple window-shopping. He couldn't be entirely sure. Couldn't make out the face perfectly. He was pretty sure though, from the gait—flat-footed and weary but willing, a little too much spring in the knees, like she was marching in sand. Regardless, accurate or not, he knew that the sliver of face he did manage to pick out would be affixed in his memory thereafter: a placeholder to use in thinking about her, how she'd ended up, until whenever he might see her next. Same crooked, over-crowded teeth, same asymmetry about the eyes, but puffier from sleep loss, and some of her defiance stripped down, transformed to a look he was more accus-tomed to in his customers. Surliness twisted together with gloom and self-defeat. Not quite sullen. All of which had been so refreshingly absent about her in the earlier days, when he was first getting to know her. Weekly or bi-weekly she'd drop in to chatter at him and visit her grandma's old stuff. Junk, really, some of it maybe worth a few dollars—TV, hi-fi with cassette player, crystal stemware, fake furs, Swiss watch, wedding band. Once upon a time there'd been a little money in the family, he supposed. Belinda would stroke the furs and hold the stemware up to the light looking longingly through it to some imagined other time in her life; roll the wedding band between her fingers, and wind the watch. He'd lean on his elbows over the display case watching and wondering about this unfamiliar softness in himself—most of the time he barely spoke to custom-ers—this choice to encourage false reminiscences. Her father had drunk away most of the money paid out for those items over the years. She'd never had the happy childhood she seemed determined to imagine for herself.

Part of it was her looks, of course. Until her smile revealed the mouthful of wayward teeth anyway, she was picture perfect. After the smile, you liked her even more because . . . well, he wasn't sure. You just did. Your heart broke a little and you leaned closer to hear, and knotted your hands together to keep from touching her. Another part of it was her age—barely sixteen when she started visiting—and a kind of vulnerability about her that invited speculation. What if I took that girl in. What if I made of my devotion to her some private novena . . . raised her up right, treated her like the princess she might-could be, the daughter I never had. Already though, she seemed more than halfway aware of this perceived innocence and vulnerability as a means to an end, as she was dawningly aware of the effect she had on men, even at that age, and willing to use either indiscriminately in ways not entirely at her command, making every interaction with her hard to read and harder still to believe. So he did nothing and said only slightly more. Smiled and nodded, "Sure," whenever she asked to see the watch again. The ring. The stemware. He asked her how she was. How the job was going. School. The boyfriends. *Nada! Got none! I'm saving myself for Mr. Right.* Kept her talking, so he could watch her and try to get a read on whatever it was that made her so quintessentially herself—the voice, the quick smiles and hair tosses, quirks of expression. When she announced that she was expecting, and twins, he didn't blink. Didn't let on how this meant essentially the end of her life. He smiled and slapped a hand on the countertop. "Well, get those glasses then. We'll have a toast. Straight root beer no chaser, for you. Who's the lucky guy?" And when she went on beamingly, looking like some drugged angel, about the day she'd fallen asleep at the lake alone, and how the sun had literally taken her off, carried her to a mountainside somewhere she'd never seen—*Ferns the size of ponderosas, giant flowers and shit, orange trees, I swear!*—and wrapped her in its rays until she realized it had gone inside her, like right inside, and was making her feel so, so good she couldn't stand it, so that when she woke she knew what had happened and what was coming . . . "I don't care what anybody says," she said. "Don't care if they call me a liar or nothing. I ain't never been with no man and that's the God's honest truth. Don't believe me if you don't want to." He played along. Knew immediately it was the one thing he could do for her: believe in her impossibility and preposterousness and ask nothing more. *The sun*, he said to himself sometimes at night, watching his face in the mirror as he flossed and brushed, wondering why she'd chosen him, of all people, for this confidence. Or maybe she said the same to everyone. *The sun!* He shook his head and spat. Pointed at his own reflection, his sagging cheeks and his hair gone the color of metal underwater. *You are a fool, Ron Santos.*

Later, when the pregnancy started showing, she visited less and less. Occasional Fridays and weekends. Busy, he guessed. Keeping to herself. A few months before her due date, she came around with the man. The one he first wrongly assumed must be the father, and who he gradually, grudgingly deduced was another lost soul from the Wenatchee Lighthouse Ministry down the street—another fool drawn to her and hoping to take advantage of her perceived vulnerability. "Really?" Ron asked, when the man produced the violin in its weatherworn, beaten case, asking for money. "Play me something, huh. Haven't had any music in the store for years."

"Can't. Fucked up my hand." Here he held up the hand to show the twisted ends of two fingers, the scraped knuckles and busted nails.

"I guess someone's missing a few teeth then. Played a jig on his face?"

The man smirked and said nothing. Winked at Belinda.

"You know the terms, right? Thirty-day payments. Twenty-two percent interest." He looked inside the case long enough to be sure it wasn't empty. That the violin was real and all in one piece. Then snapped it shut again and slid it lengthwise across the counter.

The man shrugged. "I need the money. We need the money. I'm a stick around a while this time. See if I can help out Belinda. You know. Make it all good for her." Here he'd reached an arm around her and squeezed with those twisted fingers. Ginger-haired, and younger than Ron had first thought. A few wrinkles around the eyes. Whiskered like a feral cat.

"You the father?" Ron asked.

"Hell no. Just met."

Later Ron would study the name—James McCandless—and the rest of his info for clues, but he wouldn't call the police to run a check on missing violins or ask around at other hock shops in the region, because although he was sure it was stolen, he couldn't stand to add one more trouble to Belinda's life. Name her as potential accessory to a crime? What would the courts even do with her babies? No.

Later still, during subsequent visits from the two of them together (three or four total, he guessed—no more), he got the rest of the details . . . some, anyway: itinerant field laborer, from a semi-wealthy family on the east side, near Spokane, but either temporarily slumming it or disowned. Convinced that his violin had a devil's face and voice and that in all the time he'd lugged it around since "finding" it, he'd never slept a single night straight through. "Thing's haunted, I swear. I scratched out all the names and identifying marks inside with my knife when I heard someone say that's how you undo those kinds of curses. But it didn't help none. Made it worse! Man! The batshit crazy dreams I had. First thing God told me, day one there at the Lighthouse with Belinda," here he'd looked sideways at her, nodding foolishly, basking in her attention, "He said, You get rid a that devil's plaything, James. No more false idols. Get good and rid of it and come back when you done that. Then we can talk. That's when I come in. Few days after that anyway. Belinda said you'd do right by us."

As soon as he knew that James had moved on and left Belinda for good, he vowed it: he would make the calls. Report that violin as likely stolen, maybe from the parents. Do whatever he could to help track James down and arrest his skinny ass. Until then, he'd say nothing. Even after the first thirty days, then sixty, ninety . . . he kept the violin in back. He had loaned them way too much up front—a hundred and fifty dollars when he'd be lucky to sell it for two or three.

"Five hundred bucks," he told them now, the two young customers in shorts and sandals, from the west side of the state. Both spectacled, one balding on top and thinner, arms sticking out of his green T-shirt like mantis arms, with black-rimmed plastic glasses—Karl, he'd said his name was—the other shorter, thickset. Denis. *Are you thinking what I'm thinking*, the first one had said, seeing that violin. He was bouncing on his toes. Couldn't contain his excitement. I believe I am, said the other, peering up over his glasses. *Let's each write it down on a piece of paper, separately. Blind. See if we agree.* Here the shorter one had looked to Ron on the other side of the counter. He had stubby eyelashes that made Ron think of a baby bird's eyes, and a florid pinkness in the cheeks that might have come from drinking but in this case probably not. Probably came from believing himself to have found hidden treasure. *Got a pen or pencil?* he asked. And then they'd turned from each other, wrote their answers like kids taking a test, glancing Ron's way like he was meant to be some kind of proctor or judge of their reliability, and exchanged the papers, folded in half.

"Fuck me," the first one said. "Right to the year, we named it."

"Not a surprise. Not at all. It's so distinct. But God the thing's a mess," said the second.

"Like someone left it in the rain for a month."

"Left it in the rain and tried to fix it with a pickaxe!"

"A toothpick."

"With his goddam teeth!"

"And some string."

"Some shoe polish. Jeez."

On and on they went, riffing, trying to make it sound so much worse than anyone could see it was. Ron closed up the case and leaned all his weight on one leg in the corner of the counter furthest from them, arms folded, waiting. "Five hundred bucks," he repeated. "Cash only."

"OK. But do you have any idea how this violin came to be here? Like who brought it from where, and why?" This was the second one, Denis. The one with the jaw and stubby eyelashes. The one who'd pay.

"Not a clue," Ron said. "Can't even remember the first detail." He shrugged. "Must've been years ago now. It's clean though. We check everything."

He watched the sunlight skating around the parking lot as they left, refracted into columns through the pine pollen and dust. Watched them all the way to their car, putting the violin in the back seat, high-fiving each other, starting up and rolling away. Junk hunters, they'd called themselves. Junk-shopping their way through central Washington. *Got any old violins?* He wondered briefly if they were lovers. Nah. Old friends. Hobbyists of some sort. That was the vibe he got. Wondered half-incongruously if Belinda had been telling him the truth, any part of the truth, but coded for his ears, about being impregnated by the sun—blacked-out drunk? Drugged and raped?—and wondered if she herself believed any of it. And why. Why such a tale? And why was he fated from here on, like it or not, believe in it or not, to think of her every time he noticed the sunlight sparkling its way through any form of airborne particulate, and to wonder about the sun making love to a sixteen-year-old girl on a wacked-out hallucinogenic mountainside. At any rate, he'd have a story for her when she came back. If she came back. Maybe he'd share a little of the profit. Yes, he told himself, he would do that. Or just give her back some of her grandma's stuff for free, whatever was left. Or both. Meanwhile, it was some relief having that old violin gone. One less worry on the list. One less betrayal on the horizon. The wad of cash in his pocket didn't hurt either. He fanned through the bills a final time—mostly fifties—counted them out and thunked them on the countertop, watching as they curled halfway over themselves to the shape of the shorter man's wallet. But if this was his whole takeaway from the deal, he felt . . . gypped. Shorted somehow, and annoyed, because the pleasure of money did not equate with the loss of her presence. If he could just know where she was.

—

Not long after moving to Spokane, Maurice fell into a stretch of lucky days so far beyond anything he'd experienced to that point in his life, even as one good thing eclipsed the next, he knew that to look too closely at it or to place his faith in any isolated action or magical connection that might cause his luck to renew and extend itself into the future, would be to risk its undoing. There would be time enough to search out a cause later. To wonder. To look for sources of renewal. Meanwhile, there was the daily dream of his violin-building school, funded beyond his wildest expectations by the bloat of educational resources being dumped on colleges across the country, especially on the west coast, stocked with wood from Europe and Canada, beautiful wood of the highest grade, and state-of-the-art tools and machines, all available practically for free to anyone who wanted to learn. *I think I've died and gone to heaven,* he told any old friends he could contact up and down the coast. *You must come here, and soon. The money can't last, I'm sure, but meanwhile. You must come. We can make our own Mittenwald. Our own Mirecourt. A city of violins! I swear, it is not an exaggeration! For now, the money doesn't end.* And everywhere he went—pawn shops, estate sales, auctions, garage sales—the luck that seemed without end, the hunches that paid out over and over, the leads from strangers, fine instruments falling on him as if out of the sky. *Shaping a violin, handling a violin,* he told his students in each beginning class, *is the closest you may come to feeling the physicalized shape of destiny. Feeling the angles and boundaries of an object whose form mirrors destiny. Because the form of every violin is in fact a perfect, mathematically, harmonically sublime invention, yes, but it is also the shape that is commensurate with its fate. Think about it. It has to be. Each violin will live how many hundreds of years beyond the days in which you build it. That is its destiny, that shape which you give it with your own hands and which you can feel in the turn of your knife, your gouge, but never know.* At times this awareness came with a vertiginous spinning. At other times a stillness or plunging sorrow, a feeling of time occurring in layers, layers upon layers really, and shapes moving just beyond his reach, touchable but also eluding him in the evening light, like the scent of pine on the cooling evening air. And through it all, he seemed always to know in advance: where to look, what to buy, who to talk to. He had never before been so lucky.

So it was with a feeling of luck that has just slid past its prime, luck cresting a high point and beginning its downward tumble, that he found himself alone with Gary in the sweltering heat of Gary's downtown apartment one night, high up enough to see out over the city and not be seen, pretending to enjoy another of their infernal cigars together on the back porch and relating to him the story of the latest violin he'd found at an estate sale, earlier the same day—*Pressenda, not a super high-value instrument right now, needs some love and care, a few little things to fix, but give it time! He'll have his day in the sun too, I assure you. No better workmanship anywhere, ever, I promise*—and which he'd decided, in a fit of sentiment and generosity while driving over, finding parking, and then flying up the steps two at a time to Gary's apartment, would be his gift to Gary. A symbol of his intentions to commit, to stand by him indefinitely. Through law school and beyond. What cued the feelings of luck cresting and falling away, he couldn't say, but it was something in the density of the clouds on the horizon, the deeper hue of colors there and a whiff of winter in the air, or maybe the cigar smoke burning his sinuses, or maybe some fundamental way he really didn't get Spokane, and with that, an echo-reminder of the widow's words to him, selling him that violin for a hundred dollars—*I don't know about any violin building school, no. Never heard of it! Our kids played some music in high school I guess, but beyond that anyone's too busy. Who has the time. I believe it was his granny Granoski's uncle, his mother's side that is, played it somewhere around the San Francisco Bay Area? That's some years ago! They said he was quite good, I have no idea actually, but now it just doesn't seem worth the trouble. So we're selling it as-is, along with everything else, probably a loss, I know*—some vague menace or finality about those words that made him realize how it was all in fact inconsequential. A dream. The school, his days and nights with Gary, this crazy luck and love and salaried pay. A dream that mattered to no one but him. Like all dreams, he supposed. And it wouldn't last. Soon enough, he'd be cut off, cast out and living by his wits again. *Boom times always gotta come to an end, Mr. Valloger,* the widow had concluded. *I say. They always do. First it was the silver mining brought my husband's people up from California. Then it was the wheat and the nickel. Timber I suppose. Now it's education, you say. Well, it'll go as far as it goes, I guess. Long as the government's paying.*

Maurice stubbed out his cigar though there was still a good two inches of smoke left in it. Drained his glass and tipped back in his chair, anxious to shake these feelings of malaise. "Come on. I bet it's cool enough inside now," he said. As usual, alone together, they spoke an ad hoc mixture of French and English. Frenglish. Mostly French. "Let's go back in. I want you to play! See how it sounds."

Gary nodded. "A minute. Sure. Not quite done." He drew smoke and settled deeper in his chair, cigar held close for the smell of the burning wrapper. Sipped his drink. There was something he wanted to say, evidently. He lowered the glass and reached a hand to slide fingers through Maurice's. Brought the back of Maurice's wrist to his lips and held it there, breathing in and out deeply. "You know," he said, "why is it we can't ever seem to say . . . this is good enough. This, right here, right now." At first he'd thought maybe Gary meant specifically his hand, the back of his hand, but quickly realized he meant much more. Meant everything. "It's pretty much perfect, right? A night like this. So what's all the striving for? What in God's name are we always chasing after, trying to accomplish?" Here he'd looked over at Maurice blinking earnestly, and it was a moment before Maurice could register the fact that Gary was crying. Not a trick of the fading light, not a sham. Gary was moved to tears somehow by what he was saying. And then he pushed the heel of his hand under his eyes to wipe away tears, laughing, sniffing, and overplaying the feeling to undercut and show it simultaneously. "Boohoohoo. Anyway. Goddamn legal torts," he said, sniffing again. "The crap I was reading today. Gives me such a headache even to think about it." He drew on the cigar. "I need a little longer to forget. Few minutes. That OK with you?"

"It's perfect. Whatever you want."

In the days ahead he'd carry this memory with him alongside hazier memories of the music and lovemaking that followed, the unseasonal rain tapping at their windows and blown in through screens close to dawn, and their rush half-naked out into cooler air to grab anything they'd left on the porch—a hat, pair of shoes, reading glasses. So maybe that's all it was in the first place, he'd told himself. A drop in barometric pressure, not some grandiose looming change of fortunes headed his way. Not a reversion in fate's pattern carrying him around the culminative point of his present life like the bee-sting in a finely purfled violin corner, dropping him . . . where, he couldn't say.

Five months later he was on his way back west to Seattle.

The school had failed and closed shop. Funding gone, he'd locked away its tools and supplies indefinitely. Mountains, boulders, sage, and pine trees receding in his rearview as he drove west, sinking, fading, and for years after bumping up again in his memory with the smell of the summer nighttime air, lavender blue-black sky, like the needle of Gary's stereo caught at the end of a play—click-click-click-click-click—all those nights together, listening, too lazy and tranquil to get up yet, change the record . . .

So how was he supposed to do this again? Start all over. He didn't see it.

TIME
AND
LEGENDS

One

In the last weeks of her pregnancy with us, our father says our mother developed a set of faint scrims, ghost marks on either side of her belly, each shaped more or less exactly like a violin f-hole. And in the center of her belly, a seam like a loosely furled upside-down violin scroll centered on her belly button. "A sign," he insisted, though to our knowledge our mother did not share either his perceptions or his readings of them. "Sign of nothing," she'd say. "Sign of a bladder shrunk to the size of a pancake and lungs halfway up my throat. Twin boys kicking to get out." Our father would not be talked out of his belief: "No, no, no. An indication from the universe! They will be good, these boys." This was in the days before cell phone photography and the habitual archiving of important life events in a stream of instant-access visual data, so there are no pictures to prove, one way or the other, which of them was right.

The labor was hard and nearly killed our mother. For months afterward, we're told, we didn't see her. First blood loss and then a rare form of infection held her hostage. Then a life-sucking post-partum depression. By the time she returned to us . . . our recollections from early childhood, let's say, do not align with pictures of her we've seen from before our birth—spinning in polka-dot dresses, smiling avidly, eating cake, smoking slim cigars, looking defiant on a walk up Mount Baker. Of this time, the time of her recovery, we know only that our father was as attuned to her as he was to the instruments on his workbench. And perhaps this is all those transforming marks on her belly foretold, if there were any such marks: not greatness for us, her sons, but a time of life for her where she'd have to be at our father's mercy and requiring of him all the patience, skill, and care of a fine stringed instrument. Among clients, colleagues, and apprentices he became famous for an uncanny awareness of all changes in sound (or lack thereof) coming through walls and floorboards from our rooms above the shop—a sixth sense, some said. A certain look, a stillness would settle over him and then you knew what was coming. "Watch out," they might whisper, or just exchange nods and knowing looks. Once, twice, three times a day, he'd drop whatever he was doing, fly through the half-lit back storerooms and up the stairs to her, calling her name—"Marie! Marie?" In this way he was able to keep her from killing herself one time that we know of. And even after any real danger had passed and she'd returned to better spirits, a washed-out, faded version of the woman she'd once been, or so she always insisted, but *herself*, more or less, he was still prone to alarms. Still, he'd drop a gouge or knife mid-stroke, stand aside, hands slightly upraised, and make a dash for it up the stairs. "It's all right, Karl," she'd tell him. "I'm not doing anything. Would you like some hot tea?"

—

Violins are a sorcerous, sexist, and deceitful business. Aside from the curious marks on our mother's belly, real or imaginary, our father was sure of our significance not just because we were his firstborn and only boys (the difficult labor, among other things, ensured there would be no others after us), but because we were the youngest grandsons in a family line of builders—like Guarneri del Gesù and Niccolo Amati before us, grandsons of renowned builders whose best instruments bookend the golden age of violin building in Italy and whose work, together with Antonio Stradivarius, shape and define the violin to this day. In our father's mind, there was no question but that we would join him at the bench as soon as we were old enough to be trusted with a woodworking tool.

Our grandfather by this time, never the most graceful or prolific of carvers, had been sidelined to the front of the shop where he alternately robbed or scared off customers, and, whenever possible, ran an appraising eye over instruments coming and going. "Look again, I beg you," he'd tell our father. Despite his advancing years, he never lost the knack for making a canny misidentification of an instrument and finding ways of wringing a little extra money out of nowhere. "So you change the label! So what. Who's going to know? Worst case, if we don't sell it here, we send to my connection in Shanghai. Micah. He, I guarantee, can find you a buyer in no time."

Most days, afflicted by recurrent hemorrhoids and gout flares in his feet and ankles, he sat over his cane with his one remaining friend in the world, our god-father Maurice Valloger, another small-time instrument dealer our grandfather had at various times swindled and invested in heavily in order to prop up and help keep in business, possibly out of sympathy, possibly so he could ransack him at the end (depending on who outlived whom) for the most prized pieces in his collection—a Bergonzi violin and some bows our grandfather then thought were much more valuable than he later came to believe—and for his supply of so-called ancient tone wood, smuggled from France to the United States near the end of World War Two and supposedly straight from Luigi Tarisio, part of Tarisio's final buyout of the Stradivari estate from Stradivari's destitute and dy-ing son Paolo in 1775. "Real wood," Maurice insisted. "Stradivari wood! From the workshop of Antonio Stradivari!"

I remember them sitting over the checkerboard, trading stories—notorious customers, fussy customers, customers they'd loved or hated, deals they'd part-nered on, famed instruments they'd seen walk in the door, missed opportuni-ties, and opportunities so fantastic they could not account for them in any way other than by invoking the Almighty. And though he never so much as stood to acknowledge Maurice's appearance at the shop door, most mornings, 11:30, coffee and newspaper in hand, the third consecutive day Maurice failed to show, our grandfather wouldn't be talked out of his alarm. "Marie, Marie, take me there now. Please. I'm sure it's nothing. Let's be positive though. His phone, he won't answer. He never does. Please, let's make sure. Oh, Mauricio." And later, his worst suspicions confirmed, the days of sitting by Maurice's bedside following the heart surgery and eventual death . . . A man he'd loved and hated, partnered with on countless deals, robbed and pressed into disagreement at any possible chance, loved to call a fool as much as he'd loved to fool him—turned out, he was our grandfather's truest kin and last connection to the old ways. Our father, who never loved buying and selling violins nearly as much as the feel of wood under his fingers, who lacked our grandfather's cunning and fondness for *the deal*, was in most ways not the man our grandfather would have preferred to leave in charge of the family business. But there was no choice. No other son stepping up.

Our father's violins in these years, the years immediately after Maurice's death and the beginning of our grandfather's gradually declining health, were some of his best. From one of his most respected clients, a concertmaster at one of the major US symphonies of the day, a signed picture and personal letter describing his attachment to the instrument our father had built for him during this period hung by his workbench for years: . . . *Many things in this life come to be ours in ways which seem in the end to have had little to do with real choice or provenance or will. Is this house my own because I live in it now and pay the mortgage? These clothes, because I wear them? I think not. There is but one object in my life which I consider myself to truly and fully own, and to which I can say I truly, fully belong, and that is your master model Guarneri Plowden violin. Kudos to you, monsieur, and may you build many more violins such as this one which has both opened and contained my heart . . .* Until it yellowed and one day slipped its tack to fall into the no-man's land of dust, dirt, wood chips, and other debris trapped in the gap between his bench and the wall, forever stranded from the signed picture of the man who'd written it. "Hey, when did that disappear?" our father asked. No one had an answer. Presumably he'd read it enough times by then to have memorized the most important bits, and would have weighed this against the trouble of moving heavy items to locate it; possibly he would have concluded that it was time anyway. Those words had expired or served their purpose. "Gravity wins," he liked to say. "In the end it always wins." Other instruments from that same period earned him prizes—a viola, which won gold at the VSA for tone; a violin, for its varnish and its tone—and, in turn, some attention in the Seattle papers. Whether this pleased him more than it embarrassed him was difficult to say, though later we overheard him with our mother after wine with dinner, in the kitchen complaining loudly that the reporters could have at least gotten the attributions right. "They were Guarneri copies. For Christ's sake, why does everyone in the world think only of Stradivarius?"

—

Our parents met in the community orchestra where our father sat in the back of the second violin section, his fingers calloused in all the wrong ways and generally in a bewildered state of revolt against the work of bowing and fingering an instrument he was more inclined to take apart, and our mother in the rarefied if nerve-wracking position of solo bassoonist. He was there, so he said, to keep himself tuned in at the local level—to be reminded of a certain unpolished love for music which he said was the real lifeblood of the calling. If he could, he avoided any mention of his work; he didn't want the extra hours repairing dreadful instruments on the cheap for new friends he'd never be able to turn away. The ease with which our mother's blue-gray eyes absorbed him over the tops of music stands through slow passages of symphonic semi-discord, and anywhere there was a long enough rest—leaning out of his seat until he was almost standing, so she always said ("I was trying to hear! I love the sound of the bassoon and needed to know if you were any good," he'd counter), in order to watch her lips enfold the double reed and cheeks puff with air, the vein on one side of her forehead pulsing subtly into view—tells another story, of course. Could she have anticipated anything like what she was getting herself into? A Cinderella whisked away to a townhouse palace of more and more violins—nothing but violins? *Life in the violin ramparts continues apace . . .* we'd see written on half-finished postcards from her to college friends, high school friends, friends we'd never met. Or, *The boys grow like weeds— like double-weeds! Ha ha. Karl's won his second (!) round of VSA gold medals and looks to be on track for hors concours status (French for so-many-gold-medals-you-can't-compete-anymore) by decade's end—huge accomplishment for those in the know, though outside Planet Violin, a splash of precisely zero consequence, I realize . . .*

We don't remember her playing the bassoon again until later—sometime in grade school—one afternoon, when strains of her regal, somber *oomph, oomph, oomph* reached us through the ceiling of the shop where we sat with our grandfather and his pancake ears, doing homework and listening to his ruminations.

"What's that?"

"Some kind of ancient hunting horn?"

"Is that Mom?"

"Farting bedpost," our grandfather answered. "Mating call for the tragically weak minded. Watch and learn."

Within minutes our father drifted into the front room to stand with his hands on his hips, gazing fondly at the ceiling as he moved his head in time with her notes. "I'll be! How many years now since we heard that? She must really be feeling better," he said.

"There you have it. Lesson for today, finito," our grandfather said. We fought to restrain our laughter. "Would I ever tell a lie?"

Guessing the probable cause of our laughter and some of the meaning behind his father's words, our father stared a moment and rolled his eyes. "Oh, only so long as you draw breath. Do I even want to know?"

Our grandfather shrugged. "Mr. Hors Concours. Since when do my words matter so much around here?"

"That's assuming there was ever a time that they did," our father said, winking in our direction and heading back into the shop.

"Touché," our grandfather called after him. "Touché . . ."

In the following weeks and months as the volume of her playing increased, occasionally joined by friends on other woodwind instruments—flute, oboe, clarinet, sometimes a vocalist—weaving brokenly through measures of what sounded to us like court music from another century, our grandfather's mood sank ever lower. He didn't move his head with the rhythm like our father; the moment the music started he'd draw a long breath and stare stonily into a corner of the room, seeming never to let the breath back out. As if he were willing himself to be transformed to some unhearing substance. "Of all the goddamn things to spend my last years on earth listening to. Of all the ways to die."

"You're not dying, Grandfather."

"Not soon enough, no."

Eventually, he went back into the shop where the sounds of machines and men working helped to drown her out. He'd assist with orders or just stand around with his hands in his pockets, griping and pestering our father and his apprentices with advice and observations. "I wouldn't do it like that. Watch out you don't cut that too flat across the top, kid. Took me years to unlearn that bad habit. Did you have any particular pattern or model in mind with this arching or were you just . . . winging it? If I were you . . ." His strategy, if he had one, must have been to make enough of a pest of himself that finally our father would have no other choice but to relent, tell her to stop the *infernal sonic disturbance from above, driving away clients,* in order to get him out of their hair. When the music stopped he'd pad back out to his spot by the counter, hands draped over his cane and eyes on the front door, waiting for whatever was next. "Boys . . ." he might begin. "Did I ever tell you the story about the Alard Strad, the time it came into the shop where I was working? This was 1940-something, Sacramento, right about the same time I met your grandmother . . ."

Or he'd digress at length on the subject of Vuillaume, a scurrilous trickster-saint, gifted with supreme, innovative violin building skills and a knack for making copies, and copies of copies, so perfect they fooled even the most educated players and collectors. "He'd make you a Strad ten times over. The Messiah? No problem. He made dozens of Messiahs. And Paganini's Cannon, too. All with wood much the same as what's sitting in that man's workshop now. So you see what he has. What I've given your father . . . a gift and opportunity second only to the supreme bequeathal Tarisio left on his death to Vuillaume? And what favor does he do me in return? Torture me with the noise of bassoons?"

—

Like most violin deals, our grandfather's final deal with Maurice Valloger was sealed with a handshake, in accordance to terms agreed upon and known in full only by them—no witnesses and no formal accounting or paperwork. Sometimes he said it was a 5% commission on top of a consignment fee, other times it was 10% commission and consignment fees, with all other proceeds to be paid to the estate, exclusive of profits over and above pre-arranged pricing which also changed, depending on which ledger you looked at, Maurice's original, our grandfather's revised version of it—*Such handwriting! Who can read a word of it? And the smudges! It's no wonder he couldn't keep his business running*—or any of the subsequent ledgers once all originals had been permanently misplaced. Whatever the arrangement, we know that it left our grandfather blurry and weepy, possibly because, in a final gesture of mercy and largesse, he'd allowed Maurice to believe himself to have gotten the upper hand. Possibly because the pleasure of having finally laid claim to those most prized items of Maurice's after so many years, and in such a dramatic, end-of-life scenario, was also overwhelming. Regardless, left-handed or right-handed, because of the heart catheter and

IV drips, our grandfather couldn't say and didn't care to remember, he and Maurice had shaken hands on it, and this was what mattered.

For a while Maurice's Bergonzi violin sat in the display case in the front room, until it went out on approval and from there, for a time anyway, God and our grandfather only knew; his bows sifted to various bow cases on shelves and in drawers around the shop, each stickered with encrypted price tags on the frog, all to be eventually resold, on and off the record, or passed on to other dealers abroad and in the US. The Stradivari tonewood blanks, sealed at the ends, tagged and labeled—enough for at least twelve violins—went on a shelf in the storeroom, some of the pieces frosted with mildew-stains, all of them brown-black from oxidation, dry and deeply figured, a few of the tops worm-eaten. Our father claimed not to see anything special there. But we caught him sometimes, long silent moments alone standing by that shelf, hands on his hips, lost in thought. Wondering, maybe. Daydreaming. Trying to feel his way to a connection back through the centuries of violin making to the one man whose name has dogged, belittled, obscured, and inspired awe among all who take up any aspect of the violin life, since; trying to know something about him before cutting into his last known stash of wood. Measuring himself against an invis-ible potential. Wondering if he was good enough. Saving it for the right day, the right instrument. Or thinking it was a fraud and a sham—a pile of old wood from nowhere, whose fake-sanctified origins Maurice had somehow convinced our grandfather to believe. Wondering what kind of trouble it would eventually bring on us all and how to control the damage, in advance. He shook his head. He sighed and made some clicking noises in his mouth and bent to retrieve whatever supply or wood piece he'd come for in the first place.

No fault of Maurice's he was born with a weak eye and a gullible, unlucky streak in place of most of his internal organs. But he was from a long line of respected Parisian dealers and luthiers, trained by and much intermingled with the J. B. Vuillaume family of lore, enough to have inspired our grandfather's unconditional respect, and this, we were also never to forget. "You see that man, what he represents?" he'd say to us, watching Maurice fumble at the door with his cane and coffee and his newspaper. "That's two hundred years of Euro-pean violin history in his genetic makeup, right there. *Two hundred years* of European violinistic excellence and ingenuity, right there in one man, one pair of shoes. Eh? Look hard because you won't see it again anytime soon my boys, not around here. Now let's find out what we can talk him out of today." Whether he truly believed in Maurice's Stradivarius wood was, most of the time, anyone's guess. We knew only that he believed enough to make sure he acquired it, and enough to feel that the story of its origins (despite variations in particulars with each re-telling) should be beaten into our heads by repetition, as well: a late-night raid on Vuillaume's shop by Maurice's great-great uncle, Michel, to extract payment for instruments of his that Vuillaume had sold on consignment and for which Vuillaume had never paid him. An overturned donkey cart in a back alley; flight up a canal by moonlight, and across the French countryside; wood stored in the basement of a country church, some of it ruined by flooding and freezing, and later at a family friend's vineyard for decades . . . half a century . . . more. And then the war. Maurice, poor young orphaned Maurice, the last in the Valloger line of violin almost-greatness fleeing ahead of Hitler's troops with only that wood and his Bergonzi (disassembled to avoid notice) and other items our grandfather had long since fleeced him of. "It's real, I tell you," though our experience had taught us by then that the more he insisted on a thing's truth, the likelier it was pure fiction. "Real Stradivari wood, straight from the source. From one man to the next, over rivers and oceans, concealed in a shithouse and as packing material in crates of dressmaker's dummies, and *boom* right here in our shop. Right there! Now why doesn't your father start already . . . make me a nice a little copy of the Lady Blunt or the Messiah. Tell me what is it he's waiting for? Does he think I'm getting any younger? I want to hear! I want to see the old wood sing! How much longer?"

—

The wood sat. Apart from those moments we'd caught our father standing wistfully alongside it, hands in the small of his back, taking a measure of himself against the impossible, metaphysical ideal of Antonio Stradivari, maybe, or just trying to ease the muscles that were forever cramping or threatening full seizure, the result of too many hours bent at his bench—no one paid it any mind. Occasionally our grandfather inspected to be sure it was all there. Part of his routine check of shop inventory: glasses at the end of his nose, pen, stickers, and notepad in hand, he'd go around muttering to himself, licking the tip of his pencil and making his adjustments and computations. He'd sigh and shake his head and hum and suck air through his teeth. His hope, we supposed, was to discover that some of the wood was gone—secretly or unsecretly put to use in the construction of a new violin. But if apprentices knew of its significance or whereabouts, none of them gave an indication. Always they went straight for the higher, better-lit shelves, not the shelves of stained and cruddy-looking blanks breeding shadows and cobwebs. Some nights, reading, doing homework and goofing around in the attic room where we slept, one or the other of us would pretend to hear the wood speaking through the floorboards and heating vents—words drifting up to us in a voice that was like a creepy old Italian or Frenchman back from the dead, or like our grandfather and Maurice, sometimes cleverly insulting each other, more often narrating descriptions of girls we liked in the grandiose style of one the Hill family violin biographies from which our grandfather so often read aloud to us: "Our observations upon the general characteristics of her tits and comparative analyses of the distinctive features of these in comparison with her elbows and her ass are based upon years of professional experience . . . the beauty of her bodaciously curvaceous waist and resultant anxiety that should be manifest to all men observing the manner in which she farts and picks her nose is most instructive . . . observe the fluting of her nostrils though, smooth, with a surface like that of clear still water . . ."

Once, on a midnight raid of the kitchen for leftover birthday cake (our fifteenth), we went so far as to sneak past our grandfather's bedroom at the head of the main floor stairs, and down again to the shop to see. Everywhere our flashlights touched, there was the old, familiar world unanimated by our mood of giddy half-spooked hilarity—the same framed poster-illustration of a dog and a beach ball from a vintage Guinness advertisement much loved by our mother; our grandmother's portrait, also framed, sepia-tinted and leaning on a motorbike, goggles on her forehead and a leather cap like Amelia Earhart's; the ancient porcelain urn of rose petals from our parents' wedding on a stained and unraveling doily made by our Canadian great-grandmother; our grandfather's shoes outside his bedroom door, laceless and swallowing darkness in the shape of his much maligned and gout-infested toes—none of which did anything to dull our mood of excitement.

And in the storeroom, nothing. Only the wood.

"Dare you."

"You first."

In my mind were images of Stradivari from the few drawings and paintings of his likeness in books our grandfather had loaned or given us over the years, none verified—*Portrait of a Violin Builder thought to be Antonio Stradivarius:* A balding, bearded guy in knickers and leather apron, shirt with puffy sleeves gathered around the wrists like pajamas, bulbously huge and over-calloused hands touching the top of a violin, like God in Michelangelo's Sistine Chapel. Which of us reached first I don't know. Possibly both at once, possibly for the same piece, drawing out instead several blank sets together with a noise of clattering wood on floorboards, each of us glaring and *ssshhing* the other, laughing, then lifting them to look more closely, only to realize all over again, as we had when we'd first seen the wood coming into the shop, that really there was nothing magical or special in any of it—just wood after all, corroded and satined by time; a musty, resinous redolence I imagined might strengthen or turn sweeter if you were to scratch the surface; a peculiar, radiant coolness to the touch as if the centuries of its age had somehow condensed and super-cooled elements in its core—when a voice, but not the creepily accented voice of a dead man, and not coming from the shelves or the wood in our hands either, but from the top of the stairs, reached us. Our grandfather's voice. As if he were telepathically connected with that wood and could be jolted from sleep at a single touch. As if he were wired to it in the backs of his eyeballs, always on call.

"Who the hell's down there and what do you want? State the nature of your business! Hello!" And then under his breath, "Damn cat. Hey! Is that you? Anyone down there?"

We had just seconds to replace the pieces and duck further into the storeroom before he'd get to the landing and the light switch there.

But no lights came. There was only the flip-flop sound of his slippers descending and then padding across the hall, closer to where we hid. And then nothing. His wheezy nose-breaths in and out as he stood admiring his plunder. A sigh. Another sigh, deeper. "Oh, Francesca," he said. "Francesca." This was not our dead grandmother's name, or a nickname we knew of for her—it was in fact a name we'd never heard him say aloud until then. "Francesca, Francesca. What do we do?" And then a noise from the back of his throat which was hard to tell from laughing or crying, possibly neither. We stared at each other in the half-light, fighting to hold back the laughter and mouthing—*Francesca? Who the fuck?*—when I noticed: under my brother's arm, a blank of Strad maple, tucked innocently like a book. Like he was just a studious kid on his way to class with some weird-looking tall and narrow art book. Following my gaze, he shrugged once, knotting his eyebrows and giving a quick headshake to dismiss concern and assert his fundamental innocence. *No big deal*, he mouthed. Anyway, the look said, we're in this together. Come on. We'll figure it out, put it back later, if anyone notices. Or not . . .

When our grandfather moved on from the wood to the front of the shop and from there back to the workshop, switching lights on and off as he went, squares of illumination doubling and brightening back through shadowy doorways to where we hid, we made a run for it—back up past his room reeking of feet and the menthol compresses of Chinese herbs he sometimes wore at night to ease his joint pain; up again and sliding across the living room floor silvered in moonlight from the front picture windows, fake bearskin shag throw rugs floating like clouds in a midnight sky, like reflections of clouds in a moonlit lake, and surrounded by our mother's heron-legged collapsible music stands, open and musicless, and up again, the final creaking flights of narrower stairs to our room.

What would he do or say? If he burst in now. What would we say back? I had no idea.

We leaned at either side of the doorway, listening and waiting. I watched my brother's Adam's apple, and swallowed once reflexively with him, realizing as I did that I'd also been synchronizing my breathing with his, as if that would help us to avoid notice. When we were younger, the only way most people told us apart was by the rooster's comb of semi-transparent and faintly feathery hair growing under Nick's chin; I never had a corresponding ruff. Now, with both of us shaving every third or fourth morning before school, that distinction was gone, and others had taken its place—the development of bones and muscles through early puberty skewing us unevenly in frame and physiognomy, one broader in the forehead like our father (me), the other smoother, svelte, and heavy-lidded like our mother or possibly our grandfather—though still we were mostly alike. Alike enough people mistook us for each other all the time.

"Francesca," my brother whispered.

"Oh, Francesca!"

"The wood I've got for you . . ."

"Old wood."

"Real wood."

And both of us together: "Stradivari wood!"

For some time after, in our respective corners of the room, we didn't sleep. I saw him in the semi-dark, rising to tuck the blank beneath one end of his mattress and then the other, and minutes later getting up to stand in our closet doorway, snapping down the pull-chain light so the room filled with harsh brilliance. Inside, he pushed past busted suitcases, hats and pajamas, boxes of old school assignments, a deflated inner tube, a game of Chinese checkers that made a roiling, spiraling racket of glass on tin as he lifted and moved it, looking for somewhere to hide that wood.

"Nick! Light!"

On the balls of his feet he hunched quickly back across the room, pulled the chain, and went again to his mattress on the floor beside the south-facing dormer, under quilts and pillows, where he flung himself down and seemed instantly to have fallen asleep.

"Happy now?" I asked.

He wouldn't answer. It wasn't a question requiring an answer.

And long after his breathing had slowed and become regular, I lay awake picturing that wood blank at the back of our closet. I'd heard the theories, of course: wood of Stradivari's era was so dense and perfect because of the Little Ice Age affecting the trees he harvested . . . because some of it had soaked for years in a brine of seawater and kelp . . . because it grew from a stock of wood that was afflicted with a rare fungus late in its growth cycle causing it to be less porous and therefore stiffer. Had heard, too, the stories about Stradivari divining tone by tapping on the trunks of live trees with a mallet and rushing out at the first rumbles of thunder to stand on a hill overlooking the forest, listening for the sound of particular trees split down the middle by lightning strikes in order to know which were best for tonewood and where to cut next. Legend. All of it. And here, supposedly, like a tombstone marking the end of the line, the end of time and legends, at the back of our closet under abandoned Hot Wheels cars, Legos, train sets and God knew what else: one of the last remaining pieces. Not a violin yet, maybe never a violin. Only some wood. Each time I felt myself slipping off, I saw it there . . . felt it at the back of our closet, calling down lightning strikes. Summoning past and future. Opening a passage into the next years of our lives. One minute I was sure we'd find a way to backtrack, return the wood before our grandfather noticed, and go on with everything the same as ever; the next I was just as sure this would be impossible. Like in the stories and fables we'd read or heard read aloud when we were younger, where a man or woman attempts to shift the pattern and course of fate by getting rid of the one object that most defines them—donkey, slippers, magical ring—eradicating the one trait by which everyone knows them, the birthmark, the beautiful hair, tattoo, only to be caught in a trap of infinite and escalating repetitions.

I'd return it myself. First thing. Before anyone else was even awake.

That was the thought that finally sent me off. When I awoke, my brother was already gone.

Two

By this time, age fifteen, we had seen more than our share of beautiful old violins. Guadagninis, Maurice's Bergonzi, Vuillaumes, a Strad, Amatis, and many others, including a quartet of unattributed instruments, slope-shouldered and troll-like, thought to have been built by a luthier from the ancient Brescian school (or else by Vuillaume posing as a Brescian) before they all died from cholera and were mostly wiped from the history books, thereafter to be eclipsed by the great Cremonese builders. Whenever an important instrument made its way to the shop, either for a repair or for a show-and-tell visit with the proud owner or instrument dealer, we were called in to look, learn, and admire. A form of impromptu worship minus kneeling and smoke and confession; a lot of talk about lines and measurements, modeling and tool-marks taking the place of prayer, final sermon usually delivered by our grandfather. "Boys!" he'd yell, if we were upstairs or in the front part of the shop. "Come see. A firsthand knowledge of fine instruments won't fall on you from out of the sky any time soon, I'm told. Put away the games and homework, on the double!"

But never had we seen a violin from the Guarneri family of builders. We knew about them, of course—Piotr, Antonio, Andrea, and especially the great Giuseppe Guarneri del Gesù, the last builder of the Golden Age of Italian violins, and our father's personal all-time favorite among Golden Age Italian violin builders. The one after whose work he'd patterned the majority of his own work. From our grandfather we'd heard the wildly romantic tales of jail-time and barroom fights, fights in central squares, a love triangle ending in a double homicide, prolonged wandering in poverty and inebriation, all so often attributed to del Gesù; and from him we also knew all of these stories to be untrue, many times debunked—embellishments on known events from the lives of other builders from other times having nothing to do with the great del Gesù. And yet because of the central mysteries of del Gesù's life—that he managed to put off seriously applying himself to the business of building until the final ten to fifteen years of his short life, and then, meteorically, fantastically, and with a religious fervor to earn him the name del Gesù, *of Jesus*—those apocryphal stories still somehow persisted in collecting around him and being wrongly attributed to him again and again as if he were possessed of some terrible, erroneous power of magnetism. "This we call an epic, historic rumor," our grandfather explained. "An epic, centuries-old form of gossip. Because no one knows the real truth. Why did del Gesù wait? What was his real problem and why do the heads of his fiddles look sometimes like dying maniacs, other times like starving dogs or monks or something mystical? There is no rhyme or reason. Was he in a big rush or was he a genius . . . or both? Maybe his wife or his blind father was carving his scrolls. Maybe he just had money troubles. Serious money troubles because Stradivari was sucking up all the oxygen in the universe, even then. But really, who knows? Not you. Not me."

The day after our nearly botched raid of our grandfather's wood, we were given the unlikely cover of a surprise visit from a notable expat Russian soloist who'd been away from the shop and out of town for years—much of his twenties and early thirties—and was home again for a family visit. David Kushnarov. "News, big news, yes," he said. "I will tell all. I am soon to be married man! Yes, yes, I know. But this is nothing to do with why I am again here today." We did not remember him, though he insisted we had been much in love with him and had followed him around for days and hours when we were younger *like imprinted little ducklings* . . . imprinted cherubs, laughing at his jokes and antics, every time he pulled off his thumb or cracked his nose, found a quarter behind his ear or hung by one finger from a door jamb—none of which impressed us now as deeply as his pop-eyed insistences and the thickness of his eyebrows arching up and down with each exclamation, wooly caterpillars trapped in a cragged landscape of forehead, the brow bones thickly oversized as if extra lobes of logic and intellect were packed there above his eyes—though I admit: when he fell to the sawdust and shavings on the shop floor and started pumping out pushups, first two-handed, then with a hand behind his back, and last with claps between each repetition, straining and making a noise like a stuck door, and again when he stood laughing and wiping his hands on the knees of his khaki trousers, swatting at his pecs, veins beating in his forehead and mouth open to show stumpy, tobacco-lined teeth, gapped in the front, square-tipped white tongue just behind that, I felt something: a dim haze of almost-recognition and familiarity washing over me with the smell of his expired cologne and deodorant interpenetrated with sweat—old world sweat, I thought then, though I had no basis for such an association; sweat from the old country, garlicky and tinged with an ancient mossy funk—evaporating as quickly as it enveloped my senses.

I do, I wanted to say. *I do remember.* But I didn't. Not really. So I said nothing.

With him was a Guarneri violin, on loan indefinitely from a private founda-

tion, annual renewals with no pre-set return date—an investment in him, and in
themselves, the foundation had informed him; a way of advertising their wealth
and power via largesse, promoting good will and cultivating international cul-
tural capital all at the same time—and which he wanted to leave with us now for
the duration of his visit in town in order that our father might make castings of
it, take measurements and otherwise, "Imprint its exact essence upon your mind
and heart. Not knock off," he said. "I do not want cheap look-alike copy. No-no,
I want . . . how do you say . . . an exact replication. Clone? I want this exact
violin again, but new because you see." Here he ran a finger under his nose and
slapped his hands at his sides. "She is not mine. I have her on loan only so long
as this foundation says, but. I am no longer talk of town, violinistically speaking.
Yes? A concert here, a concert there, but nothing like in old days when I am ev-
erywhere guest of honor, and so you see how it is only a matter of time, so many
more days or weeks or maybe months before I am called. Ding-a-ling. She is not
yours anymore. Guarneri lady? We must have her back. And so . . . and so. What
to do then if I am parted forever from this, the love of my life?" He shook his
head. "It cannot be. So many hundred thousand or millions of dollars I do not
have, and anyway, she is not for sale. And this is where you come in, because you
must help me. The man with superlative touch. The Guarneri master!"

Our father had built on commission for him once before, years earlier—a
Strad copy that had helped launch his career and on which he'd debuted with
symphonies and in concert halls around the world, now lying dormant under
the silk in the double-case beside his beloved Guarneri lady. Would our father
mention it? Ask after it? This seemed unlikely. He stood with his back straight
against the edge of his bench and hands clasped behind him, one foot pointed
toe downward at the floor, heel resting against the inside of its opposing ankle.
Like Saint Sebastian, I thought—from one of our mother's coffee table art
books: Saint Sebastian pinned to his bench by invisible arrows, and with an ex-
pression on his face as balefully obscure and world-weary (though nowhere near
as pious) as the original. It was for his back, I knew—a standing position to ease
the pain in his lower back, or make him think he was easing it anyway—and
much as I might have wished for actual arrows to pierce his cruddy old sneakers
(grey with green racing stripes on the sides and tears along the toes and a source

of continual embarrassment to us) I knew he was neither martyred nor a saint, and his shoes . . . (*What do you want?* he'd ask, if I were to say anything about them. *My lucky shoes! I ran track in them when I was a little older than you. Still good. Still got some good tread left in them. Forty bucks they cost, back when forty bucks was a lot for a pair of shoes, not that you'd know or care about that.*) A greasy lock of hair slid across his black-rimmed glasses and he made no move to push it aside. Green T-shirt he'd probably slept in, hair smelling of sleep too, and hands most likely sweet with smells of coffee, cinnamon and the huckleberry scones our mother had made for breakfast. Outside the sun shot rays of light through the clouds and haze, illuminating raindrops on the window glass beside his bench and causing blurred, miniature reflections of the room to form in each drop as they spun and slid and continued to fall across the glass.

"Sure," he said. "We can do that. We can try. I can't of course guarantee a sound like a three-hundred-year-old violin. It might be better. It might not be as good at all. Almost certainly it won't be the same, exactly. In fact," here he finally pushed the hair aside and stood straighter, both feet on the ground, hands clasped in front, "I'm going to propose that all three of us try. Guy, Nicky, and I—we'll each make you a copy and you can choose. Which do you like the best."

"I can only . . ."

"Of course, whichever one you like, you pay for. Or none. Doesn't matter to me." He waved a hand. "We've got orders and the boys need the practice. Right? This will be a good project—for all of us. A learning experience with a real-life outcome and a new model we can each of us gain a little take-home knowledge from."

We had seen Guarneri's violins in pictures and catalogues—had read detailed descriptions in the Hills' biographies of all the brothers, father, and grandfather—but until that day, had never seen one in real life. As it worked its way around the informal circle we'd made at the side of my father's bench—watching as first our father and grandfather then one of the better apprentices held it by the neck and turned it side to side, admiring from all angles—the soloist went on in his sing-song English: "The varnish to me is of utmost importance and here I will tell you why. I will let you in on little secret . . ." But we were too absorbed in looking to give him our full attention. His words fell under the

ground of our reverence, a kind of counterpoint to which our father occasion-
ally cued a headshake or grunt, eyes lifting toward the soloist, blinking as if try-
ing to remember why he was there or bring him into focus—and then as quickly
turning from him again. Everything he said had to do with his pre-performance
ritual of caressing the violin around the shoulders and front and back plates,
pressing lightly with fingertips and feeling how each part of the violin corre-
sponded with some detail of his own physical anatomy—heart, belly, shoulders,
kidneys—until he was literally at one with his instrument and ready to step
into the spotlight. Ready to go *deep inside* and make himself one with the music,
one with the audience's apprehension of that music too—all of this entwined
and evinced through tone and vibrations in the air, and all of it no longer his.
No longer having anything much to do with him. The varnish, he felt, had a
magnetic, anodyne effect in achieving this transcendence, not cosmetic, and
therefore our replicas must appear exactly as the original or it would not work
at all. "These dimples here and scratches everywhere on the back. See? Every
one. Every single one. A part of my heart. My soul. So please. No mistakes."

As always, in the presence of an old, semi-important instrument each of us
had retreated into his own private reverie and self-examination having to do
with history, wood, pigment, the passage of time and shrinkage of wood fiber,
all physical attributes of the instrument itself calibrated in accordance with the
inscrutable and ineffably shifting sense of self-worth (or lack thereof) at the bot-
tom of our endeavors and driving us on—*Could I make that? Could I do that? Would
I make that choice? How many flaws and mistakes do I see, and why do they even matter? Look
at those fucked-up corners*—and set against the seeming unlikelihood, seeming im-
possibility really, that this relic of two hundred and sixty years past was intact and
still completely itself. Was still, after all these years, really just another violin. A
bunch of original parts with new pieces (fingerboard, pegs, tailpiece, neck, some
doubling on one corner, etc.) carved and re-carved and assembled in exactly
the same manner and in accordance with the same shapes, principles, patterns,
methods, and limitations that defined and contained our own work daily. Red-
dish brown finish like cognac, scuffed corners, wood worn almost bare on one
shoulder and lower bout, tightly grained top with the tell-tale strip of darkened
resin-impregnated grain down the middle, present in so many of Guarneri's tops.

Look, it's just a violin, I wanted to say—*I mean, a really, really nice violin, but all the same just a violin*—before passing it to my brother and watching him, to see if he registered it in anything like the same way. If he was able to *imprint* back through the centuries to some unique or mystical quality in the violin's material and construction. I watched his lids drop and eyes narrow. Saw his hands, so like mine but not, one on the neck, the other bracing one of the lower bouts, then the fingers floating around its outline, quickly tracing something I didn't see. "Magnificent," he said.

"Please," our father said, handing it back to the soloist, lifting his eyebrows.

Immediately taking his meaning, the soloist bent to retrieve his white hankie and bow from the double case where our father's old Strad copy also lay. He wound the thumbscrew of the bow quickly, tapped its tip in his palm and cleared his throat once; stood with feet wide, eyes closed, the fingers of his left hand, ring, index and middle, pressing once the left side of the violin's front plate as if to take its temperature, and then tucking it at his jaw with a minute shake of his head. "A piece composed by her most illustrious owner and namesake, the greatest violinist of all time—Henri Wieniawski," he said. "The *Legende*. You may recognize." He inhaled sharply, a hissing-rattling noise like wind through a field of wheat or a sword rattling from its sheath, air whistling through his distended nostrils and the caverns of his massive sinuses, and lunged into the music.

As he played, I don't know if anyone else in the shop was similarly affected. Maybe it was only his hyperbolic descriptions of tonal and esthetic perfection and their interconnections through his body and spirit which had opened me to a physical appreciation of his playing; maybe it was seeing how he touched the violin where it would have a heart if it were alive, before playing, but I felt myself, watching his fingers and bulbously oversized forehead, the movement of his eyes under closed eyelids, the faintly whip-like movement of the bow, carried away to a giddy state of hilarity verging on grief, at times embarrassed for him, at times fighting tears of my own not to look a fool—*too much, too much feeling*, I wanted to yell at him, *stop!*—as if there were invisible strings in me vibrating in accord with the notes he bowed and fingered. He didn't stop, and soon I found myself absorbed in the rain on the window, the light reflecting all of us in miniature, Planet Violin in each of its drops, as a way to distract myself from whatever it was I was undergoing.

—

Wood is not a mirror for the soul or a prism through which anything worthwhile about a human life can be seen, our father often said. *Period. That's our job, carving these blocks of spruce and maple to the various shapes and forms of antiquity. It's all so musicians can pour out their most intimate, unintelligible feelings. We're just the carpenters. The drones. No, we're priests with the tools of a carpenter making objects for people to fuss over and fetishize and sometimes to transcend all that crap. Well, and we're also mathematicians. Sometimes philosophers . . . who the hell knows. Definitely not artists of any kind.* For a while, until it vanished, Nick and I hid that Stradivari wood blank in our closet or under one of our beds, moving it from place to place to trick each other and keep it from being found. Some mornings before school, I liked to take it out and stare into its grain, thinking *mirror . . . prism . . . antiquity* and trying to feel through its eel-slick surface some sense of wonder commensurate with its origins: the decades of dumb, vegetative growth on another continent followed by darkness; the Italian men who'd ostensibly cut it and sealed its ends so many hundred years ago; the fingers that had touched it, quartered it, smoothed it, and felt in it whatever dreams and plans people those days made for fine violins. I tried to remember what I'd felt, hearing the soloist play, too—bits and pieces of melody; his subtle rocking movement forward and back, not quite in time with the music—to make sense of it all. But not much came to me. Just wood, I thought. Just old and dense. Just music.

Meanwhile, we went ahead with our efforts to map and sketch the soloist David Kushnarov's Guarneri, the ex-Wieniawski, and in every way possible prepare ourselves to make violins in its dead likeness. Whenever Nick and I weren't at school, doing homework, or helping out around the house we were busy drawing and making measurements: numbers corresponding with graduation to the front and back plates, a topography of points and nodes set within the outline of a violin, plotting every idiosyncrasy and variation in thickness and arching; lines bisecting circles to diagram the exact asymmetrical proportioning of shoulders, arching, corners, bouts and f-hole placements. Because this was before the days of more advanced photography and cheap photocopying and other technological advancements which would have eliminated intermediary steps, we were forced into a hand-drawn, painstaking intimacy with every aspect of that violin's construction and geometry—a laboratory and inner-sanctum of secret knowledge and private obsession. Long before the day we picked wood for the tops, I was anxious to carve. Of course, these were not our first violins. Under our father's watchful eye we'd independently completed work at every stage of construction on instruments that had gone out of the shop bearing his label, several times over, and had finished our own instruments top to bottom several times as well. We'd been doing his rough carving and most of his linings and purfling for what seemed an eternity. We were years from the confident sweep of his final, signature knife strokes and tool marks. What was fast and simple for him might be light years beyond us, might in fact take us hours longer with jigs and chalk, but we were good. We were ready.

Afternoons he was not busy with other obligations, David Kushnarov occasionally visited—to check on our progress or to have a spare hour alone with his Guarnerius, playing in one of the upstairs rooms. From our father's sudden stillness at the bench, his glare over the tops of his glasses at the sound of the soloist's voice approaching from the front of the shop as our grandfather's efforts to distract him with stories and facts and trade secrets were brushed aside, we registered his aggravation. "Damn, damn, God damn," our father would mutter. "How can he expect us to get anything *done*, always popping in like this. When'd he say he was leaving town again?" But the moment his rolling gait carried him around the corner and into the room, arms wide, the necks of his sheer dress shirts always open a button past modesty—our father transformed. "David!" he'd say, beaming, as if he hadn't realized until that moment the imminence of his arrival. "Karl!" And for seconds they'd stand like that, each with his arms open in welcome to the other, before closing the distance and ending with a backslapping embrace. "Always good to see you. We're getting close now. Really close. Would you like to see? Just settling a few details. But today? Absolutely! She's all yours to play. Strung up and ready . . . Guy? Nicky? Can one of you please get David's instrument from the vault?"

So it was a surprise but not a shock, the afternoon I went upstairs to make a late lunch of sandwiches for everyone and found him on the couch with our mother, their heads bent over a music score on the coffee table and the fingers of his left hand darting and pressing rhythmically along his right forearm, both of them humming and tapping fingers and feet, swaying their heads to a rhythm, like pieces of seaweed caught in a current. "Da-dya-*da-da*-dya-*dya*," David sang, his voice rising over my mother's as hers sank to a note like purring. "No, that's not right, right there." His hand closed on hers to stop her and then he was stabbing his fingers at the coffee table in time and counting to illustrate his point. "Again, again, we try again!" She laughed and in the few seconds before either of them registered my presence in the doorway, looked at him with an expression of what I took to be such unguarded affection, the only word I could think of to help myself understand what I'd witnessed was one I'd heard occasionally at school and on TV—*gooey eyes*. Eyes with a quicksand undercurrent of lustful affection to suck you in. I was embarrassed for her, afraid that he might not return the feelings; equally afraid that he might. Worse: whatever she felt for him and his stunt-flying fingertips, coiffed curls, and the sweet, penetrating strains of violin sound that seemed to surround and follow him everywhere with wafts of his cologne, his impossibly muscular pecs and mostly hairless chest, I felt it too. Who could blame her? How could anyone *not* be carried away by such feelings in his presence? I was equal parts aroused on her behalf, drawn to the brink of private giddiness and delight, and terror stricken. If she loved him, then . . . what?

When they saw me, the light drained from the picture and both of them froze. "Why hello, Guy!" my mother called, waving with the tips of her fingers. "We're sight-reading, sight-singing some music I just got from the library! But David doesn't have his . . . doesn't have anything to play, so we're pretend reading. Imaginary reading, which is just great because, you know," and with a breath and a lilt in her voice like she'd just made a discovery, "you can't make any mistakes!" As she spoke she shifted subtly from David on the couch so their knees and shoulders no longer seemed to me bound in a force field of positive or negative magnetism—or maybe my perception of the situation shifted. It was hard to say.

"I'm just getting sandwiches," I said. I flapped my hands at my sides and then shoved them in my pockets and jogged a leg up and down like our grandfather, just to have something to do. I shrugged. "Don't let me wreck anything."

"Oh, you couldn't! Nothing to wreck! It's all up here." She tapped a fingernail at her forehead.

Soon enough, as I retreated to the kitchen to lay slabs and strands of pastrami and cheese on bread with mustard, pickles, and horseradish for our late lunches, I heard them counting each other in again, humming and singing nonsense words in counterpoint, stopping, laughing, trying again, but something had gone out of it. We were accustomed to hearing our mother referred to as beautiful, exceptional, even cosmic, particularly by our father, and had grown up with a background sense of her beauty being somehow a function of his devotion to her—also part of an unconditional deference from our grandfather, which was harder to pinpoint or grasp since in his case it also seemed to include an equal apportionment of exasperation and aggravated impatience—but mainly we had assumed it must have something to do with *us*; that it was all somehow a reflection back on us, like a giant, invisible equals sign hanging in the air between us, twin genius boys and inheritors of the family business, and her. Those bare shins tapering from the knees to the scroll-like bend of her toes, the *gooey* blue-gray eyes, red mouth singing nonsense rhythm syllables or opening around her double-reed . . . for the first time all of this occurred to me as if I didn't know her. As if I had no part in her life. Why was she here? What kept her from going, after all? Like the chatoyance in a fine piece of wood, polished to draw the figure toward the surface and make it more three-dimensional, flickering and receding ever deeper into the grain, her separateness and will shone and receded. Something you could see and admire but never touch. Chambers within chambers, inside the grain.

"Sandwiches?" I called to them. "I'm making some . . . easy enough to do a couple more for you."

If they heard me they gave no indication one way or the other.

━

From that day forward I was always attuned to David Kushnarov's actions and whereabouts. So long as his Guarneri sang from an upstairs room—his preferred concertos from the Romantic and late Classical period, Bruch, Brahms, Sibelius, Mendelssohn, Wieniawski, Mozart, and occasionally Bach—so long as sound poured from windows and open doorways down the hall or more dimly through vents and floorboards overhead, silvering the silence, floorboards sometimes squeaking and squeezing arrhythmically as he rocked side to side or bent forward at one knee, lunging subtly like a portrait of a man in a swordfight, eyebrows arched stiffly into his massive forehead (all things I'd witnessed when I'd been sent to get him, ask a question, find out his opinion, tell him of some new development), or stopping suddenly to tune—pinching, flicking, plucking, pulling at each string with the pads of his fingers to fine tune, and finally resuming with a skitter of notes at the top of the fingerboard . . . so long as any of this was audible to us downstairs as we went about finalizing preparations, I didn't worry. My focus stayed with the work at hand, at times even aided by shapes I apprehended inside the music—weird paisley birds and spirographically swirling oddities like seahorses' tails or the necks of stallions, like what I sometimes saw on the insides of my eyelids falling asleep at night—and I felt myself transported to a state of near rhapsodic attentiveness. But if he was visiting and I heard no music, if his violin was back with us for more scrutiny and measuring, closer analysis for color and varnish opacity, mapping of major marks and scuffs for antiquing, I'd feel myself stranded in a no-man's land of hesitation and inattention. Anxious. I couldn't think. I pictured them laughing together. I saw his knees and shoulders, knew the heat of his skin in the too-open V of his shirt collar and then it was all I could do to keep from dropping whatever I had in hand and rushing upstairs to confront them, confirm my worst suspicions or stop them before it was too late.

There was no point looking to our mother for clues. The patterns between her and our father were too worn and familiar to read. Standing beside him after mealtimes as he rinsed plates for the dishwasher, kneading the perennial kinks and knots and sore spots in his shoulders and neck as they talked and she finished the ends of his sentences to speed him up—was she any more or less kind, more or less impatient? And what would either prove? Making mock-pouty faces at him across the table as, between bites, he gave the usual litany of screw-ups and delays to work, and later whipping him with the rat-tailed end of a towel if the litany didn't stop—any difference? Skirts that swirled and flared in a way to flatter the curves of her ankles and calves; form-fitting sweaters with bright buttons and silk placards. All the same as ever. She'd recently joined a women's choir and in addition to the woodwind group was preparing pieces with them for an early winter recital at the community center. Holiday favorites and show tunes. Often as not she seemed lost in a haze of hummed parts, eyes focused into an imaginary middle-distance as she repeated under her breath lines that caught her or stuck in her head—*In egg-shell-cease Day-OH . . . day oh, DAY-oh*—all of which could have signified heartsickness and longing for David or could, as the notes also seemed to convey, just indicate distraction and excitement about the upcoming show. Her hair in a braided rope down her spine or swept up in a scarf or hair band, absorbed and reflected light in its strands the same as ever, swaying with the sound of her heels on the floorboards and causing our father to stop and look after her. "Isn't it just great?" he'd say sometimes. "Seeing her like . . . *this?* Again? It's so . . . She's really," he paused looking for the right word, making and unmaking a fist. "On."

"Yeah, she's *on* all right. On something good, by the looks of it," Nick would quip.

"On love."

"Yes, that's exactly it, Guy, isn't it? Love. It's always love makes us do anything."

Our grandfather, for reasons of his own, had developed a special attunement to David's activities and whereabouts, too—maybe, I thought at first, he was moved by the playing; maybe in his own way he worried about something between David and our mother; without a doubt, he hoped that customers dropping in, hearing the music and noting his hushed and reverent yet offhanded mentions of the soloist's name and Guarnerius—often delivered with traces of scorn, as if any explanation were beneath him—would feel encouraged to part with money for things they'd never intended to buy: an overpriced second-hand Italian violin case lined in silk velvet, ridiculously overwrought as a sarcophagus; also, hunks of rosin shot through with gold, silver, and other precious metal salts, priced at four and five times their actual value. But mainly, as it turned out, he was laying groundwork in his campaign to make David request the use of the Stradivari wood in one or more of the copies we'd soon begin carving. This we learned gradually from the splotchy reddening of our grandfather's face and his uncharacteristic silence when David started up playing; also from the way our grandfather would stand suddenly to limp from one room into the next, muttering and stabbing his cane at the floor, cursing, as each piece wound to its conclusion and another opportunity for saying something about the wood seemed imminent or seemed about to pass him by. It wasn't long before we began catching him idly positioned in doorways leaning on his cane, sidling along hallways or perched on an old camping stool outside whatever room David had chosen for the afternoon, jingling the change and nail clippers in his pocket or snapping open and shut the tin of lemon and mint suckers he always carried beside the dirty handkerchief in his shirt pocket—"To sweeten the deal!" he'd say, swirling them at us, if we asked, "Remember! Because what sucker can resist a sweet sucker? Eh? Keep them with you at all times! Here, you want one?" But only as his propaganda began drifting back to us in bits and pieces, in lemon-and-mint-smelling words from David, did we know for sure: *But wood is of utmost importance as well, yes . . . but old wood for old copy is most logical in this case, is it not? I hear tell of your most fantastic store of immaculate and highly regarded old wood from centuries ago. Is not true?*

All of which was predictable enough.

What none of us predicted or anticipated, the day we were to begin construction: several of our grandfather's knives, gouges, planes, and fingerplanes, freshly edged and arrayed on the bench he'd used mostly to collect clutter and boxes of old receipts and correspondence for going on two decades—the snakewood and Koa knife handles made by him and custom fitted, chipped and marked around with his ancient finger grime, working edges all mirror slick and gleaming—beside a set of black-brown Stradivari wood blanks. His bench surface cleared and ready for work. Smells of coffee brewing and the glue pot heating. So he'd been up for hours already making preparations.

"What?" he said, meeting our father's stare and headshakes of dismay, incredulity. "What? It's a free country, last I checked. Anyway, you think I can't still show you a thing or two, Mister Hors Concours? Think again! I got a few tricks left to share! Watch and learn!" He lifted the knife closest to him and slid its blade across a thumbnail. "See that edge? Baby, I'm back!"

"Good God, no!"

"You want *God's* help now too? Like I haven't done enough already around here? One last violin in the world for me. That's it. Is it so much to ask? I even got my own plan. Look!" Here he held up a full-sized sketch of a violin on newsprint, as rudimentary and wavering through its arcs and lines as anything we'd drawn in grade school. "A nice Carlo Bergonzi Strad model, like the so-called one from Mauricio, rest his soul. All right? I won't even touch your . . . your . . ." He couldn't seem to find the words. "Molds! Castings!" This came with an explosion of saliva. "Your tracings and nonsense. None of it! See? I got my own here." Again he rattled the drawing at our father.

For an answer our father shook his head, groaned and slowly lowered his chin into his hand. "For crying out loud," he said. He pushed up his glasses to squeeze the bridge of his nose between his thumb and the knuckles of his forefinger, crossed his arms and let out a breath. Time, efficiency, and productivity—what he called *the only knowable coordinates in our daily struggle against gravity*—elements of each: these would be foremost in his considerations. Would our grandfather's chatter and use of shared tools and space and general sloppiness around the shop add only time or aggravation into the equation . . . what quotient of either? What would the consequences be? How much was too much? And why was he doing this?

Because of the time of year and because our father had said we were over-due a little victory-lap fun after the weeks of hard prep work—most recently drawings with compasses, strings and pins, scotias and half-arcs and inverted arcs because, as he said, *We don't just measure! Anyone can measure. Makes no damn difference! We have to know why!*—our final practice had involved carving paired enlargements of Guarneri f-holes in jack-o-lanterns using the exact asymmetry of David's Guarnerius for a model: the left slightly skewed and higher in the face than the right, the right with a crease in the center stop to widen the opening. These were still arrayed on the window ledge—mine, Nick's, our father's—the skins withering along the cuts, Nick's charred with smoke and paraffin residue around the top. *Waste of time,* our grandfather had said, the day we gutted and carved them. *I got some old shoeboxes and other garbage upstairs too if you want to do more handicrafts later. Fools,* he said, ducking out of the room. In a rare display of solidarity with us, a reversion to childhood maybe, our father had catapulted a spoonful of pumpkin guts after him followed by a wedge of cut flesh. *Macramé,* our grandfather called back over his shoulder, continuing on his way. *Beadwork and needlepoint! Like that'll come in handy.* Even half-rotten, our father's pumpkin still stood apart from ours, taller-seeming for its confidence and rigid grace, the off-handed elegance in its angles. Again and again I felt my eyes drawn back there, remembering, waiting for him to speak, annoyed at the delay and disappointed in myself for not measuring up.

Finally, he straightened, blinking and breathing again. "Boys?" he said. He pointed a crooked finger at the doorway. "A moment alone, please? See if you can make yourselves useful upstairs? We'll only be a second."

"They can stay! They can witness the shame and humiliation you'd heap on an old man, a man who gave you everything, taught you everything . . ."

"Boys?" he repeated, still pointing, nodding. "A moment?"

When we returned, all was normal. Our father's favorite radio station played in the corner—oldies and classics until the game later in the day, if there was one. One of the apprentices was inspecting his own latest work—a neckless, un-varnished viola—taking on and off his eyeglasses to see it up close and at arm's length. "Do you see it now?" our father asked him from the other side of the room. "You have to learn to perceive these things for yourself. I won't always be there telling you what's real and what's not. OK?" The apprentice continued his inspection, shaking his head, then replaced the viola on his bench and walked out of the room. An exterior door slammed and next came the sound of his feet in the gravel. A single curse.

Our grandfather had slid on an old apron and was at the sink flat-grinding our 1200-grit whetstones—a job, along with window cleaning, normally re-served for the newbie apprentices. This was telling in itself: A first failure and indication that his edge-sharpening might not have gone as well as first glances indicated. But more telling: The wood sets had all been switched. In place of the old wood on our grandfather's bench was some new stock from our father's sup-ply of "practice wood"—coarse-grained spruce and less-figured maple—and on our father's bench, and our own benches as well, sets of old brown Stradivari wood, stacked and ready to be worked.

"Don't ask," our grandfather said, winking and grinning. So he'd gotten his way after all. "You could shave with my knife if you had anything to shave. Punks! Mashuganas."

"But, Dad, are we . . ." my brother began.

"Yes. That's right. The three of us will be using the same wood. The so-called . . ." Our father coughed and cleared his throat but seemed unable to bring himself to say it. "Never mind. But remember. These are faithful copies. They are not forgeries. Understood? We're not in the business of making forgeries here. Ever, under any circumstances. It's a very, very stupid idea. Do I make myself clear?"

Three

Ours was a mongrel family, never church-going, brought up on a catechism of violin lore, facts and practices, rather than any formal belief system. All our lives we'd heard of our grandfather's famously divided parents, barely able to speak the same language well enough to disagree on what was right or wrong, or in accordance with which faith to raise the seven children—her Italian Catholicism or his Russian Orthodox Judaism? When he was thirteen and old enough in appearance to pass for eighteen our grandfather struck out on his own, eventually faking his way into a ring of racketeers stealing, re-selling, and delivering hooch, cigarettes, and sundry goods around Sacramento and the San Francisco Bay Area. One day, his meet point blown by an inside informant no one had suspected was on the take, he learned of a sixth sense for trouble he hadn't previously known in himself. So he said. *You hear these stories of guys who know better with their hunches and superstitions. Well. And you think it's a bunch of malarkey, bunch of hooey, until one day, it happens. You come up the street and you see. Something's not right. Those tipped-over flower pots—not where they were last time. The door open like that? That window? The angle of that shade inside? Nuh-uh. Something's wrong here. Not going in. No way. It's got to be a hunch, like a feeling in your blood. Anyway . . .* Instead he took off down the block and into the first store he saw, a violin shop as it turned out, where his mother had rented instruments for several of his younger siblings over the years and where he was known by the owner for having occasionally come around with late or partial payments from her—cash, loaves of bread, jams and jellies, once a silver necklace. *Truth be told,* he might say, in some versions of the tale, *Maybe he was a little sweet on the old lady. Who could blame him? She was a fine-looking dame to be sure.* He held a finger to his lips and then cut it across his throat to signal distress, turned to where the owner pointed—the stairs leading out of sight to the basement storeroom—and down he went. There he waited much of the afternoon among crates of old parts and tools and busted violins, watching peoples' legs pass in the windows above, waited until a rap on the floorboards gave him the all-clear. And in those hours, knowing nothing of what went on above—was the drop made, extra money extracted, shots fired, his pals arrested and booked?—only the drip-drip-drip of a leaking pipe to keep him company, he experienced a kind of reckoning and transformation. *It was those violins,* he'd tell us. *Nothing special mind you, but for me they were an Aladdin's lamp. Maybe because of my situation or because it was my first time seeing so many in one place, all used up and put to pasture for spare parts, I don't know. A mystery for which, to this day, I have no answer. But I heard them in the silence like they were speaking to me in words and music—legends, poetry!—all those ugly, unloved violins, and if I so much as touched one its whole life would spring into my mind's eye like a moving picture. Like I was right there. All the good times and bad times and the dead people who played them . . .* Weddings, funeral marches, concerts, fairs, parties, quiet evenings alone—the details changed with each re-telling. But always, by the time he emerged from that basement storeroom he had, in his words, seen the light. *I had no sense before then how short a life is. And seeing it, what I knew like a thunderclap was this: I could change my ways, or I could end up like those busted fiddles. A whole lot of nothing. The choice was mine. And so in honor of the objects that had already saved me in my hour of need and delivered me from the benighted ways of my youth, I decided. Then and there. To the store owner, a man I'd known since I was this high and to whom I now already owed my life once, I said four words and then four words more. I said, I must thank you, and then, You must teach me. This, he did. From that day, I never looked back.*

Our faith, if we had one, was and always had been violins.

And to that point in my life, it was a faith I'd never questioned or given much thought. If our father said, *Tap the wood here, like this, light taps, quick. Listen for how quickly it responds,* we did just that. Or, if he said, *Cut the ribs from the maple billets and scrape them to one millimeter . . . Now we split the top and bookmatch the grain so it's like identical pages of the same book running backwards and forward—like you two! Twins! Bookmatched! So who's backwards today? Guy, are you backwards? Ee-kin, raa oo-y? Nac oo-y keeps zdrawkab?* In all of it, a mixture of science, geometry, superstition, metaphysics, guesswork, habit, tradition and luck, we followed the advice and instructions of our father exactly. Over and over. How to flex and tap around a mostly finished top, feel for the irregularities; how to cut a channel, which tool to use to shape your f-holes; how to wind our fingers in cloth for French polishing. And whatever task I was at, in the corner of my eye was my brother, my near double at the opposite side of the bench we shared, his actions and movements mirroring my own, sometimes a step or two behind, a step or two ahead. His knife paring along the curvature of a c-bout, scraper peeling up shreds and ribbons of spruce, elbows locked, puffing at the wood surface to blow away dust and shavings; his weight rocking back and forth like mine, his saw biting through wood. No Aladdin's lamp for us in any of this, no visions beyond or behind or inside the wood. No voices or sixth sense. Even at the final stages, rubbing in finish, watching the bars of color in the back flames light up and transform, deceptively alive and three dimensional under the surface, all those summers and winters of wood growth, decades soaked in sunlight, cold and rain, heat and snow, permanently on display—nothing. Only the gradually resolving shape of the one thing in the world we knew as well as we knew each other—points, arching, bouts, waist . . . another violin.

So it was a surprise for me the afternoon we began rough carving our backs for David's Guarneri copies, when with each push of my gouge I began notic-ing an unfamiliar buzzing-tingling sensation through my arms and shoulders, heat like a hand pressing up the back of my neck. Also a kind of precognition, as if I knew everything before it happened, felt it in advance—our grandfather coming into the room, waving the new portable phone from the shop at us and shouting, "Don't answer! It doesn't work anymore! I'm finished with these people!" as he dropped it into the bath for his whetstone and we all paused to listen for the end of its chirping, underwater burbles; the light outside shifting through tree shadows, brightening suddenly and fading with a burst of rain; my brother sniffing and pausing to rub his nose on the shoulder of his T-shirt, and sniffing again—as if in all of this I was some future projection of myself, going back over actions I'd already finished in order to witness and bring to completion a few remaining pieces. Maybe it was all David's talk about the physical interconnections between himself and his violin—picturing him playing this violin someday and seeing his fingers, hearing the imagined tones pour out lush and full of feeling. Maybe it was some magic inherent in the so-called Stradivari wood or, more likely, all our practice and prep work and our grandfather's buildup and hype, getting us finally to use his wood in a few instruments: I felt like I could have closed my eyes and still known exactly how the grain flowed and where to move next. A kind of relaxed and drowsy almost-autopilot, but more than that.

"Good, good," our father said, and I knew from the rest of his body language what would follow. "This is pretty nice wood. I had my doubts, but this is just fine." His billets, of course, were the best of the three—tight, silky spruce and shimmering maple of a pattern most closely resembling the Guarneri original.

Is this the real life, is this just fantasy, I heard in my head, and seconds later "Bohemian Rhapsody" came over the radio. *Caught in a landslide, no escape from reality* . . . Everything was the same as ever, really. Another day in the shop. Another afternoon roughing blocks of wood to the arched bug-back shapes of some new violin backs. All that had changed was me. I muttered this under my breath to make it more real somehow or reveal it for the falsehood I was half-convinced it must be. *All that's changed is me . . . All that can change . . .*

"Guy?" our father asked. "Pay attention to where you're going there. OK? Everything all right? You need a break? How about we all take a little break time. A little tea."

For an answer I stood back, let the weight fall through my forearms to my wrists and closed my eyes. Felt through my wrists for where to move next and leaned into the wood, but the feeling was fading or my conviction in its rightness. "I could do this with my eyes closed," I said. But I couldn't. Not quite.

"Yeah, well, but it'd be better all the same if you didn't. OK, pal? Better for all of us if you don't blow right through that piece of wood or chop off a couple fingers. Bad for business. Plus it makes a mess. A bloody mess. Ha, ha. Let's have a break now."

Upstairs our mother and her woodwind friends were also on a break from rehearsing, sipping plastic cups of sparkling cider and eating nuts and crackers with cheese and salami and shrimp cocktail, so there was a general mood of festivity—of things having reached a high point or broken chrysalis of feeling—an air of unexpected, intercepted celebration. Soon I found myself backed into a corner of the kitchen counter, balancing an empty paper plate and plastic cup in the palm of one hand, caught in conversation with an oboist I knew slightly from previous post-rehearsal mixers—an older woman in a woven purple tunic with oversized beaded chunks of something like bone around her neck, ornate tribal talismans from some other time and place. Between her questions and horsy, contagious nose-laughs I kept noticing the cheese stuck between her teeth with granulated crackers. I knew she wouldn't care even if I were to point this out to her. *I'm sixty five. Why would I give a goddamn what anyone thinks of my appearance, kid?* she'd told me more than once—an attitude I found pleasing, much as I also disbelieved it. A smell of booze surrounded her, further affecting me with a kind of expansive merriment—an expansive lack of care—until I found myself rambling at length and with completely inauthentic authority about our work and the history of the wood we were using, Salabue and Tarisio and violin lutherie in general, laughing with her at each unexpected turn in the narration. "They're *copies*, maybe even copies of copies, who knows, but they're not copies, if you know what I mean. We don't do forgeries. Ever. I'm not sure of the exact difference, but it's a difference. The most amazing thing though, the strangest thing . . ." I was having trouble finding words. "I've been doing this all my life, right? Making these violins? And I've never had such a solid sense that nothing's changed in all the hundreds of years since Amati. Like really . . ."

"Listen, listen," she said, a hand on my arm. "What you have now? It's a gift. A real gift, a mitzvah, this life, this total and complete *direction* and dedication from such an early age. I can't tell you enough. I was in college before anyone put an instrument in my hands. *College!* Imagine how my life might have turned out otherwise. I still remember the day." And as her words continued spilling one over the next, her eyes brimming with feeling, a narration too personal to really appreciate, our mother floated in to my rescue, backing us further into our corner in the Formica, an arm around the woman's shoulders, squeezing and shaking her hard enough that some of her drink splashed over the cup rim.

"Are you all right, Guy? Is everything all right here? Is Elizabeth boring you to death? Honey. What you need," she shook her again, "you need some boys of your own to —"

"Good God! I've got boys of my own! Three times over. I only just got rid of the last one! Thirty-five and still living at home with his mother! No! No more."

And as their heads bent together, the top of our mother's touching Elizabeth's above the ear, laughing and continuing to talk without removing their eyes from me, there was again the feeling of something in my mother shimmering just out of reach. A flickering of longing like chatoyance, some quality under the surface of apprehension, hers and mine, and again I was left wondering how long? How long before she awoke to a realization of it or would she ever? Would it stay there just under the surface, flaming and iridescent as the colors in the back wood of a fine violin—never to be touched or let go?

"Excuse me," I said, showing my empty plate as an excuse. "Must forage for sustenance." And as our mother called after me with instructions about leftovers in the fridge and what to leave, what to eat first, I made my way blearily downstairs and back to work.

—

I had ideas. Maybe it was a type of metempsychosis, like what Pythagoras and his followers believed in—something too alive and animated in the reincarnated fibers and substance of the wood we were working, causing me to slip around in time. Kicking me forward and back incrementally. Or if not the wood, the form of the violin itself—some cumulative effect of making them all my life, like what I'd explained to the oboist, Elizabeth, the afternoon we started carving our backs: thinking about them, drawing, touching, hearing, smelling them, looking at pictures of them, activities that had to eventually engender time travel, making you envision the souls and fingers of people in whose hands your violin would live its many lives, the same studies and pieces of music resurrected through it centuries into the future, another kind of metempsychosis . . . or back in time just as many hundreds of years to the principles and practices underlying construction, mostly the same now as in 1742. The same tools and problems. The same form. Every violin essentially descended from the same set of stencil shapes, yet no two violins exactly alike, no two days spent making them ever the same either. How could you *not* slip around in time through the process of making one, and cease to be yourself? When my brother's head cold exploded through my sinuses shutting down airways, plugging my ears and making me feel as if a marble had stuck in my throat, I wondered if maybe that was all it had been in the first place—a biological premonition related to the virus and its imminent attack on the weakened walls of every cell in my body. For a few days, as the virus propagated, it had given me feelings of omnipotence and vision, a zoomed-out sense of connection with transcendent otherworldliness. In fact, I was only diseased, and in the weeks that followed, crippled with snot.

Still, the feeling persisted. The day I put to the final test our outlines of the distinctive Guarneri f-holes from David's "Guarneri lady" and began carving them for real—measuring, sketching, drilling open the eyes and finally cutting in with my saw—I focused on a mental image of David as detailed as I could make it. Conjured him just beyond or beside the grain of the wood until I swore I felt the fabric of his most recent rosette-patterned dress shirt smoothing taut against my neck and collarbones and rippling with each inhalation, my pecs swollen to twice their normal size moving under the fabric, fingers, lithe and clever acrobats ready for anything; felt the weight of his forehead and eyebrows, the waxen wave of hair going back on my head like a helmet, tucked above his little square-tipped ears, mine now, fuzzed with stubble, the lobes polished until they shone, the channels leading in, winking obliquely open, black, waxless, receiving sound. All an effort to imbue my work with his physicality, to put *him* in the violin somehow, an effort so intense I was almost unsurprised to discover him actually standing beside me. Landed there as if delivered out of the air on a string (or maybe it was my deafening congestion), hands on his hips and waiting for me to finish what I was doing so he could ask his questions. "Is good, I think! You do final moves now! Soon she will sing!" He made a fist and then relaxed his open hand on my shoulder sighing deeply, his breath on my cheek making me remember days I would have registered the smells of meat and garlic from his lunch, his after-lunch cigarette and coffee. Now, not a thing. A humid, dampness fluffing my cheek, a recollected sweetness at the back of my throat making me vaguely queasy. I ducked from him, drew my blade a few more strokes, spun the plate and started cutting my way back toward the eye where I'd entered. "Horrible racket, yes?" David asked, hands covering his ears, laughing. "Such shrieking from wood! It's good to remember how she responds to this most intimate violation, cutting, cutting, and yet without cutting—no sound! It is, how do you say . . . ironic?" He leaned on his heels, surveying the shop, nodding. "But your father, is he not also to begin work with final touches to top?"

"Oh, he's done already. He's way ahead. Always ahead. See for yourself." I pointed to where his top, back and rib assembly rested in clamps together, awaiting glue. "Anyway, he's sick—everyone's got it. Except Nick who had it first and is back at school." My voice echoed, stuck in my head, making me wish to be alone, to be done speaking, and at the same time wish just as fervently to be better again and speaking freely. "I'm just rough cutting today. Nothing more, without him to check my work. Plus . . ."

"Marie, your mother, is too unwell?" I nodded. "Please, you give them from me well wishes and remember poultice of raw garlic and potato vodka from old country with a chicken soup is most—what is the word . . . efficacious . . . I love this word. Eff-ee-*cay*-shus for recovery, yes? This is the same in my language as . . ." And here he said something in Russian, a burst of consonants and breath with throat-scraping sounds. "What?" he asked, eyebrows raised, evidently misapprehending my look of pleased bewilderment. "You know this word? You know Russian already? Little prodigy! Of course! It is in your blood, like this making of fine violins, from centuries ago. We know so much more than we can know! Like Henri Wieniawski too. Eleven years old when he graduated from Paris Conservatory! Eleven! The youngest in all history, and he barely spoke French! I will tell you, years ago, when I first played her, my Guarneri lady, I never stop hearing him. Have I told you this already? Like I was not even playing! Wieniawski's voice, his touch still so much trapped inside. Now . . ." He shrugged dramatically and again came the explosions of Russian sound, vowels overweighted in a buzzing storm of h's and ch-sounds flapping like grounded birds in a hailstorm, like our father's backwards talk—this time a whole string of them, sentences or a paragraph softening in emphasis toward the end with a quizzical and poetic uplift as his eyes grew even more distant and fogged with tears.

"I am forever blessing you in all things important in this life, as my teacher once did for me." Hands joined at the sternum like a man in prayer, he nodded and backed up a few steps to leave the room.

Later, alone with my mother, across from each other at the kitchen table over vat-sized metal pots of steaming water strewn with lavender spikes, yarrow, eucalyptus stems and floating blobs of camphor oil, bath towels draped at our necks and used Kleenexes littering the table between us, I tried to conjure some of the feeling left in me from David's words—to see if he'd been right. Had I understood? What had I understood? *Little prodigy . . . we know so much more than we can know.* Somewhere in my brain, his words must have left a residue of memory and comprehension. I buzzed some sounds between my lips and at the back of my throat and tried to remember, searching my mother's face as I did—the scrolls and rivulets of water on her cheeks, two drips on her chin that hung and didn't fall, the dampened eyebrows and water-slicked forehead, bones showing at her wet hairline and eyelashes made stumpy from water. "Honey," she said. "Please, use a Kleenex if you have to bring anything up, OK? Do you need a fresh Kleenex?" She glanced at her watch and back at me pushing the tissue box closer, and only then the drips fell, immediately replaced by two fresh drips. "Good God, the cure is almost worse than the disease, isn't it? Thirty more seconds and we steam again. Last round."

"I think David is in love with you," I said.

"Wait. What?" She looked at me as if she couldn't quite decide who I was. "What did you just say? You mean David *Kushnarov?* The *violinist?* Guy Gary Marcowicz!" And here she became momentarily unable to restrain her amusement, eyes crushed with laughter as she reached a hand for me and quickly withdrew it to her chin, her neckline, pressing with the edge of her towel at her mouth to stop herself from laughing more. "Honey, if he even . . . if David could love anyone but himself, that is, I'd be the last one to be let in on the miracle. Please! He's charismatic, but don't be fooled. Men like him . . . his kind of charm does not automatically everyone's Romeo or Lothario make him. OK?

In fact . . . never mind."

"What?"

"We need to steam again. Submerge!" and with that she drew her towel over her head like a tent and leaned in, breathing deeply in and out and cursing. "Jesus, mmm. God. Get your head under there, Guy, close as you can stand it. It's good. Steam is good. I know you're cheating." Again she reached for me and only then did I follow her example. Lowered my face to within inches of the water and pulled the towel over, waiting for relief—waterlogged, sinus-burning relief. "I need my *voice* again," she said. She slapped a hand on the table and sang a few cracking notes. "God damn it. What am I going to do? Here's a thought. If David loves me why doesn't he offer to join our little group? For fun. Help sing with us, or play in the recital. God knows we'll need it." And seconds later, "You have an imagination, Guy, you've always had a good imagination, but if I were you . . . I wish you'd put it to better uses. Write me a song or a poem. Don't worry so much about peoples' love lives."

Again, I heard his words buzzing in the back of my mind, the blessing which had or hadn't lodged itself in me, its meaning forever obscure and transforming as it unfurled, replicating, finding its way deeper.

"The midnight steam team," our father said, opening and closing a cupboard, opening another cupboard. "Hey, where's the . . . Hey, honey have you seen my . . .?"

"On the counter. I put it out for you already. Take two capsules with plenty of water and then it's your turn with the steam." Her voice echoed strangely against the steel of the pot and the water, muffled and tinny. "It's the only way."

"Oh no, it isn't," he said. "The only way for me is back to bed." Next came the sound of water running and steady glug-glug of him drinking. "But look at you two. Little pupae. Larva. Like those, what did they call them . . . tent caterpillars? What are you guys germinating under there anyway?"

"Snot," I said, and "Love for you, dear," my mother said. We'd spoken almost at the same time.

"You all definitely need to get your story straight."

Does not everyone's Romeo or Lothario make him, I thought as we surfaced, alone again, faces streaming water. She was telling the truth. Her truth. So long as our mother loved anything or anyone, that love would have to be returned exclusively. And if he loved her, really, who could blame him?

Four

I'd never thought of any violin as having a gender, until the day we finished assembling David's Guarneri copies in the white. Only then, it dawned on me how much I'd been thinking of his original, finished "lady" as mostly masculine all along: the rusty, Kreisler-like red-brown coloring, broad edges and shoulders, blond-white blushing through the crown of the scroll where the volutes had worn smooth as a balding man's forehead, patches of pigment that had shifted and concentrated over the centuries into black smudges ringing the fingerboard and chin rest like a beard or heavy five o'clock shadow. These had left me with impressions of masculinity—somberness and sobriety, which I must always have associated with David, but without thinking about it and without designating the violin male or female. And only by seeing her exact likeness, made by my own hands and lacking any varnish or stain, did I suddenly understand: beyond the coloration and pigment, in the arching and elongated corners, slim ears, and throat of the scroll, lay something elusively, luminously female. I felt what David must have known all along, and I understood maybe why he so rarely referred to her by her proper title, the ex-Wieniawski, but only by his pet term, "lady." With this came glimpses into the feelings that must have caused his involuntary blinks and shudders, his fondling and guttural sighs whenever he'd first reunite with her after any time away. I wanted to rub my fingers into the wood of my copy to claim something beyond the grain in that smooth gold-brown surface, before any stain or varnish could light it up in ways to please and misdirect the eyes.

This was the same day, as it turned out, Alene Valloger made her first appearance in our shop.

By the time we met her, our grandfather must already have worked some magic to contravene and convert to his own advantage the rage and frustration that had driven her an ocean and a continent's distance to find him, coming to a peaceable enough detente that on the face of it, they appeared old friends. Old lovers, even. "Gents," he said, coming into the shop, an arm hanging on her shoulder, "I'd like you to meet the driving force behind all our endeavors and the one to whom we owe a debt of gratitude for most if not all of the important contemporary innovations of our trade—the woman on whom the sun would rightly rise and set in the violin world, if there were a violin sun that is, or a world to go with it: great grand-niece of J.B. Vuillaume and executor of the Maurice Valloger estate! Alene Valloger straight to you from the streets of gay Paris." We'd been hearing their voices from the front of the shop for some time by then, but without really giving them particular attention—without registering anything beyond the usual in what we heard. Just the typical song and refrain of our grandfather's salesmanship. The mellifluous hook-and-flow of comments to reassure, entertain or divert, the deeper undertones to assure sincerity, stammered apologies and admissions of defeat as needed, usually beginning, *But, but, but, but* . . . Nothing new, nothing we hadn't witnessed a hundred times before. Alene was only the latest in a string of unlucky customers, not by a long shot the worst or most gullible, probably—though from the blinks and nervous smile, her wide-set eyes and way of casting around the room as if anticipating applause and loving regards, we could tell at once she was Maurice's blood kin. Also, and not inconsequentially, in all other regards by far the most striking (younger than our parents, I guessed, though maybe not by much), even beautiful "client" of our grandfather's we'd ever met or seen. Our father stood frozen at his bench, possibly unable to focus beyond the light spun and magnified in her red-gold hair, the slim outline of her legs through the material of her dress backlit by the shop windows, the deep overbite so like our mother's. "Charmed. Charmed, charmed," she said, making the rounds to each of us with a light scuffing and tapping of heels, wafts of intense French perfume, and steely body odor accompanying her as she offered and simultaneously withdrew three cold fingers for us to squeeze in the edges of our palms. "It is magnificent, this work. Such industriousness. I love the feeling of these shops. These woodworkings. May I see now?"

"Of course! Of course," our grandfather said. "We've used the wood I spoke of earlier, the special tone wood from the, uh—" here his voice dropped to a lower register, as if the restraint and decorum required in mentioning anything connected with The Great One so pained him he could barely say the name aloud—"Stradivarius estate. From Maurice, as you know. Your cousin. You know the story. The wood is of course real. We've verified its provenance yes, and so to make the copies most letter perfect we're using it here in the construction of these three violins, all flawless to within a millimeter of a millimeter. As I said. But. Work remains. They are not yet finished or set up, as you see. No antiquing . . . Other details to be filled in . . ."

"If I may," our father cut in, finally having sorted himself out enough to fix our grandfather with his most incredulous and despairing look of loathing. "What *exactly* is going on here? *What* are you talking about?"

"Why—the copies we're making, of course!"

"OK, because for a second . . ."

"Don't be foolish . . ."

". . . it sounded like you might be about to sell something out from under the customer whose money we've already collected as a deposit for one of these violins?"

"Not at all! No one's *selling* anything, Karl. Listen and learn!"

I stroked two fingers along the shoulder of my copy, feeling the ripple in the grain and flaming of her ribs, the smoothed edges of the channel and the upwelling at each corner like a perfectly tuned note or the feeling caused in a note, the ridges in the grain of the top running out at the sides; too embarrassed for them to listen any further, I sank through the surface of their words, thinking, *I don't care, I don't care, this violin is mine, it's not even for sale . . .* These were unlike any violins in the white we'd seen or made, because of the age of the wood—gold-brown rather than off-white, and consequently in need of no ground coats. Probably. Of course, it's impossible to know how a violin will sound from touching and looking at it, but I had the intuition with this one, fingers zeroing in on a slight divot formed around a tiny knot at the edge of the front lower bout, that it would sing with a fine, strong voice. Stronger and finer than any I'd made to that point in my life. A voice like wire and light—like the color of the light in Alene's hair seconds earlier, or the feeling it had given me, seeing her there, backlit by the shop window.

"This one I especially like," she said, materializing at my side as if my thoughts had somehow been amplified across the room to her, so I was again surrounded in her smell and unable to think past that or resist her effect on me. *Pheromones,* I thought. *She's drenched in pheromones. God help us all.* She lifted the violin from my hands and turned it front and back, made a clucking sound and spun it again, tilting her head and handing it back. "It's very special, I think. This one, its destiny will, how do you say, it will rise to the stars? Impossible to know, of course. *Petit chou!* You are so young to have made such a lovely and exquisite violin!" Next she inspected Nick's, tousling his hair, nails flashing through his mop of curls as he blushed and averted his face—"*Cherie!* So lovely!"—and moving last to our father where her over-demonstrative clutching at her heart with both hands, staggering backward as if in a swoon, holding his violin at arms' length and then hugging it to her chest and groaning—all seemed sure to wreck itself on the shoals of our father's cool reasonableness. His usual stoicism and reserve, skeptical blinks and shrugs and refusal to accept or be taken in much by flattery.

"It is pretty good," he said. He scratched at something on the back of his neck. Blushed and held out a hand to take the violin back. "If I say so myself. Thanks. I'm not *un*-proud of it, anyway."

"It will be a very, very lucky person, man or woman, who gets to play this for the rest of their life! Bravo, monsieur! Bravissimo!"

Through it all, our grandfather watched as if straining to see from a distance, blinking, lips moving, the color drained from his cheeks. He hadn't shaved in a few days and this only accentuated the effects of his blanching, his jaw outlined in a murky sheen, the edges of his lips and chin etched in fuzz so his mouth appeared crimped and more inward-collapsing than normal. I wondered if he'd forgotten to put in his teeth again. "Please," he said at last. "Ms. Valloger. Shall we? A little tea, or maybe we could walk out somewhere? Just around the corner—Mauricio's favorite lunch spot back in the day, rest his soul. There, I know we can find a decent cup of soup or a hamburger. Talk to our heart's content. Yes?"

With a light tapping of heels, door jingling open and closing again, they were gone, and for some time after, as the sound of their voices faded up the gravel walk, the smells of her perfume and skin dissipating, we seemed to have forgotten ourselves.

Nick set his violin back on the bench with a clatter. "*That's* a dame," he said, affecting a tone like our grandfather's and laughing a little too loud. "That dame was a real *broad*, tell you what. What the fuck was she on about, anyway?"

Our father stayed at his bench as if superimposed in space, stranded and unable to reintegrate with his surroundings, eyes twitching between parallel focuses in some other dimension—a cut-out figure of a man in a bewildered state. Then he was shaking his head, reanimated. "Oh," he said, again, "Oh. This will not be pretty. Boys? If ever the time comes that I'm such an embarrassment to you that you can't find it in yourselves to stop me and just call me on my bullshit, whatever it is, you're too weak or can't find a way to do it? Please, just take me somewhere nice and quiet and shoot me. Hold me underwater until I'm dead. Seriously. OK? My best guess, what's going on here—and sadly, I'm pretty sure it's all too accurate, though the particulars . . . the particulars—" he shook his head, "—your grandfather has just convinced that woman, that poor, long-suffering, jet-lagged, Frog . . ." He nodded now, evidently agreeing with his forthcoming assessment. "For now, he thinks he's got her convinced that we're making copies of a violin she once owned. A family heirloom she's been calling about for years now, and which he's probably sold or lost somehow without her ever having seen it, and without ever paying her one red cent. Or red franc, as the case may be. A violin that may never have been whatever he claimed it was in the first place . . ."

"You mean the Bergonzi? From Maurice?" Nick asked, always one to underscore the obvious, nodding with our father until I felt I had to get in on it as well, bobbing my head in a rhythm with them.

"That's right. The so-called . . ."

"But," Nick said, again underscoring the obvious, turning his nod to a head shake. "These aren't Bergonzi copies at all. The fake labels we stuck in there don't even say Bergonzi anywhere."

Our father squinted at him. "You think she cares or knows the difference? Really? You think *anyone knows any goddamned thing at all about violins?* Sure looks like a copy of an old violin to me! Right now that's all she knows, and all *he's* trying to do is stall for a little time. He needs to come up with a bunch of money for her. Fifty, sixty grand probably. Maybe more. Who the hell knows. Probably more. Maybe five hundred thousand. He'll figure it out. Send her packing. Or not.

As long as I've seen these, these, these petty criminalities . . ." He dropped off. "Sometimes I swear it's really a wonder we're not all in jail or shot up by violin thugs and loan sharks."

—

That our grandfather was being stepped on and played with in the same ways he was always playing with customers and clients—undervaluing and discrediting their instruments in order to sell them later for ten and twenty times as much money as he'd promised; withholding payment to consignors until threatened with his life; concocting stories to make the weakest and most questionable un-papered, undocumented pieces entirely alluring—that he'd been backed into a corner by people scamming him in all the same ways and using the same lies and tactics, but for larger sums of money, none of this occurred to me until the day of Alene's visit to our shop. Until he as much as told me, when I caught him alone afterhours in the workshop the same day, an inverted cone of light shining over the bench where our Guarneri copies sat waiting for stain and finish and other final touches that would make them all but indistinguishable from the original. He crouched with a hand on one knee, magnifying glass and dentist's mirror in hand. Because all three were without endpins I assumed he would already have looked inside them, like seeing through a spyglass, trying to find secret, identifying marks anywhere hidden there.

"You must help me, Nicky."

"Guy," I corrected him.

He stared at me over the tops of his glasses. Blinked once and in a way to reveal the depths of his despair, made a noise in his throat between keening and growling, like the night he'd almost caught us pinching wood from his stash, and when his eyes popped open, was himself again. "I know who I'm talking to, kid."

"OK. So what do you want?"

"You must show me how and where your father marked these instruments, because I know him. I know he will not let these violins out of here without secretly signifying somewhere permanently . . ."

I shook my head. "Nope. No secret marks anywhere. Real as the day they were made in 1742. But you see the other label inside there, on the neck block, right? As far as I know, that's all they get." The insides of our violins had each been stickered with sooty and acid-aged fake Guarneri labels featuring his signature script, *Joſeph Guarnerius, Cremone, 1742,* alongside double-headed scepters in a Roman cross pattern like a snowflake, and del Gesù's usual *nomina sacra* Christogram—IHS. Beyond that, on the neck block inside, was our own everyday label to make it plain for anyone looking even only a little closely that these were copies. Not real. Ours. Made in a violin shop in Seattle, late twentieth century.

"Listen, kid. I wasn't born yesterday. Labels do not last two seconds in the real world. Everything your father knows, he knows from me. Now, there's probably a hundred reasons you can't tell me where these violins are marked, and a hundred more reasons why you must. I'll let you in on a little secret, OK? I'm stretched as thin as a flat dime. My friend Micah in Shanghai with the Bergonzi and other so-called antiquities from Maurice? Not so much of a friend, as it turns out. A friend, but with a nasty habit of putting any profit he makes straight up his nose. So. But where else am I going to unload an unpapered instrument everyone else in the world wants to cut down—smear it this way and that way, say it's nothing, it's garbage, it's fake, and give me a nickel so they can make a mint. Please! I have eyes. I can see what it is! And I know what they'd also sell it for, the crooks! I'm not some gypsy born two days ago! From their own books and catalogues, you look and see for yourself! A Bergonzi, through and through. Nah. So you tell me, how am I supposed to make up the difference to that pushy French dame and her lawyers all of a sudden? Huh? Flew over on the Concorde to talk about money? I'll tell you. These violins—these copies of ours . . . We sell to my friend—another friend, not Micah, never mind who—connections in New Jersey, he has. Maybe the Bergonzi too, if we can get it back. So he pays us obscene amounts of money but nothing like the money he gets later and cuts us back into once they're papered in Austria by kingpin Dietmar Machold, and then sold back to Mr. New Jersey through Chicago as real Guarneris. Or if not Guarneris we aim a little lower, so what. Doesn't matter. Something Italian. The guy, Mr. New Jersey, he wants Italian. For his symphony orchestra there in Trenton. Anything Italian. And old. Twenty-six million he's spending! Now you tell me anything that's wrong with that kind of money."

I would like to say that my faith in the ways of our father was unwavering. But I also had a dawning sense of life outside the windows of his atelier, his shop, his monastic hermitage of violins lovingly picked over and carved by hand and set adrift on the currents of commerce and music, little boats sent down the music river to be picked up and played by whomever; hopefully to retain some feeling engendered in the playing—love, joy, release, grief, celebration—some sonic residue of humanity's best and worst accruing in the grain to be carried forward in such a way so that one day, hundreds of years in the future, a master-piece might emerge out of it. Who knows? Would mine or Nick's or our father's violins be most favored, most valued on their own merits? We would none of us live to see.

"How can we be so sure?" I asked.

"Sure! You want to talk about sure? For starters, David's ex-Wieniawski? His Guarneri lady? He has no intention ever to return it. This is a given, which maybe you've already figured, and certainly your father has. If he hasn't, he's a bigger fool than I thought. David will not be parted with that violin, the love of his life—it will go on with him always. Value, schmalue, he does not care. This is the psychotic and petty nature of violinists. Do not try to understand or to get between them and their instruments that they love or sometimes suddenly hate, only pay attention, and see what you can do, wherever the chips may fall, and how to make a little bonus cash on the side if you can. So, pretend Guarneri number one goes back to a vault in Los Angeles with Mr. David Kushnarov's blessings and thanks. Most likely this will be the instrument of your father's, meaning no offense, but it will be a matter of exact likeness, and he has some years on you in this regard. Real Guarneri gone. Poof. To be played by Kushnarov the rest of his life and then who knows. Fifteen thousand dollars to your father for his efforts, a little more to us to keep quiet which we split fifty-fifty if you but tell me where those marks are. All very cheap for the acquisition of a rare Italian gem, no?" He snapped his fingers. "Which leaves the other two violins for us to make a bank. Think on that a minute. Meanwhile, I'll tell you a little story, I'll let you in on a special secret of the trade, to give you some indication of my trust and as an illustration of just how loving and thoughtful people in the violin busi-ness can be. All right? A far cry from anything we're undertaking here . . . But.

What some friends of mine and I used to do back in the day? We'd watch the obits for symphony players with fine old violins—these we knew of, from sales and repair records in this shop or that shop, connections we had all over the west coast, those days," he stretched his arms to illustrate, "gents who survived through the World Wars, barely got out alive, lost everything and maybe set up a new life over here with some lousy American symphony. I shouldn't be telling you this. Anyway, before anyone else could figure out and make the rounds, file for insurance or what have you, we'd pay a little visit. A little phony house call. *Oh Mrs. So-and-So, I'm so sorry for your loss, but I'm here to help. I knew your husband in the camps. I knew him from his time in Los Angeles or San Diego. Like a brother to him, I was! Loaned him so much money,* choose your dollar figure, choose your year, doesn't matter. *I got him started on his way, back then, because he was like a brother to me, because I believed when no one else did. Such music! Such a talent. And you know what he said to me, when last I saw him? He said, This instrument, Bernie (or Harold, if it was me, Mauricio once, Mannie, Charles), when I die I'd like it to go to you and yours. Please, just knock at home when the day comes, God forbid it should come too soon, and tell my wife. She, I guarantee, will help . . . The least I can do to repay you—this violin shall be yours."* He guffawed and continued. "Did we try a dozen times if it worked only once? Twice? What do you think? Why else do we read the papers to see who's alive and who's dead today? And where's the harm? No one I know ever got hurt by a little pure violin profit. Nice free Tonini I got, that way. A Goffriller, Montegnana, Testore, and once a rare French thing we never did figure out what it was. Sold it as a Derazey. All that money gone now anyway, so what, who cares, and nothing by comparison with what we stand to gain now. So what do you say? Here, I've already told you enough I'd have to kill you if you walk away. Ha! Are you in or are you out? You want the rest of your life to look like your father, some poor schmuck cutting and scraping and bending wood to keep food on the table, a roof over your head, so a few people can say *thank you for your services* at the end of the day if you're lucky? What kind of life is that."

"But there are no marks," I said. "That I know of."

Again the odd noise in his throat as he stared at me, in the throes of whatever agony of suspicion and desperation had ahold of him. "You're a good kid, Nicky," he said finally. Put a hand on my head to tousle my hair and grab my ear, twisting lightly before letting go. "Good of you to listen to an old man's ramblings, which by the way, bear in mind, nothing I've told you just now is true, right? Lies, all of it. We go on from here the same as ever . . . the same as when you stole my girlie magazines and put those exploding things, the pop-rocks, into my cigars, and that time you tried to rob from my wood pile. OK? We forget all about it. But as soon as you see anything, you tell me. Now go to bed."

"It's fine, Grandfather. But I'm not Nicky. I'm Guy."

"I know who you are, kid. You can't put anything over on me."

Every day, adding new coats of color and varnish, bitumen and chimney black along edges or smeared into scratches, breaking down the new sheen to a hazed satin, adding more, through the aura of chemicals and solvents, always the first thing to enter my senses was a smell of metal and French perfume. I couldn't say if it was my imagination, the result of breathing so many fumes and worrying all the time about what my grandfather had told me until my sleep ripped open—dreams invaded by thugs and walking, talking violins, fires, chases through underground tunnels, if I slept at all—but I had the feeling each afternoon, taking her from the light box and starting in again with the work of mirroring her finish to David's Guarneri lady, that mine were not the last fingers to have touched her. I looked for evidence. Of course, no sign. No finger-tracks through tacky oil and color. No surprise pigment blushing through the finish. Only that smell. And the sense that I was not alone in my obsession. All of which caused me, in small ways and bigger ways, to begin taking my own direction with her appearance—to break from the pattern so that however she turned out, she might not be confused with David's Guarneri. So she might be herself. I went too light on the pigment one day, causing her to turn dull orange in the light box, and the day after, amber again with another coat. I misapplied bitumen in some areas to suggest a wear pattern less insistent than the one we'd mapped to the tenth of a millimeter—slight whiskers and no five o'clock shadow, no scratch marks in the c-bouts. I underpainted with oil on the back varnish so the bubbling effect of center wear went subtler, thinner, and to my eye more appealingly delicate; gobbed and blotted the button with gooey pigment and unstuck a patch of color on the right lower back bout to match it, exactly the same size and shape, like the Guarneri Cannon—an echo of one of its most notable eccentricities (though placed differently), which I'd only ever seen in pictures. Through it all I let instinct be my guide. Daubing up color and varnish, rubbing it in, watching the flames darken and shimmer, go multi-dimensional, I listened for the voice in my head saying, *Stop.* Or, *More. Go heavier here.* I held her at arm's length and asked myself, *What do you want to become? Who are you, really?*

"Guy's losing his touch," Nick said. "What exactly the fuck are you doing with that brush?"

"What does it look like, ass-boy?" I said, lunging at him to smear his arm and back again to dodge a retaliatory brush swipe.

"Hey-hey!" Our father peered at us over his glasses. "Knock it off. That's expensive stuff. For Christ's sake." And then, looking again, "Guy, are you deliberately throwing the game there? Any particular reason?"

"Like we don't already know which of these instruments is going to look and sound and play the best, Dad. Give me a break. Duh! Look at yours. Now look at mine and Nick's. OK? What *game* are you even talking about?"

"Well . . ." Our father put down his work and came to stand between us, hands on his hips. Exhaled as if this was all exhaustingly beneath him. "I'd say Nick's giving it his all. Yours is . . . Well . . ." he lifted my copy from the bench and as he did I had the dizzying sensation that it was me he lifted—my ribs and back pressed in his fingers, my head spun and puffed at with his nose breaths, my neck stroked for smoothness and scratched at with a thumbnail where it joined to the ribs—a little bubble in the finish there, where I'd rubbed it off unevenly. But it wasn't. It was just a violin and I was myself still, watching as my father checked it over. I breathed once in and out to remind myself and maintain composure. Looked at my feet—the wood chips and dust and curls of wood on the floor. Someone needed to sweep soon. Whose turn was it anyway? Mine? Nick's?

"It's an intriguing interpretation of . . . something," our father said. He pointed at my pigment-blot echo of the Cannon, eyebrows raised in question.

"Really?" Picked at it like a scab and sucked his lips, nodded his head. "OK." Considered it from another angle. "OK. I guess you could leave it. But as a *copy* I'm not sure, overall, if it's within the margins of what we were . . . without completely stripping and redoing all of the varnish, that is, which of course, I don't know that it'd make a difference anyway. It's not what the customer ordered, really." He turned it again; again, shook his head. "I mean, it's fine as its own thing. You can't *do* bad work, Guy. I've already told you that. Maybe we could make it like the Artiste Model in our new line? Charge a little more as an upgrade?" He angled it under the light, spun it again. "Modeling and arching are spot on. But . . ." He set it down and shoved his hands in his back pockets. There on its side again on the chipped and gouge-scarred butcher block of the bench, it was just a violin. Nothing different, nothing special. Some unusual flaming in the back wood and nice horizontal figure in the grain of the top which I hoped might make for better sound—might add a little stiffness and resilience, amplifying its voice. *Stay like that, leave me alone,* I thought, willing it to remain separate, not attached randomly to my feelings and senses. "Current odds on Guy to be our next 'lady' in waiting?" He scratched his head. "I don't know. Slim to nil, to be honest. Though you never know. Could be the long-shot, dark horse just waiting for a break along the inside coming into the homestretch . . . Now." He dropped the fast-talking radio-announcer impersonation. "Nicky-dog," he said, lifting my brother's violin and spinning it under the light. At best it was a crude imitation of our father's imitation. Anyone with eyes could see that. "Huh. Still hard to say. Looks to me like there's still plenty of dog left in the fight for that puppy . . . ha, ha, ha."

We looked at each other and at our father and didn't laugh. No one had called Nick "Nicky-dog"—because of the ruff under his chin—in years now. Since grade school, maybe.

"Oh, you guys," he said. "Come on. It's a joke! For Christ's sake. Lighten up a second, OK? First-world problems! We're making violins! Why always the long faces? So, look," he raised and lowered and raised his glasses again for a closer inspection of Nick's violin, " . . . right here, Nicky, what do you say we do a little better to hide that doubled corner purfle and the cut marks, like on the original. Go big with the soot. Black it right out *then* clean it up. Whatever you do, don't be hesitant. Go hard or go home."

Another favorite saying of his we were all but sick to death of hearing.

———

Final steps would involve over-reaming and filling and re-reaming peg holes to match our scrolls exactly with the ancient and over-tended original. Until then, our pegboxes were sleek and sealed as shut fox snouts. Over-thinned on both cheeks to match the original, the ear on one side of the scroll drooping subtly as if it had come too near a flame, started melting and later re-solidified, forever dissipated and off axis. Because of the over-thinning, the process of reaming and re-touching would be delicate, painstaking and aggravating work. A final task I did not look forward to. Besides, I liked her look, unpegged and mute along both full cheeks. Mixed in with my other nightmares now came dreams of drilling holes in the pegbox . . . scroll crumpling, shattering, bending, a splintered, crazy, plasticized mess to be hacked off and redone. Our father standing by, *What is wrong with you, Guy? What's happened to you? Are you actually trying to wreck everything?*

No! I love this violin! Why would I try to wreck it?

So it was a surprise but not entirely unexpected, early the day we were to begin this process—to ream oversized pegholes and bush the holes with scraps of old wood so they'd have the look of a repair job done sometime in the previous century; varnish, color, and drill through again for our new pegs—to find him at his bench, visor loupe down and prepping our violins with an unfamiliar tool. "Close that door behind you boys," he said, without looking up. "Close please, and lock." No other apprentices were present and our grandfather had either gone out or was asleep in his dyspeptic funk, dreaming of debts and stolen violins and money falling out of the sky. Only hints of singed wood mixed with the usual lemon oil, naphtha, glue and varnish smells of the workshop. "I debated telling you about this long and hard. Your mother and I both debated, and in the end she won. The voice of reason. Because we all should know. I'm engraving a little something for us each so we'll always have a way to identify these violins. Have a look." By this time we were at his side to witness the needle-fine scribe between his thumb and forefinger pressing lightly into the inner channel of Nick's pegbox where what looked like a miniscule image of a head or maybe a tiny boat resolved out of the grain beneath Nick's miniaturized initials, NLM, and the year. "All I can say. Thank God I paid attention. In that section on miniatures? At art school. My one semester. At U Dub. Very fussy. People who burn this kind of detail on toothpicks. Have my highest regard." He puffed at his work between burn marks, dipping the point of his scribe in heat from a gas burner without looking before leaning to draw another dot or dash. "Should have been a tattoo artist, huh." Watching, I was convinced that I would never possess his skill or steadiness in all known aspects of woodworking—his confidence and unerring sense of when to stop, when to add a last touch and what that last touch might be. It made me want to bump the back of his chair, kick one of its feet or jostle his shoulder, anything to make him screw up just once, drop his tool, burn through, blot out details. "Very fussy. Very tiny work. What do you think?" He sat back finally, handing Nick his violin and the visor loupe with it. "Look through that. You'll need it," he said, rubbing fingers through the stubble on his jaw. "Phew!" He sniffed at his underarm. "That's some work."

Both of us watched as Nick hunched closer to his scroll and began grinning, bobbing his head and laughing. "Amazing," he said. "Holy crap!" The effect was not unlike hearing someone singing with headphones on. He angled the peghead slightly and moved it closer to his face. Laughed some more. "Really, really super incredible! How the . . .?"

"Well. Next, we just black it over, like always, so no one knows—not that anyone would think to look inside the channel of a pegbox, right? So this way, should you ever suspect foul play, should any of us ever see this violin on the market advertised as something it isn't and feel like making a stink? Unstring it. Wipe away the blacking. Voila, hidden in plain sight, your mark that only we know about. Nicky the dog. Initials and date. And Guy, for you a lucky rabbit because . . . I don't know. Seemed right. Sorry one of his ears got a little fudged there. Almost looks more like some kind of space alien."

When it was my turn with the visor loupe, warm still from our father and smelling faintly of his hair and skin, I saw that the head in Nick's scroll box was in fact a dog—some kind of Labrador in three-quarter profile, earnest-eyed, ruffled and gazing into a scene where I easily imagined surf and blowing wind, a sunset, our grandfather in his flip-flops. We'd taken a trip like that once, to Hawaii, our grandfather's treat, and the whole time he'd done nothing but hide from the sun with sugary drinks, reading the paper and smoking cigars, congratulating himself at every opportunity for having paid for everything. Around Nick's date and initials was some shading to suggest a background like a headstone, making the numbers and letters pop almost three-dimensionally. "Incredible," I said, though I'd been determined not to duplicate my brother's enthusiastic gibbering. In my violin, behind my initials and the date, a similarly hazed rainbow background caused the same three-dimensional effect. And the rabbit of course was not the least bit fudged. It looked exactly like a microscopic fingernail copy of the Dürer watercolor of a hare I'd loved as a child and had hung over my bed for years in grade school—as doleful and mysterious in the peghead of my copy as it had always seemed to me in that print, and provoking in me the same longing to reach through the centuries and rub my fingers in the pale fur of its belly, to know whatever caused its melancholy. Too beautiful to black over. Shifting and angling it slightly for better light, one of its eyes winked open and shut at me and I swore its front paw lifted as if in greeting, but looking again, all was fixed and set as before. Exact to the last detail, stamped into the wood.

"That is truly incredible," I said. "How in the heck? That, like . . . for a second it was so real I swear it was moving!"

"Trick of the eye. *Trompe l'oeil*. You like it?" Our father laughed. "You can do it too. Just takes practice. And patience. And practice. Anyone who's willing to learn."

Nick pressed the nib point of the scribe to his thumb callous. "Hells yeah! I want one of these."

Our father nodded. "I figured. But the main thing here . . . and I hope, it goes without saying. This information stays among the three of us, forever, or as long as any of us draws breath and can remember. All right? It is our mutually known checkpoint which, as long as only the three of us knows about it, should work as a fairly foolproof assurance to keep us honest. Right?"

"Well, us and mom," I said.

He shook his head. "She knows *that* they're marked but not where or how."

"So what's in yours," I asked.

"What's in my what?"

"Your violin. Scroll channel."

He stared at me, the mounded gray of his irises absorbing me, their faint encircling ring of blue like spilled ink, magnified behind dusty, thumb-printed glasses, as he placed this question alongside some internal measure, deciding what to say. In the back of my mind the image of that rabbit still burned. Its little wink at me and slight paw lift of acknowledgment. "That's for me to know and you to guess at. I've blacked it in already. Why?"

I shrugged. "Curious."

He nodded. "Good. Curiosity is good, so long as you can keep on the right side of it. Now let's get to work with drilling some pegs for these pups, and be *done*! What do you say?"

Later, working the reamer in the cheek of my peghead I became aware of her smell intensifying around me—her metallic body odor and French perfume. *Not real—get over it*, I told myself, rotating the reamer handle into the wood, blowing to clear the channel, sniffing, knocking the metal teeth of the reamer clean, inserting and turning it again. On our first passes we'd go just a few millimeters too wide. Then, waiting for glue and varnish to dry, we'd shape our pegs in the little box like a magic pencil sharpener for converting ebony blanks to perfectly tapered and fitted friction tuning pegs. *Focus*, I told myself. *Get it done.* The wood of the cheeks, in addition to being thinner than we'd ordinarily cut a pegbox, was oddly light and brittle because of its age, the shreds and chips of wood looking to me more like old toast and cinnamon chips than normal shavings. *The last I'll see of you*, I thought, brushing clear my space on the bench and again rotating the reamer handle. *Good bye and good luck . . .*

"This is most excellent, this one, I think!" David said. He put a hand on my shoulder and squeezed. "I love that you have made her this much different from others. Yes? She is magnificent. These colorings!"

How I'd missed the sound of his entrance—his voice rolling ahead of him from the front of the shop, his feet rumbling down the stairs or the front door jingling open and shut—was one mystery, easily enough explained by the intensity of my concentration and the fact that our grandfather, gone on errands that kept him out of the shop all morning, had not been around to run his usual interference. The other mystery, the unmistakable smell of Alene's skin and perfume surrounding him, permeating the air around him and interpenetrated with his own cologne, was answered more vaguely by something in his posture and demeanor—an outward re-shaping, as if he too had been slipped into a magic conversion box, magic pencil sharpener to fit and taper him to new purposes. *Wild imagination, my ass*, I thought. *Super Lothario.* Beyond that, an image in the backs of his eyes resolved all too quickly and easily for me into a scene of him and Alene kissing . . . on the hood of a car, maybe, or in an open doorway. The pale blue blazer he wore over a checkered sports shirt enwrapping her, or later draped over her bare shoulders as an impromptu bathrobe to become further saturated in her smell. *Really*, I wanted to ask. *Can you just not keep your hands off anyone? Like, she could practically be your daughter, if you had one!* But maybe I was all wrong. Maybe I was letting my imagination run, looking for reasons for her to have stayed in town so long. Maybe they'd met for coffee. Or passed each other in a hall somewhere and bumped shoulders. She wore enough of that perfume it was almost plausible.

"Thanks," I said. "I'm liking the look."

"Yes! I am liking so much as well. She is almost alive!"

"Who knows how it'll sound though, right?"

"May I?" And again as he lifted my violin I was lost to an internal gyration of scale and perspective I couldn't control—his fingers pressing my sides and back, spinning and lifting me to a stubbled lip to fit his nostrils at my sound hole where he inhaled once sharply, and again. "Mmm!" Again he sniffed. "This smell. Like perfume. If you could bottle and sell forever I would wear nothing else! To me is like inception of life, miraculous tonic, all good and inspiring things, this," he inhaled, "wood and new violin varnish. Mmm."

I pushed with my hands on the edge of the bench. Knocked my reamer again to get out a few last embedded chips. Anything to distract myself from the sick feelings of being handled and spun around, sniffed at and hollowed to nothing. "You mean, linseed oil?"

"Whichever it is. Yes. But I love this smell!" He set the violin back on the bench with a rattle of distant music through her ribs. "Soon!" He made a fist and nodded his head. "Yes? Yes?" Again came the Russian words, both hands on my shoulders, chin leveled with mine—the soft explosions of sounds. Only as he stood back from me, hastily brushing aside tears with the back of a wrist and removing a wrinkled hankie from his inside jacket pocket to blast at furiously and with a laugh like barking, did I identify the emotions that had possessed him and which he must have meant to express. "Look! I am like a baby. What you have done to me!" And before I could stop him he'd gathered me against him, enfolded in his arms exactly as I'd pictured him doing with Alene—like the signals had crossed somehow and by picturing what I'd meant to admonish or dismiss I'd somehow brought it on myself—pressing little kisses up and down my neck like a prickly, tender cephalopod, before thrusting me back at arm's length, hands still on my shoulders, laughing and shaking me. "You!" he said. "Magnificent one!"

———

Every time I started down the stairs to our grandfather's room to tell him where the marks hid, willing myself in advance to become someone flippant and unconcerned, someone with a voice that went straight at its purpose like a blade—*Yeah, in the scroll channel, under the blacking . . . you'll need magnification to see*—I'd remember my rabbit and stop. I'd see the pale fur of its belly and the little paw lift of recognition it had given me, or which I'd imagined—its baleful expression of fully expecting to be blacked over, ignored and later gouged out, never to be seen in this world—and I'd stop. *No*, I'd think. *Can't do that.* Nick's dog I might have sacrificed. Our father's mystery mark, maybe. But that rabbit? And no way to deliver one without the others. So despite our grandfather's long looks at dinner, raised eyebrows behind our father's back, his hands turned out at me making the universal sign—*Come on, give me something to go on here! Please!*—I shook my head. Nope. Can't help. Got nothing for you. That rabbit was me somehow, or had been stamped into me so I couldn't betray it even if I wished to.

The day of the trial our grandfather showed up in his best duds—new tan loafers with tassels and unmarked leather soles probably saved aside for years in his closet, pressed wool slacks we'd last seen at Maurice's funeral, blue ascot tucked at the neck of his one tailor-fitted hounds-tooth shirt, eyebrows trimmed and his hair slicked at the sides so his head appeared compacted and shiny, some of its luster restored. Smells of shoe leather, mothballs, Brilcream, and aftershave surrounded him. Before any music he stood in the center of the living room and raised a hand for silence. Our mother and Alene sat on the couch leaning together and talking, each with a drink in hand; our father was in a chair by the window looking out and up at something—a passing bird or cloud maybe—legs crossed at the knees and at the ankles, stray rays of sunlight illuminating him in a way to show his beard shadow and pallid skin tone, as if he'd been flash-frozen; Nick and I on stools dragged in from the kitchen counter. We hooked our heels at the highest rungs and felt how the spinning seat cushions still wobbled and gave subtly under us, as they always had, and remembered wild games of spinning each other until someone flew off or the stool fell over. From below came the trudging footsteps of some apprentices on their way to join the fun. Bowls of dip and crackers, cheese slices, olives, and sliced vegetables stacked in rows on a plate, sat untouched as a still life on the table before our mother and Alene. The soloist, David, appeared torn between again re-examining the three new violins on the closed piano top and diving into the dip or the veggies for sustenance before playing. In the end he went for a single celery stalk which he chewed up in a bite, wiping and re-wiping his fingers on his pants leg and thereafter eyeing the food on the table, occasionally leaning toward it but never taking more, while our grandfather cleared his throat and snapped his fingers—"If I can . . .

"People? Please?

"What we're about to witness here is the resurrection of a sound and style . . ." He paused, waiting for silence, backtracking to find the right words, " . . . the resurrection of a spirit in sound and music and lutherie which, for going on three centuries now, has lain dormant. Asleep! Nothing, but *nothing* like it has been seen or heard in all these centuries! Wood from the original store of Antonio Stradivarius given new life in original instruments cut to the exact proportions and specifications of his most illustrious contemporary and successor, Guarneri del Gesù. A marriage, if you will, of the two greatest violin builders ever to live, whose work we still think of today as representative of a polarity in ideals . . . whose work could not have evolved from more opposing ethics, temperaments, goals, and esthetics to a more opposite ideal in the construction of a violin. The one, Stradivari, a meticulous and flawless builder, always accurate to within a hundredth of a millimeter, a superlative craftsman whose instruments to this day are the be-all end-all measure of perfection. The other, Guarneri del Gesù, an artist of free and sweeping proportions and . . ."

"He was a drunk," our father said. "Simple. And poor. Stradivari made all the money."

"There are theories," our grandfather continued. He glared at our father.

"And there are facts," our father said.

"In honor of this bold marriage of styles and the resurrection of materials unheard now for centuries . . ."

"If it's real," our father broke in again.

"Please! In honor of this most momentous occasion, I will tell you now a story as true today as the day it was told to me by Mauricio Valloger, rest his soul, and will leave you to make of it what you will. Believe or don't believe, as you like. But I will tell you this as well: *believing is always better.* The wood from which these violins were constructed, all straight from Stradivari himself to Luigi Tarisio via Count Cozio di Salabue, and from there to the great-great uncle of our esteemed guest Alene Valloger, none other than the great Jean-Baptiste Vuillaume, one of the finest builders ever to walk the earth, and from there directly to Mauricio, rest his soul . . . all of this wood is known to have been inhabited by the spirit of Stradivari's first wife, Francesca. This we know from Stradivari's letters to his sons Omobono and Paolo, outlining events—the same in each instance—wherein the unexpected death of his wife caused the wood in his workshop to become spontaneously harmonically enlivened and to begin singing to him of its own accord and in a heavenly voice as if to give comfort, or maybe to alert him to the imminence of her death as she lay breathing her last and he worked on in his shop. The music is said to have contained the spirit of his dying wife and to have issued with it a command in her voice—that all who take up this wood must be pure of spirit and intention, and that if they are, then the music issued from any violins made of it will be unsurpassed in quality and perfection. Notes to fill a cathedral with ease! Tones to hang at the back aisle of a two-thousand-seat auditorium, no amplification, as sweet and crystalline and bell-like as if the listener were standing only two feet from the source! A richness and tonal superiority, voluminous, complex sound and an ease of playability that with the passage of time will only deepen, mature and improve and . . . In a word, the absolute and sublime perfection in a violin. This same wood, so we're told, which was used by Stradivari in the construction of his final masterpieces including the Messiah and the Rode and some others of unusual merit, and referred to by him in his writings always as *The Francesca Tone Wood* to honor the presence of her spirit trapped there. Never surpassed or ever to be surpassed *in the history of violin making*, period! Because in the grain of the wood . . . in every fiber of the wood is the undying love of Francesca for Antonio, and Antonio for Francesca . . . the same love that called out from her dying heart to his and enlivened the substance of Stradivari's work so that he must drop his gouge and run inside to say goodbye. The love that, given shape by the maker and later summoned by the player, will allow music from these violins to penetrate even to the deepest and most inaccessible regions of the heart . . ."

Nick nudged me. His breath touched my ear. "How much of that scotch did he have? He is spinning this crap harder than I've ever heard him spin it."

"Oh, Francesca . . ." I whispered back.

But in truth, for once in my life I had no idea if our grandfather believed anything he was saying—if his legend-spinning was authentic in his own mind or calculated to achieve some other motive at its end. Well, always some other motive—*always*. Legend-making and hyperbole always went hand-in-hand with crookery and shenanigans. But why, and how much of what he was saying did he mean for anyone to take seriously? How much had he convinced himself to believe? Any scenario seemed as likely as another. *Believing is always better.* Yes, but I had never heard him sound quite this deranged. Had he finally and irrevocably slipped a mental gear? Gone a tick closer to stroke or full-on dementia?

"All of this," he continued, "was told to me as straight as I tell it to you now, today, first by Mauricio's great uncle, whose job it was to inventory and catalogue and safeguard this wood in Vuillaume's shop—wood so transparently significant in its powers and value even Vuillaume was mostly too afraid ever to touch it! Never, in all the long years of its life in his shop, was it used in the construction of a new instrument, that we know of—never, because Vuillaume regarded it as untouchable, his *bois terrifiante, bois noir, bois fatale*—all of this as told directly to Maurice and by Maurice to me as I now lay it before you. The wood of Francesca and Antonio Stradivari . . . legend or fact. Do with this as you like." And at that, he ducked down onto the couch between our mother and Alene, snapped up a cracker with some dip in a shaking hand, and leaned back in his seat, a palm on either knee, chewing and waiting.

No one spoke. The sharp intake of breath from our father to presage words we were sure must follow and could mostly guess at in advance—*And so ends to-day's visit to La-la Land,* or, *And that about wraps up today's edition of story-time with luna-tics*—was intercepted by stern looks from our mother and a headshake to silence him. David raised his hands and held them apart as if measuring something in the air. He shook each at the wrists as if to remove drops of water from his fingers, raised his eyebrows and looked from our grandfather to our father and back again for some kind of approval. "Yes? Yes? Shall we?" he asked finally, and made the few steps across the room to where our violins sat on reflections of themselves in the gleaming black of the closed piano. He lifted one—our father's, we saw—flicked fingers across the strings, raised his bow from the piano with a clatter of wood on wood and quickly tuned. Played a scale up and down, three octaves, his eyes shut and a smile compressing the corners of his mouth, then a nod. "Is good! Very good. Balanced! Fantastic." Next a skitter of notes from high to low and the opening motifs of the Mendelssohn violin concerto, soaring, singing, repeating phrases here and there, bearing down with a buzzing intensity to see how hard he could push, where the limits were in each register, the pressure required to make the back plate open and vibrate. "Very nice!" he exclaimed, and switched to a familiar Bach partita. All pieces we'd heard through floors and walls for most of a spring, summer, and fall on his beloved Guarneri lady. He paused to admire the violin from all angles, to press with his fingers in the points where he'd told us months ago he felt a special metaphysi-cal connection with his instrument, to feel around the ribs, his eyes shut and an expression of grave sagacity on his face. "Yes, yes," he concluded. "Is most perfect. Exactly as I wished for. Bravo, bravissimo!"

Our father nodded and otherwise didn't stir from his seat by the window. His legs were still twined together, double crossed at the knee and the ankle, his cup still full and untouched on the window ledge beside him, his napkin wadded in his fingers and twisted to a bowtie shape. Only then it dawned on me that he'd never even taken off his apron. "It sounds like a violin," he said. "That's for sure." He allowed himself a smile. "Not bad at all. Young still."

"In time . . ." our grandfather began.

"Yes, yes! She is baby still," David cut in. "We must let her breathe and grow. Many hours she needs to imprint with sound, to impregnate wood fibers with feeling."

Our father nodded again. "Without a great player," he shrugged, "a violin is nothing. There's no mystery about that. No spirits hiding in the wood or any of that crap. Just a lot of work." He shook a finger at David. "Don't play it against the ex-Wieniawski for a while, is all I can tell you. You'll only be disappointed."

"Not so, not so! Never disappointed. Meanwhile," he set our father's violin back on the piano top. "Most balanced and sweet, perfect sound. A blank slate for new beginnings. And a perfect look-alike." Next he lifted Nick's violin which he chorded across quickly with the same opening phrases, scales, and arpeggios, and then lost himself for a while in one of the Beethoven Romances, again pressing to find the outer limits of the violin's volume and sonority, high and low, and to wake up the back plate. While he played, I felt myself drifting, my eyes following a panel of wallpaper that appeared to be in the process of separating from the other panels, blistered at its edges, a slight bulge and discoloration of failed glue in the topmost corner of the seam near the ceiling. It would be good, I thought, letting my eyes hang there in the torn corner of the wallpaper, to get past this Guarneri thing—this seemingly unending obsession with David and his violin and the Stradivari wood and our grandfather's desperation—get back to some of the more ordinary stuff that had occupied me in the months and years prior. Schoolwork and chess and choosing a good shirt to wear every morning before school; the walk through rain and sodden pine needles, fall leaves slick on the cement, jumping puddles and rushing not to miss first period, the tight feeling in my legs and burn though my throat and lungs chasing uphill after a girl I knew who lived a few blocks over and who would occasionally talk to me if the timing was right . . . if I caught her at the exactly right moment and told her something funny; prosaic worries, too, like the older kids hanging around the chain link fence at the back entrance, smoking, and what they would or wouldn't choose to say as I passed, if they noticed me at all. *Freak. Faggot. Get a life.* It would be good. And not good. A relief, and a letdown, because . . . Here my thoughts left off. I didn't know why. Regular life. *What's so great about regular life?* Nick's voice was so clear in my head at first I thought he must have said it out loud, but a quick glance told me he hadn't said anything. He was listening— evidently not pleased with what he heard, judging from the way he kept pushing aside his hair, biting the skin on his fingertips, breathing too fast. My best guess, zeroing in on it and analyzing the tone, was that he'd left too much wood in his top or bass bar, misgauged something with his f-holes. Nothing unfixable, but nothing that easily fixed either. The sound was smooth and balanced but some-how distant—as if it were coming to us from beyond a partially closed door. "Is nice this one, too! Very sweet. I am not in love . . ."

Next he seized mine at the lower bout and I had to sit back hard against the wall, pushing down at the rungs of my stool to orient myself as the world spun over and flattened. *No,* I thought. *Please, not this again.* The light stretched across the room to me and as sound reached my ears I felt myself lift with it and spill out. Only the feeling in my fingertips, all the residual, vestigial sensations of my hours upon hours connected with the grain of the wood in that violin, ringing and tingling through my nerve endings, kept me in any way mindful of the world. Notes of his that should have vibrated in my ears or corresponded to registers in my voice or larynx, or deeper at heart or gut level, instead felt placed throughout what would have been my body if I'd had one—back, stomach, shoulders—all parts of me lighting up with unbearable pleasure, an agonizing joy of release. *Please,* I wanted to beg him, if I'd had a voice, *it's too much! Stop. Please just stop!* But the notes poured on and I was emptied of myself through them until looking down I saw that even my hands and arms had vanished. Nothing left by which to know myself. Our mother and Alene on either side of our grandfather on the couch moved their heads in a rhythm with the music that now played through me, and in the looks exchanged between them, smil-ing, swimming with feeling . . . I knew. Good. It was good. Our father kept glancing up as if he meant to stop the show, critique or analyze, a finger about to be lifted in objection, but then thought better of it, shaking his head, went back to stroking his chin and gazing at the floor. Nick yawned. Picked at something in his nose and flicked it aside. Our grandfather stared straight ahead as if he were seeing into an abyss, into the beyond, looking for all the world like one of the stricken, flabby, naked demon figures in our mother's books of Hieronymus Bosch paintings, about to be boiled alive, flayed, or dropped in a vat of serpents and molten lava. What was he thinking? The music shifted and with it my perspective inverted so I no longer saw anyone in the room but instead felt the weight of years through the building, the timbers and old horsehair plaster of rooms that hadn't been renovated yet, beyond the peeling panel of wallpaper, the dead stale air of tenants long gone, our voices at all ages, shouting at each other and dripping bathwater from the upstairs bathtub to the first-floor room we once shared, floors tracked over and worn silver by us and by the feet of people long departed . . . and again another shift so I saw sunlight, clouds, rain, heard birds singing, a rattling of wind in leaves, and felt my way through rocks and soil to a source of sustenance where I could drink and drink a course of lifeblood to a spine that swayed and swelled, stretching up to the light until . . .

The music stopped. In every nerve, a searing sensation of having rejoined myself—of having been sucked through time and snapped to life. Again the familiar outline of my skin and bones, weight of my circulating blood, nerve endings etched to known sensations, scents, familiar limits. Had anyone even noticed?

"This!" David exclaimed. "This violin, I must have this violin! It is me. It is my voice all these years that I have been without! How could you know? Cherub, most gifted young prodigy! How is possible? Is not possible! That you should know from inside my head these most intimate sounds I have always wanted and now must not live without? It is me, this violin! I love it! Yet how have you done this?" And again, scrubbing at his cheeks with the back of a hand to wipe away tears, he raised his bow to draw it across the strings. "Is perfection!" he said. "Listen!" This time, by an act of will, focusing in my mind's eye on an image of that rabbit in the peghead and waiting for its paw lift of recognition I was able to stay with them, anchored in myself, and to hear, my body still lighting up with sensations but at a distance. Another Bach partita, perfect as clockwork and humming with feeling—courtly, stately, weeping. It was, after all, as my father had said, only a violin. Balanced and smooth and sweet, crying in all registers; a set of tones mirrored to some previously inaccessible concept of sound in David's head or heart, but otherwise mostly the same as other violins. "Yes!" he said, at the end. "I will buy this one and also these other two violins for students and for perpetuity, as investment. It is too good. Today you have made me very, very happy man! Three times happy! Yes? All three. I must have them."

Our grandfather stood, his hand already out, ready to seal the deal. "Done!" he said, closing the space between them.

And with a clink of glasses and sudden outpouring of human voices around the room, David playing a few notes and replacing my violin on the piano top, laughing, lifting another, playing, talking again, Nick leaning to my ear to whisper something about Stradivari's wood—*He had so many kids and wives, you wanna know why?*—this much of our story ended.

Later, alone by the piano and running a forefinger along the outline of my scroll a final time, letting her colors absorb somewhere to the roots of my eyes and otherwise imprinting her exact likeness in my soul—her crackled and hazed reflection in the black of the piano more like a stain soaking through darkness, as if the piano itself had been lit from within—I'd have my moments of private farewell. *Not mine, not mine, goodbye, so long,* I'd think, following the smooth curves of wood under my finger. As soon as I turned away, I'd be committing to a life of following this pattern again and again. I knew this. A life of always filling the void between having and longing with more and more violins made to be sold, used, taken from my hands and lost in the world. *But not yet,* I thought, a finger still magnetized in the turns of the scroll, the smooth join of neck to fingerboard, until finally looking up, I caught our father's eye on the other side of the room. So he'd been watching. He nodded knowingly and smiled. Crossed an arm at his waist and bowed slightly, still beaming, his greatest show of respect. No words, ovations, fist-pumping, back-slapping welcome to the club. Just that nod and the little bow to say, *I understand.* Nick was nowhere in sight. With our grandfather, I assumed, fetching cases for the new violins, to pack them up and send them on their way. Counting money. Saying that other goodbye.

—

That in the years to come, our mother's radiance would slip ever further un-
der the surface of her beauty and elegance, her chatoyance of longing and un-
realized potentials dulled by the passage of time until it was visible only to our
father and occasionally to us in her music or in loving looks between them; that
our grandfather's final years would be spent in an agony of unpaid debts and at-
tempts to extract money from violin crooks in Austria, Shanghai, Chicago, New
York, and New Jersey, money owed him for violins and bows he'd passed off as
antiquities, some real, some not, as the outer ring of a worldwide violin cartel
collapsed around familiar names we'd grown up hearing all our lives, toppling
some giants, leaving others broke and temporarily shamed out of work, with
plenty of room for new crooks to stake a claim; that my brother and I would go
on with our lives the same as ever, bending, scraping, carving, gluing, joining,
finishing, until one day in his mid-twenties Nick would look up suddenly, know-
ing he'd never really had the touch, *the knack, or the obsession,* as he put it—*the
natural ability to feel my way through a piece of wood, the love for it*—and say, "You know
what? I'm out of here," and would hang his apron by the door where our father
would leave it and where, every day for years after, it would serve as a reminder
of his absence for one or the other of us, pushing it aside to reach the light
switch it partially blocked, until the day it would suddenly vanish and reappear
laundered and tied shorter at the neck by a new young apprentice—a girl this
time, with questing dark blue eyes that affected me in ways I had not been af-
fected since the afternoon hearing David's violin—and whose first questions for
us, *Where would you like me to store my tools, or should I just use yours?* would alert us to a
presumed almost permanent place in our lives thereafter; that our grandfather's
final heartbreaking calls to New Jersey with the tax-evading pet store magnate,
who'd "bought" and never paid for our grandfather's real and fake antiquities
and who now faced a prison term longer than his life expectancy, would finally
rupture something in our grandfather's heart to spring the last few cords of his
sanity, causing him to reel around the shop in a stooped and staggering manner,

complaining about who had stolen his shoes and why must our mother always burn the onions, so many onions, until we understood enough to rush him to the hospital for cardiac care and his remaining days and hours alive; that the rest of the so-called Stradivari tonewood would be mixed together with newer wood blanks in the construction of violins to pass from our shop into the world, unremarked; that my brother would later return to the fold, though indirectly and never in full, always with that little buffer of indifference, the shrugs, stutters, and grimaces borrowed from our grandfather and calculated to keep you at a distance, VP of an international, boutique-style investment firm specializing in fine art and violins, and a very busy family life with two stepsons and twin girls of his own; that Alene Valloger would vanish from our shop with the soloist David Kushnarov and his three new violins, never to be heard from by any of us again, though in pictures of him later viewable on the internet she is often at his side, the same overbite and wide-set, aloofly solemn eyes, and always in his hand is the violin I made for him or another, the exact double of the ex-Wieniawski Guarneri which he claims to have been gifted by a most talented but unknown and undocumented modern maker in Cremona; that all of this should come to pass in the next several years of our lives is of course nothing. A blink, a drop, a personal side note, obscure footnote, endnote, or addendum to be mentioned in passing with the lives of the violins that came through our hands and passed from there into the world.

So, one day in a hundred or two hundred or four hundred years, presuming there are violins still and people to play them, after too many changes of ownership to count, slipped ribs, varnish fixes, replaced fingerboards, new bass bars, glue joints reinforced . . . One day scraping and blowing at the inside of the scroll to bush and re-ream those same pegholes that once tortured my dreams, a repair person somewhere, a young apprentice anywhere in the world using some of the same tools we used but maybe not speaking English to describe his or her experience, will glimpse my father's rabbit resolving and emerging out of the blacking beside my initials and the date from so many years prior to conflict with whatever remains of a label inside. *Guarneri.* Will they think it's a Guarneri? Will anyone know? *What is this*, they might say to each other and pass the violin around for a look. *Wow! Check this out! What's the story here? Why these initials and this mark? Crazy. What is that. A rabbit? Get the book! Let's look it up and see if we can find a match anywhere. Had to be someone! But what a whack job. Look at that asymmetry! Oh, these cracks, we'll have to fix. That's nothing. But who would have made anything on this pattern, and why? It had to have been on purpose. Damn though, I'll bet it sounds good. Where did it come from? One thing for sure, it's really old. Maybe really, REALLY old . . . who knows.*

Because after all, what is the scale of a human life beside a violin's?

What is ever to be known about those of us who made and sold them?

Acknowledgments

"The Five," Santa Monica Review
"We Unlovely, Unloved," Kenyon Review

Thanks:

For research assistance, reading suggestions, and tips and tales straight from the violin world, thanks to Morgan Andersen, Peg Baumgartel, Jonathan Cooper, and James Kytonen.

For advice on earlier drafts thanks to Louis B. Jones, Sands Hall, and Christopher Howell, and for beta-reading the final draft, thanks to JoAnna King Yost.

Thanks to Xu Xi, Jim Schley and everyone at Tupelo Press.

Extra special thanks to Ann Joslin Williams for years of friendship, editorial consulting, and endless patience reading draft after draft after draft.

For funding, thanks to the National Endowment for the Arts. For its generous support in the form of summer grants and sabbatical leaves, thanks to Eastern Washington University.

Thanks to my parents, Alice and Larry Spatz, for violins and violin lessons beginning at such an early age. Also, for musical inspiration and for endless generosity.

Most of all, thanks to Caridwen Irvine-Spatz for her patience, faith, honesty, vision, explanations of lutherie, ancient mathematics and metaphysics, and for her fine editorial sense.

Recent and Selected Titles from Tupelo Press

Silver Road: Essays, Maps & Calligraphies (hybrid memoir), Kazim Ali
A Certain Roughness in Their Syntax (poems), Jorge Aulicino, translated by Judith Filc
Flight (poems), Chaun Ballard
Another English: Anglophone Poems from Around the World (anthology),
    edited by Catherine Barnett and Tiphanie Yanique
Everything Broken Up Dances (poems), James Byrne
The Book of LIFE (poems), Joseph Campana
Fire Season (poems), Patrick Coleman
New Cathay: Contemporary Chinese Poetry (anthology), edited by Ming Di
Calazaza's Delicious Dereliction (poems), Suzanne Dracius,
    translated by Nancy Naomi Carlson
Gossip and Metaphysics: Russian Modernist Poetry and Prose (anthology),
    edited by Katie Farris, Ilya Kaminsky, and Valzhyna Mort
Xeixa: Fourteen Catalan Poets (anthology),
    edited by Marlon Fick and Francisca Esteve
The Posthumous Affair (novel), James Friel
Leprosarium (poems), Lise Goett
Hazel (novel), David Huddle
Darktown Follies (poems), Amaud Jamaul Johnson
Dancing in Odessa (poems), Ilya Kaminsky
A God in the House: Poets Talk About Faith (interviews),
    edited by Ilya Kaminsky and Katherine Towler
Third Voice (poems), Ruth Ellen Kocher
At the Gate of All Wonder (novel), Kevin McIlvoy
Boat (poems), Christopher Merrill
The Cowherd's Son (poems), Rajiv Mohabir
Marvels of the Invisible (poems), Jenny Molberg
Canto General: Song of the Americas (poems),
    Pablo Neruda, translated by Mariela Griffor and Jeffrey Levine
Ex-Voto (poems), Adélia Prado, translated by Ellen Doré Watson
Intimate: An American Family Photo Album (hybrid memoir), Paisley Rekdal
Thrill-Bent (novel), Jan Richman
Dirt Eaters (poems), Eliza Rotterman

Good Bones (poems), Maggie Smith
The Perfect Life (essays), Peter Stitt
Kill Class (poems), Nomi Stone
Swallowing the Sea (essays), Lee Upton
feast gently (poems), G. C. Waldrep
Republic of Mercy (poems), Sharon Wang
Legends of the Slow Explosion (essays), Baron Wormser

See our complete list at www.tupelopress.org